The Seven-Year Witch

Cindy Keen Reynders

Publisher's Note:

This is a work of fiction. All names, characters, places, and events are the work of the author's imagination.

Any resemblance to real persons, places, or events is coincidental.

Solstice Publishing - www.solsticepublishing.com

As always, thanks to my husband Rich and my family for their patience and understanding when I go into my office and disappear for hours. They respect my writing addiction and for that I will be eternally grateful.

June 1877
Somewhere in Merry Olde England

Chapter One

*I*t's best to travel through time naked.

Miranda Rose, novice witch of the Wysteria Hedge Haven Clan, was doing exactly that as she vaulted through cumulus clouds into the nineteenth century. Her long golden hair whipped behind her like a banner, and the skin on her face had become so taut, she feared her teeth might pop out of her mouth.

The reason for being naked was simple—travel went much faster. Also, clothes caught fire upon entering the atmosphere whereas skin simply became very hot. Hot skin she could live with; incinerated clothing and torched hair, no.

Wincing, she pulled up on her red broom handle, and braced for a hard impact. "Whoa Nellie!"

"Damn it, Miranda, I'm...just...a broom..." the Witchwright model squealed as it shuddered and bucked.

Breaking free of wispy white vapors, Miranda flew through the forest treetops and landed with a thud onto a mossy stream bank, dropping Nellie. She rolled across the rough surface, laid still for a moment to catch her breath then pushed to her feet. As intense heat rose from her bare skin, she hurried toward the water and splashed into the silvery depths. She could practically hear every pore sizzle and pop with relief.

Stepping out of the stream, she waved a hand over her body and clothed herself in soft lavender robes. Her nostrils flared with loamy, forest smells as she searched for

Nellie. When she found the broom, she grasped hold of the handle.

"You okay?"

"Sure," the broom said. "But that nearly scared the birch right out of my wood. By the way, what are we doing here?"

The broom had a memory like cheesecloth, but Miranda didn't mind explaining things a few extra times. "The Supreme Witch's Council has assigned me to find Balthazar the Wizard and the Philosopher's Stone by Halloween."

"Halloween? That's only a few months away. Tell me again, why you have to do this?"

Miranda rolled her eyes. "This is my seventh and final task. If I succeed, the old biddies will make me a high witch. If I don't, I'll remain a novice and the clan joke. It's never taken a Hedge Haven witch this long to be promoted."

"And I just *know* you're going to succeed." Nellie swished the straw on her back end. "I can feel it in my knot holes."

"*Sigillium magnifitum.*" After intoning a spell to reveal anything that had been rendered invisible, Miranda pivoted on one heel, scanning the horizon. At last she saw what she'd been searching several months for—a crumbling fortress, perched on a hill like a dark sentinel.

"Son of a monkey, there it is!" She pointed toward the edifice, straddled Nellie, and flew toward the tower. Hopefully dealing with the wizard wouldn't be too difficult. She wasn't the most proficient with her spells, even though she spent hours trying to perfect her powers.

The errors she made weren't just simple ones. For some reason, she had trouble reading her witchcraft books clearly, yet she didn't dare admit it. She'd tried glasses and other reading enhancements, but nothing worked. Her parents, who were exceptionally brilliant and traveled all over the world on archaeological digs in order to write history books, would think her a dimwit if they ever learned the truth. And her six older sisters, some of the smartest witches in the clan, would feel sorry for her if they knew her secret shame.

She didn't want their sympathy. It would be humiliating.

At least she could always find humor in her exceptional skills at messing things up. Being able to laugh somehow lessened the sting of feeling like such a complete failure.

Arriving at the castle, Miranda and Nellie hovered outside the wizard's workroom. She peered through a window at the book-lined shelves hugging the walls. Faint light spilled across the area from a tall, wax-encrusted candelabrum. A black cauldron suspended over the fireplace bubbled noisily. Nose twitching from the noxious fumes, she glanced around, noticing the hollow-eyed skulls decorating one wall.

Enemies?

Hopefully she didn't piss this guy off. His trophy wall could put Hannibal the Cannibal to shame.

Once she'd glided inside, she landed on the stone floor and leaned on Nellie. The room appeared empty, but she sensed a presence. Skin prickling with trepidation, she noticed a caged owl studying her warily with large yellow eyes. It tilted its head to the side and blinked. "Hoot, hoot."

"Crapola. Nellie, do you have any idea how to call out a wizard?"

"Beats me."

She chewed on her lower lip contemplatively. "Uh, Mr. Wizard? Are you in here? Yoo, hoo…"

A whirlwind of sparks flashed, stinging her eyes. After rubbing them, she looked up to see a small figure.

It's a bird, it's a plane, it's…a midget wizard?

She blinked several times, trying to determine if her vision was playing tricks on her. Nope. Someone in a black, star-covered cloak and a black pointed cap had appeared. His dark tousled mop of hair fell into his eyes, and a pair of round horn-rimmed glasses rested crookedly across the bridge of his freckled nose.

"Holy bat dung, you're just a kid! How old are you?"

He lifted his chin haughtily. "Eleven."

"It's hard to believe the fabled wizard who has awed generations is…" She trailed off, not wanting to insult him by saying what she really thought. *A scrawny punk.* "Well, um, so handsome."

He grinned like a kook. "How'd you like my last trick? Did I scare you?"

She gave him a thumbs-up. "Way impressive."

"Whoo, hoo. I'm bad, I'm bad…" He started moon walking around the room.

Oh brother. "Balthazar, I need to ask you something."

He squinted suspiciously at her. "What?"

"Do you have the Philosopher's Stone?"

He plucked a shiny black obsidian-type rock, about the size of a baseball, from the voluminous sleeve of his robe and held it up to the light. "Cool, huh?"

Her eyes widened. "I'll pay you any price."

"It's not for sale. See, my mom found this magic rock in an antique shop a few years ago. I rubbed it and spoke some magic words from this wizardology book. When I finished with *abracadabra*, I showed up here. I don't have a bedtime and I can conjure up whatever I want to eat. This cool wizard called the dark lord comes every day to teach me more magic. It's totally awesome."

"Maybe we can barter for it." She held a finger to her chin. "How about a lifetime supply of Nerds? You know, those little candy things—"

"Take a hike, Ms. Witchy-poo. Besides, according to my wizard books, you freaks are bad *ju ju*. I'm gonna have to banish you to the Neverlands…" He whipped out a wand and waved it with a flourish.

Desperate, she began to ramble like a fool. "No, don't do that! Didn't your books teach you the difference between a white witch and a black witch? See, I'm one of the good guys—we've all sworn to do no harm."

Balthazar hesitated, his wand wavering slightly. "I don't know…"

Encouraged, Miranda went on. "I've been assigned by the Supreme Witch's Council to fetch your stone so they can use it to help mankind. If I don't, I'll fail my final task. I'll have to wait one hundred years before I can take another exam. I'll be the oldest novice witch on the planet!"

Tossing the stone up and down in his palm, Balthazar scrutinized her. "Like I care."

"Please, you've got to help me!" Her insides knotted like shoelaces.

A wave of his wand sent a bolt of lightning toward her. As a powerful electric charge rocketed through her body, she catapulted, head over heels, out of the window.

"You little bra-a-a-t!"

For the second time that day, her extremities began to sizzle like pork chops on a hot grill. A scream ripped from her throat as she shot through the starry sky. After what seemed like an eternity, she landed with a painful thump.

Every bone in her body cried out in anguish. She didn't bother to fight back against the black wave of unconsciousness. She figured she was a goner.

***

Sir Maxwell Chadwick, the seventh Duke of Pellamshire, steered his carriage away from the pub and allowed his horse to find its own way through the foggy, torch-lit streets of London. After a night on the town with a couple of his chums, Max leaned back against the plush seat, feeling better than he had in weeks. Unfortunately, he knew his good mood would fade once life fell back into its familiar, mundane pattern.

These days, he spent most of his time in business meetings or alone in his empty mausoleum of a townhouse, battling bitter memories. Occasionally, like tonight, his friends managed to drag him out. It was a welcome respite from lingering sadness that ate at him like a sickness.

His glum attitude stemmed from several events. He'd suffered the first blow two years ago. He'd been courting a lovely young lady by the name of Catherine Fettiplace, and he thought they got on quite famously. Then he made the foolish mistake of asking her to marry him.

After that night, she'd refused to see him again. Several months later, his brother began courting her. Before Max knew it, they were betrothed, and they married shortly after. Pride wouldn't allow him to show how much it affected him. Yet inside, he'd been seething with anger.

They'd meant so much to each other; how could Catherine have thrown him over for Marley? No doubt her parents had reminded her that Max's older brother was in line to become the next Duke of Pellamshire, and encouraged her to set her cap for him. Shallow, to say the least. *Women.* He didn't think a lot of the flighty creatures.

Attempting to drown his frustration, he'd begun dallying with a string of other women. Most of them made it clear that since he was only the second Chadwick son, he was not the type of man they would consider marrying. Brutal, but honest.

He tried not to let it bother him. Instead, he simply enjoyed the sex if they offered it. If they weren't loose with their favors, he moved on. He'd made up his mind that's all females were good for.

When Catherine had died in childbirth and his tiny nephew shortly afterward, it nearly devastated him, but once again he dealt with the loss by exhibiting silent stoicism. Propriety dictated that he should feel nothing but sympathy for losing his sister-in-law. Love dictated that his heart be torn in two. Despite his own torment, even though he was still irritated at Marley for marrying the woman he loved, his brother had lost his wife. He needed to show respect.

Then while he was on a military excursion at sea a year ago, both his parents and his brother had contracted lingering fevers and passed away. Once again, his life turned completely upside down and he nursed secret guilt for having survived. His brother was the accomplished one who garnered everyone's respect. Why hadn't God spared him, and taken Max instead? And his parents—they'd been good people who didn't deserve such a terrible end. Although Max wasn't religious, what faith he had in a higher being had begun to dim.

Somehow, he managed to continue living, though the ache of his losses festered inside. He knew he had to remain rock solid, especially since Queen Victoria counted on him to assume the Duke of Pellamshire's title, preside over duties at court, and attend to the needs of the people living on the Chadwick family's ancestral lands. He wasn't mucking it up too bad, considering he was learning on the job.

Growing up, he'd been left to his own devices, and he'd found unique ways to occupy his hours outside of school. No one had thought it necessary to train him about the inner workings of the dukedom and he'd never worried about it. After college, he'd become an officer in the Royal Navy and finally discovered his place in society—serving in those elite ranks.

These days he sorely missed the camaraderie of his shipmates, the routine, and the regimented activities. He'd give anything to be back on high seas, commanding his ship, feeling the salty breeze on his cheeks as he sailed to distant shores. Unfortunately, his new duties consumed most of his time, so his military service had been halted. Max had found himself landlocked, and he didn't much like it.

A flash of light trailing through the dark sky drew his attention, and he turned to watch. *A comet?* Totally absorbed, he studied the ribbon of illumination making its way toward earth.

Ka-thunk!

When an object landed in a nearby field, his horse reared back and whinnied in fright. His coach careened through a puddle and sank in the mud, splashing cold, fetid water across his face and evening clothes.

"Thundering blazes, but this is rotten luck." He righted the carriage and patted the horse to calm it down. Wiping his face with his sleeve, he spat in a ditch, ridding himself of the foul taste in his mouth. Curious about the bright entity he'd just seen streaking to the ground, he walked into the field.

Searching his grassy, moonlit surroundings, he headed toward a line of trees. Hearing what sounded like a low moan, he held very still and listened harder. For a moment, he thought the few drinks he'd had at the Golden Hound tonight might have created a buzz in his brain, causing him to hear things. But he'd never had a problem handling a couple of whiskies, so that couldn't be it.

More than likely it was his imagination. He'd spent so many hours cooped up alone in his library, poring over his father's account journals, that he'd begun to worry his reclusive tendencies might have addled his senses.

As if that weren't enough, he would soon need to pay a visit to his family's ironworks factory near Boston, Massachusetts. Every summer, his father or brother visited the manager, his father's American friend and business partner, John Weaver, in order to review the sales figures. In their absence, the task now fell to Max. And it was a task he didn't much look forward to.

"Ohhh, owww…"

"Bloody hell," he muttered. "Either I've gone daft in the head or some poor bloke's out there."

Following the soft moans, it didn't take him long to find a scorched area containing a heap of smoldering rags. His nostrils twitched from the smoky odor as he leaned over, determining the heap was in fact a body.

Is this what crashed into the field?

It couldn't be. Humans didn't fall from the sky on a beam of light. He must have simply seen a shooting star. The unfortunate individual lying at his feet had probably been caught in a fire, though he wondered where it had occurred, since news of conflagrations in London usually spread as fast as the flames. Whatever fate had befallen this person, he needed to try and help. With the tip of his boot, he touched the bundle tentatively.

Another moan.

"By Jove, what's happened?" He hunkered down beside the individual who wore a disheveled lavender robe. When he pulled material away from a face, he was struck by the sight of long, golden hair trailing over slender shoulders.

It's a woman.

He studied her soot-covered face, and her small, upturned nose smudged with black. Long dark lashes rested like butterflies on her alabaster skin marred by dirt stains. Strips of the robe clung enticingly to her silhouette. Beneath her frayed bodice, curves hinted at full breasts and material fluttered across her shapely thighs.

His vivid imagination provided the final detail, and he realized there was a desirable female underneath all the burnt clothing. He resisted the urge to allow his gaze to linger, as it appeared she was in need of assistance. He sat down and drew her against his chest, enjoying the feel of her soft form as a smoky scent drifted from her curls.

Though he was concerned about her stricken appearance, he still couldn't shake off the effects of her close proximity. It had been a long time—too long—since he'd held a woman. Much to his consternation, he began to notice familiar stirrings in his loin that had lain dormant for months.

It occurred to him he hadn't been with a woman since his parents and brother had passed away because he'd been so preoccupied with taking care of family responsibilities. The idea of satisfying his sexual urges had been the last thing on his mind.

And this is definitely no time to be thinking of sex, my man.

Fighting back inappropriate cravings that had come from only God knows where, he cleared the thickness in his throat. This woman might be a prostitute or some other impoverished creature of the streets. Or she simply could have been the victim of a terrible crime. It didn't matter. She obviously needed aid, and he couldn't ignore her plight.

Patting her cheeks, he tried to rouse her. She shifted in his arms and nuzzled closer to his chest, making his heart melt. Who could have hurt such a stunning creature? He didn't even know who she was or what had happened to her, yet he wanted to defend her honor against the brute that had done this.

Why am I ready to defend her when I don't even know her?

Max considered the idea this could be a ruse. Perhaps ruffians waited in the shadows to assail him and steal his wallet. His gut wrenched and he narrowed his gaze to peruse the area. Fortunately, he didn't see anyone, but he still remained wary.

Considering all his current responsibilities, he really didn't have time to pick up strangers from the street, even though he hated to see anyone, or anything, suffer. Nevertheless, he couldn't just leave her here. That would be cruel and heartless.

"Miss, you need to wake up," he told her in an uneven voice, gently shaking her arm. "You've been in some sort of accident. I'd like to get you to a physician so you can be examined."

She coughed then her eyes slowly opened, the white parts nearly glowing against her sooty face. The vivid blue iris areas reminded him of ocean swells on sunny days.

"Am I in the…the Neverlands?" she asked in a hesitant voice.

"The *Neverlands?*" He chuckled. "I'm afraid I don't know what that is. I can assure you you're very much alive. However, since I don't know what happened to you, I can't account for whether or not you're injured."

With jerky movements, she felt her arms and legs, and moved her hands over her body, apparently checking herself for cuts or bruises.

Max's mouth practically watered. He would have loved to volunteer to perform the examination, but unfortunately, that would have been quite unseemly. Nevertheless, he watched her, completely mesmerized as her fingers roamed over areas he would gladly have touched and massaged for her.

Good God, man. Have you lost your mind! Get a hold of yourself.

"Son of a monkey, I don't believe it," she cried. "The wizard didn't blast me to smithereens."

The wizard? Smithereens?

Narrowing his gaze, Max wondered if she was in her right mind. Perhaps a few marbles had gone missing. The idea that maybe she'd recently escaped from the insane asylum occurred to him. Yes, by George, that had to be it. He'd best take her there so they could lock her up again.

And throw away the key.

That idea didn't sit well with him, however, and he clenched his jaw. He was determined to find out where she'd come from. "Have you found everything in order, Miss?"

She sat up, leaving emptiness where her warmth had so recently surrounded him like a billowy cocoon. He missed holding her already. Why, he couldn't say. Only that she affected him in ways he couldn't explain. Dizziness gripped his brain and his mouth had gone dry as a bone. Again, he considered perhaps he'd imbibed too much at the pub but realized that couldn't be the cause of the strange feeling that had come over him.

"I guess so."

He pushed to his feet and held out his hand. "May I help you?"

"Sure."

She placed her palm in his, sending a tingling sensation through his arm and throughout his body as she stood up next to him. When she swayed, he caught her and held her against his chest, wishing he could keep her like this for a while longer. Shock rippled through him.

You have no idea who this woman is, Max. Why are you acting so protectively toward her? You really must be more cautious—she's a stranger.

He couldn't explain it. He simply knew she needed help, and he wanted to be the one to give it to her, as outrageous as it seemed. Even though his forehead had become overly warm and he wondered if he was taking ill, he asked her, "Are you all right?"

"I'm a little dizzy. I had quite a tumble."

"Did some ruffian accost you? If so, I'll find him and give him a taste of his own medicine. I was a champion wrestler at Oxford, so I can easily give him a black eye for doing this to you. In fact, I'll give him two." His offer to defend her honor seemed a tad inflated, but amazingly the words seemed to fly from his mouth. It was as though he couldn't stop himself.

She placed a hand on his sleeve. "No, no, it's nothing like that."

"What happened?" He lifted a curious brow, trying to curtail his innate desire to scoop her into his arms. But that was a completely irrational thought. There was no question about it; there must be something wrong with him.

"It's difficult to explain. But I assure you, I'll be fine."

"I can't imagine how. You look as though you've been through hell, if you don't mind my saying so." He frowned, wondering about her peculiar behavior. No woman he'd ever known would take a beating like it appeared she had, and not be cowering in fear. Again, he wondered if this was some sort of ruse to catch him off guard...

"I appreciate your concern, Mr..."

He cleared his throat, waiting for her to pour on the ridiculous female charm once she realized who he was. These days, he'd grown quite accustomed to women fawning over him and flirting outrageously. After his brother died, he'd immediately become one of London's most eligible bachelors. Now all the matchmaking mamas were in dogged pursuit of him, hoping to snap him up for one of their daughters.

He found the complete turnabout darkly humorous, especially after all the years of genteel society girls considering him beneath their delicate, spoiled noses. Not in a lifetime could he forget how they'd shunned him. It would take a miracle for him to ever choose one of those featherheaded society chits for his wife.

"My name is Maxwell," he finally said. "Sir Maxwell, the Duke of Pellamshire." He waited for her reaction, but to his sheer amazement, her face didn't register a thing—except a beautiful smile.

"I'm pleased to meet you." She reached out and shook his hand, giving it a good steady pumping, like that of a hardy sailor.

He blinked, completely bewildered. She spoke strangely, behaved oddly, and now she didn't know who he was?

"I say, you haven't heard of me before?"

She shrugged. "Sorry, but no."

Surprise washed over him. If she lived in London, how could she *not* have heard of his family? The gossips were having a heyday, going on about the Chadwicks' recent tragedies. He'd become quite a famous topic of discussion, much to his irritation.

He cleared his throat. "I haven't had the pleasure of hearing your name, Miss."

"Oh, it's Miranda."

"Just Miranda?"

"Yes." She brushed twigs and dirt from her tattered clothing, obviously wishing to change the subject. "How did you find me?"

"I saw a streak of light in the sky and I thought something had fallen in this field. I came out to investigate, and I found you. I believe the glow I saw must have been a shooting star, or perhaps a comet."

"Yes, I'm sure you're right," she said quickly. "Thank you for stopping to help me."

"I couldn't very well leave you lying in the middle of a field, now could I? It wouldn't be very gentlemanly. You were hurt." He glanced at the street. "There's all manner of foul individuals roaming this part of town who might have taken advantage of you."

She chuckled. "Believe me I'll manage just fine if anyone tries anything funny with me. I'll karate-chop him right where it hurts." She made sharp motions with her hands.

Max shook his head, still wondering about her odd manner of speech, and her unusual conduct. Perhaps her brain had been addled during her mysterious accident. He'd heard that often caused people to exhibit erratic mental behavior.

"My carriage is nearby. If you'd like, I'll take you to a physician so he can examine you."

She stared at him like he'd grown horns and a tail. "I appreciate your consideration, but I'll take it from here."

"You really should come with me—you're in no condition to be wandering about town on your own." When she backed away, shaking her head, he tried a different approach. "If you'd like, I can summon a night watchman and he can take you where you need to go."

"No. Absolutely not! Do not call anyone. No one can know I'm here—you shouldn't even know." Her fiery blue glance pierced him like an insect pinned to a scientist's collection board.

He shifted his weight from one foot to another, observing her frazzled hair and clothing. "What are your plans, Miss? To wander through London looking like that? You'll make a laughingstock of yourself. And surely you have family somewhere that will be looking for you."

"Don't worry about me. I can take care of myself. Please just let me be."

He lifted a brow. "What?"

"I'm sure there's nothing wrong with your hearing. *Let me be.*"

"See here now—"

"Look, Sir Maxwell." She flipped a soot-stained hand at him. "Don't get me wrong. I appreciate everything you've done. But you really need to leave. The wizard could come after me again and you might be hurt. I absolutely couldn't live with that on my conscience—and the council would have my head. So please, just leave me be. All right?"

Incredible! Max stared at her as though she'd swallowed an entire roast suckling pig. The woman was truly delusional. Stumped about what to do, he scrutinized her closer. Should he leave her as she requested?

I can't. What if some scoundrel attacked her? He frowned and treated her to a stern look—one he hoped portrayed his deep concern. "I refuse to budge one iota until you agree to come with me."

She stomped her foot. "Oooh! You are impossible. Fine, then. Stay and risk getting shish kebabbed by that punk in the tower. It's your funeral. I'm not sticking around. Meanwhile, you can't remember me or what happened here tonight." She pointed at him and muttered, *"Nexus praxtor belivius forgetfulness!"*

Max could hardly believe his eyes when she snapped her fingers, and a red-handled broom appeared in her hands.

Where did that come from? He blinked several times to clear his vision, but it didn't help. To his complete amazement, she straddled the innocent household item.

"Come on Nellie," she urged. "Let's go back to Wysteria. We've got to figure out a new plan."

Gadzooks! The woman really has lost her mind; it appears she believes herself to be a witch. Stunned, he watched as she waited for the broom to magically whisk her away.

Nothing happened.

He folded his arms over his chest, seriously considering hefting her over his shoulder and hauling her to the booby hatch, kicking and screaming if necessary. Not now, but perhaps in a moment. This was jolly good fun, watching her cavort around. In fact, he hadn't enjoyed himself this much in quite a long time.

She rubbed the broom handle, and a worried expression creased her brow. "Don't tell me that punk got to you! You're better than that, Nellie. For Pete's sake, you're brand new! You should have been able to handle a little fall."

When she couldn't get the broom to do anything, she made her way over to a rise in the ground, planted her feet, and said, "Okay, I've given you a slight advantage by standing up here." She pointed the broom handle skyward. "This ought to do it. Come on now. Be a good girl."

Still nothing happened.

Growling with frustration, she stomped over to a boulder. Glaring at him over her shoulder, she said, "What are you looking at?"

"You. You're quite remarkable."

She rolled her eyes and concentrated her efforts on trying to make the broom fly.

Why in the world didn't he summon the authorities and have her hauled away? Why did he simply continue to watch her prance around as though she'd lost her mind? It was obvious that in her current state, the unstable woman might be harmful to herself or possibly someone else.

Yet, he hesitated, still in disbelief that he was seeing this. It seemed likely if he left and returned with a witness, she would probably be gone, and then *he'd* be labeled the lunatic.

Still talking to the broom, she climbed atop a boulder, steadied herself on the handle and pointed it once again at the star-studded sky. "Shoot for the moon, Nellie!"

To Max's complete astonishment, the broom began to levitate and whooshed out of sight. Staggering backward, he rubbed his eyes. In all his twenty-seven years on this earth, he'd never seen such a strange sight. A numb feeling washed over him.

Good Lord, had he lost his mind? Had he really witnessed that? Perhaps he ought to admit *himself* to the insane asylum. He couldn't possibly have seen that woman disappear into thin air.

Could he?

He looked frantically around the area, seeing nothing that could verify she'd just been there. She hadn't left a single clue. Even the blackened, burned out area where he'd found her now appeared completely normal.

"Bloody hell," he muttered as he stormed back to his carriage. Swinging inside, he flicked the reins across the horse's back and the coach began to roll forward. He wanted nothing more than to leave the scene of his outlandish hallucination.

Turning the coach around, he headed back to the Golden Hound for another drink. He needed it badly. Deep in thought about what had just happened, he focused on his horse clopping over the cobblestones.

"Ho there, old mare. Did you see what I just did? Or have I lost my wits?"

The horse whinnied and shook its mane. Whatever that meant.

Chapter Two

Miranda flew over the rooftops of London, anxiously waiting for her broom to zip into the stratosphere. When Nellie began slowing down and losing altitude, she called out, "Any time now. We need to get home. ASAP."

"Cap'n, I'm givin' her all I've got…" Smoke began to trail from the straw on the broom's backside.

"Enough with the Star Trek excuses, Nellie. Try harder. I know you can do it."

"Right. Assuming warp speed…"

Miranda rolled her eyes as the broom shimmied and shuddered. Nellie wasn't the only one who didn't feel well. Her tongue felt like a wad of cotton, her throat ached, and her limbs felt like giant, swollen sausages. To top it all off, she smelled like she'd been at a weenie roast, and she'd been the weenie.

I should have seen it coming. But Balthazar was just a kid. She hadn't really thought he could hurt anything. Next time she confronted him she'd be more prepared to meet him head on. *I just need to work my spells better…*

Finally, Nellie shot off like a rocket and began the journey back to the present. They wouldn't set any speed records, but at least they were on their way. To pass the time, she allowed her thoughts to dwell on Sir Maxwell, the duke of…hmmm, she couldn't exactly remember.

The Duke of Piggingham? No, that wasn't it. The Duke of Pentagon? No, no, no! The Duke of Pellamshire. That's it!

So, what about him? He was cute in a stiff-upper-lip sort of way with his, "May I help you Miss?" attitude. His chocolate brown, dreamy bedroom-eyes were killers.

She could only imagine what he'd thought when he found her passed out cold, dressed in nothing but incinerated clothing. He'd probably figured she was a prostitute or a nut job. Yet, being an old-fashioned kind of guy, the duke had gone all chivalrous on her and tried to be helpful.

Holy stars, he was hot. *Really* hot, as in she'd rate him as a ten on the Richter scale of mortal guy hotness. She supposed he was what women called drop-dead handsome. His dark, shining hair reminded her of a raven's wing, and he'd towered over her like a glorious Greek Titan.

She recalled how his trousers clung to his corded thighs, showing off some mighty fine male endowments. His evening jacket had stretched across his broad shoulders, making her wish she could get an itty-bitty peek at his pects.

Be still my witchy little heart.

His voice reminded her of how fine red wine rolled like velvet down her throat, tingling throughout her arms and legs. She felt it again, right now, just thinking of him. A flush crept into her cheeks and slow warmth wound through her. Goddess above, she felt like she was sitting in a steam room. Then her heart launched into a complete nuclear meltdown, like a teenage witch with her first crush.

She considered looking him up again once she'd finished with all this wizard nonsense. Suddenly it hit her. Where had her dorky, libido limbo come from? She was acting like a love-sick fool, and she'd just met the duke!

She'd always been particular about the men, mortal or magical, that she dated. And even fussier about who she did the mattress mambo with. In fact, she hadn't been with a man since…hmm, she could barely remember.

No, wait. Now she recalled the last guy she'd been crazy about—her Scottish highland warrior from the fifteenth century, Tavis McClarren. That man packed a punch underneath his kilt. He could literally knock her socks off with one single glance.

Unfortunately, she'd had to leave him long before she'd cared to. When the Scots started burning witches at the stake again, she'd high-tailed it out of there. Tavis had been great, but not great enough to make an ash out of herself over.

Ever since then, she'd been too busy to get involved with anyone—mortal or otherwise. Relationships were far too complicated. Oh, she'd dated around a little, but nothing more.

Someone usually wound up getting hurt. *Her*. It all boiled down to the fact that men found her too intimidating. Guys told her bone-headed things like, "Sorry babe, you're just too much to handle," or the worn-out phrase, "I love you but I'm not *in love* with you." And her all-time favorite, "You're too high maintenance."

When her breathing started to rasp from her throat and perspiration dotted her forehead, she placed a hand on her brow. *Too hot!* Unconsciously, she began to rub her forearm then glanced down to see it had broken out in a rash of tiny red, stinging bumps.

Her mind raced erratically as she tried to think of what might be wrong with her. Had that kid given her some sort of prepubescent wizard cooties? *Crapola!*

She furiously rubbed a spot behind an ear. Stars above, another bump! The damn rash was spreading. It felt like a million fire ants were stinging every square inch of her hide.

"Hold on," Nellie warned as she nose-dived toward the ground. "We're coming in for a landing!"

Jolted from her thoughts, she gripped the broom handle as they blasted into the present-day atmosphere of 2010. Birds flapped frantically past them as they tumbled head over broom bristles, in a freefall toward *terra firma*.

Doomed for a crash landing, Miranda braced for impact. With a sudden jerk, she and Nellie halted in midair, hovering about five feet above the ground in front of the Rose family mansion.

"Are you okay, Nellie?"

"I think so. It was like driving Miss Crazy, though. What in the whispering willows is wrong with you?"

"I think that punk wizard must have hexed me with wizard shingles. You don't remember anything about getting our butts kicked by him, do you?"

"Not a stick."

"Figures." Summoning every ounce of magic she possessed, she tried to discharge the strange force holding them. The air crackled with electricity as she concentrated.

"I'm getting dizzy," Nellie moaned. "I think I'm gonna toss my cookies."

Still dangling like a rag doll above the lawn, Miranda called out, "Peace with the gods, peace with nature, peace within. May the four winds release us, so mote it be!"

Slammed to the ground with sudden force, she rubbed her aching backside. Impatiently she waved away the lavender haze obscuring her view. A large Victorian home rose up before her surrounded by tall trees, hedges, and flower gardens, all of which had been lovingly tended for more than a century by Aunt Aggie. While her parents traveled all over the world for their research, her aunt, who'd never married, kept the home fires burning.

Clutching Nellie, she pushed stiffly to her feet, feeling as though her joints had turned to stone. She sniffed at the fresh breeze sweeping across the Columbia River. Beneath gentle bluffs, the waterway stretched across the horizon, spilling into the sparkling Pacific Ocean.

Her heart melted like a slice of butter on a hotcake as she recalled the good times she'd had here with her sisters. Their home located a few miles from Wysteria, Oregon, had always offered a safe haven. Exactly what she needed right now, along with some help figuring out what in the heck was going on with her.

By now, every inch of her skin burned with fiery patches. Feverish and dizzy, she stumbled toward the house. Hopefully Aggie would be able to offer some mumbo jumbo spell that could relieve this hellish misery.

Inside, she limped past the tall grandfather clock and passed through the parlor. In the kitchen, she put Nellie away in the broom closet, headed out the back door, and hobbled toward a large, ivy-covered shed.

Aunt Aggie, wearing a black apron, her pale hair swept into a net-covered bun, looked up from a bubbling pot on an ancient, cast-iron stove. Despite modern conveniences, she still preferred to use the old appliance to stir up her concoctions for the Rose Sisters' Soaps and Scents shop in town. After Miranda's six sisters performed their tasks for the witch's council, they'd all gone to college and now held jobs in the mortal world so they could observe and assist humankind when needed. They often returned home to spend their vacations at the mansion. Since Miranda still needed to finish her tasks, she continued to live here and worked at the shop in her spare time.

Cassandra and Elizabeth, two of her sisters, glanced up from a large oak table where they sifted herbal sachets in gauzy cloth bags. Cassie's red hair shimmered with golden-red fire as she shot a concerned look her way. "Hey sis, you don't look so good."

Lizzie, with her olive complexion and hair the color of blackberry wine, clicked her tongue. "Miranda! What happened to you?"

Aggie wiped her hands on her apron and rushed over. "Stick out your tongue."

When she complied, Aggie grimaced. "It's covered in fuzzy brown patches."

Lizzie made gagging motions. "Ick. I hope you're not contagious."

"Oh-mi-gods!" Cassie clapped her hands on her cheeks. "You've got whiskers!"

"Gweat. Whass wrong wiss me?" She cleared her throat, and a creepy sensation shot up her spine. Rubbing her serious five o'clock shadow, she managed to utter, "I thound like a bwubber-wing id-thiot."

Hurrying over to a pie cupboard, Aggie removed a large book bound in mahogany-colored leather and blew off the dust. She began thumbing through the pages. "Let me see… This says we need to hold the ceremony of the charmed woods and ask for an ancestor's guidance." She snapped the book shut, produced her willow branch wand and waved it through the air. Magical wind and the sound of wind chimes whooshed around them. A second later they appeared in a forest clearing.

They positioned themselves in a circle with Miranda in the middle. Her head began to swim, so she closed her eyes tightly and stared into the darkness.

Aunt Aggie's voice rose above the woodland sounds. "Spirit circle thrice around, we call on those who've gone before to impart the wisdom of the ages."

When the air crackled and sizzled, Miranda opened her eyes to see bursts of blue light flickering in the grove. Suddenly a plump, elderly woman in a long purple robe appeared, her long hair falling like a frosty curtain across her shoulders. She yawned and plodded toward them, her craggy old face a mask of irritation.

"What in Hades do you want? I was napping."

"Our apologies, great spirit," Aggie said. "My niece needs help."

The spirit glared at Aggie. "Knock off the *great spirit* crap, okay? The name's Ursula. *Don't* wear it out."

"Sorry gr— I mean Ursula." Aggie pointed to Miranda who was currently raking nails into her scalp, like a dog chasing fleas.

Ursula cackled uproariously. "Well smack my backside blondie, you got it bad."

"I feel wike cwap." Miranda shifted impatiently from foot to foot.

The crone rang a small, tinkling bell as she muttered an incantation then asked, "You're the seventh sister of a seventh sister, correct?"

"Yeth," Miranda said.

"And you're seven-hundred-years-old?"

Miranda nodded.

"The Supreme Witch's Council also assigned her seven tasks to complete in order to advance from novice to high witch," Aggie added. "For her final task, she's been time traveling trying to find Balthazar the Wizard and the Philosopher's Stone."

Ursula nodded. "What year did you last hang out in, goldilocks?"

Miranda cleared her throat. "1877."

Ursula shook her head. "My dear, I believe you've got seven-year witch disease. Every year around Beltane— a time of brazen sexuality—some poor witch usually contracts it because they've had a run on the number seven. Have you also recently had an encounter with a very handsome man?"

"Well, yeth actu-wy." Miranda swallowed hard. "I met this hot duke."

Ursula leaned closer. "Listen up, blondie. You must find this man and make love with him seven times. Not just have sex, understand. He's really got to *want* you."

"In other words, Miranda's got an itch only the duke can scratch." Lizzy giggled.

The thought of getting horizontal with Sir Maxwell caused a strange mixture of anticipation and dread to twist through Miranda. "How can I compwete my final task if I'm twying to get in the duke's pants?" The second she said that, flames of embarrassment licked her face and she realized she had no more regard for the man than a piece of juicy steak. Stars above, that wasn't like her at all. She had more morals than that. *It's got to be the disease.*

Ursula grinned. "All I can recommend is to work fast. And remember, every seven years the disease will flare up unless you find your one true love."

"You gotta be kidding, wight?"

Ursula shook her head. "I'm serious as a warthog in heat."

She released a hot breath of frustration. "Okay, I'll jus-th get Nellie and th-zip back in time, kidnap the duke and…well, *you know.*"

Lizzie giggled. "Problem is you look like hell, sis. He's definitely not going to want to hit that."

Miranda stomped her foot. "Thankth for wee-minding me."

"Don't worry, blondie. Once you're near him again, you'll be fine." Ursula faded away, a smug look on her face. Then she appeared once more, shaking her finger. "I forgot. If you don't accomplish the deed, you'll have to learn to live with this disease. You also won't be able to use your powers any longer."

"Impo-thsible!" Miranda's heart nearly fell out of her chest. "The duke lives in the past. How am I th-supposed to time twavel there if I can't use witchcwaft?"

"Whine, moan, complain. That's all you young designer witches ever do."

When Ursula flicked her gnarled fingers at Miranda, a dizzying whirlwind of cold air whisked her off her feet and jolted her into a black void.

***

The whiskey hadn't helped. In fact, the extra drink only served to give Max a monster of a headache. When he arrived home from the Golden Hound, he immediately went to his room, shed his clothing, and crawled into bed.

Closing his eyes, he threw his arm over his brow and tried to sleep. When that position didn't help, he rolled from side to side trying to get comfortable. *Impossible!* Nothing worked.

His mind clicked away, and heated warmth poured through him as he continued to think about the beautiful, but highly unusual woman he'd met in the meadow tonight. *Miranda.* A lovely, exotic-sounding name; and one he'd never heard before.

The woman herself was most definitely unlike anyone he'd ever met. Beneath her sooty, grime-encrusted exterior, he'd detected her unique beauty, and had been more than affected by her unusual, albeit rough, charm. For a brief moment, he compared her to Catherine. Even though he still had feelings for his brother's deceased wife, they paled in comparison to his burgeoning inquisitiveness about Miranda.

She'd captivated him with her peculiar manner. But had she really disappeared, or had he imagined all of it? His reclusive habits had possibly begun to take a toll on his senses. Perhaps he'd made up his entire encounter with Miranda this evening, much like a child concocted imaginary friends when he or she became lonely.

But I actually felt her—held her in my arms and smelled her tumbled, smoky hair.

The acrid odor wasn't exactly the most enticing of scents, but it had definitely piqued his curiosity. If he'd been dreaming, he doubted his mind would bestow a burning smell on an imaginary woman.

Throughout the night, he continued to toss and turn as similar thoughts twisted through his brain. First, he was hot, then he was cold. His head continued to ache, his throat felt raw and his breathing became labored. His skin felt as though it was on fire—as if he were a haunch of venison turning slowly on a spit.

He finally jumped out of bed and began to pace in the midnight darkness, wondering if he was falling ill. Lord, he hoped not. He didn't have time to be sick. Throughout the early morning hours, he fretted and scratched the itchy skin all over his body.

He couldn't stop thinking about Miranda. The more he envisioned her in his mind's eye, the more he recalled her voluptuous shape barely hidden beneath her tattered clothing. It taunted and teased his senses, creating heat in his groin. To his dismay, he remained wide awake as lustful thoughts kept him hard and needy.

At last he drifted off, just as dawn touched the windows with a rosy glow.

***

Miranda landed with a muffled thump, her body cushioned by warmth and silken softness. She stretched and took a deep, cleansing breath.

Incredible. No more itching. No more twitching.

As her gaze adjusted to pale morning light, she took stock of her surroundings. A large four-poster bed covered with sumptuous blankets and pillows cradled her in marshmallow luxury.

Curtains danced in the breeze of an open window and gentle sunrise filtered across dressers, overstuffed chairs, and carved benches. For one teeny, tiny minute she started to relax. Then the memory of Ursula's diagnosis came back in a rush.

As she bolted upright, embroidered sheets slipped from her naked breasts. The rest of her was also as bare as the day she'd been born. A quick perusal of her birthday suit revealed the boils and angry red patches had disappeared. Reaching up to touch her hair, she grabbed handfuls of her long, golden curls.

Relief overcame curiosity. It seemed she'd been restored to her old self—thank the goddess!

Back to exploration mode, she ran her hand across the mattress in a wide sweep. Warning bells pinged in her brain when her fingertips caressed flesh. *Who the heck is in the sack with me?* Holding her breath in anticipation, she lifted the covers and took a gander.

A pair of muscled buttocks, obviously of the male persuasion, sprawled next to her. The man's hip displayed an interesting tattoo—the outline of a blue sailing ship. *Anchors away...*

His top half must have fallen off the edge of the bed. However, what she could see looked awfully tempting, and she shivered with anticipation. Scooting next to the hunk, she leaned over, trying to get a look at his face. No such luck. She only saw the back of his head, which was covered in tousled black hair.

Could it be my duke? Her heart slammed into her ribs as she realized it probably was. *That old Ursula really knows her stuff. This gig is gonna be a piece of cake.*

Sir Maxwell sneezed, and she scooted away, watching in fascination as he maneuvered himself back onto the bed with a heavy thump. "Miranda," he muttered in his sleep as he hugged a pillow against his abdomen.

Is he dreaming about little old me?

Fantastic—this was a start in the right direction. Her gaze lingered on his strong, chiseled face then drifted down to his broad chest lightly peppered with fine black curls. The sheet twisted between his long muscular legs, hiding his groin, and the delectable main course—the thought of which made her quiver with dangerous excitement.

And dread. Now that she was here with him, she realized seducing the duke—a stranger—went against every moral fiber she possessed. But do it she must, so she could finish her final task and be promoted to high witch.

Hesitantly, she reached toward the sheet, intent on unwrapping Sir Maxwell's tantalizing package. Since she had to do this thing, she might as well try to have some fun along the way.

Her breathing became shallow and blood rushed to the nether regions of her traitorous body. Incredibly, her libido behaved like a living entity, bouncing around the room like a bullet gone wild. Promiscuity wasn't her style, but now it seemed to be the current fashion.

Erotic sexual impulses warred with her usually cautious nature, and the reasonable side of her brain dueled with the untamed side. She'd had lovers before, but usually took the time to know them better first. Throwing herself at a man didn't seem right. Considering her current predicament, she realized this situation was no holds barred, whether she liked it or not. She needed to get it on with the duke and fast. The sooner she cured herself, the better.

At what cost though?

Buzzing sensations pulsated through her like a tidal wave. Despite her better judgment, she allowed herself to give in to the passion racing through her blood. She had no other choice. Inching her hand toward him, her finger tips tingled with anticipation.

A stroke here and a kiss there and soon I'll be giving him a test drive...

Feeling completely wanton, Miranda scooted next to Sir Maxwell, gently pried the pillow from his fingers and snuggled against him, pressing her nakedness against his so they lay together skin to skin. His warmth filled her with a provocative sensation and when he moaned with obvious enjoyment, she felt encouraged. Pressing her lips against his shoulder blade, she shivered with anticipation.

***

Max's strange symptoms had finally abated, and he was having a jolly good dream—actually a jolly *wicked* dream about making love to a beautiful woman. As she kissed her way down his side and lower toward his groin, he rolled on his back, offering her easy access. Her lips felt like slices of heaven, and her tender fingertips were soft as feathers as they made an exploratory trail across his body.

His manhood leapt with excitement as her mouth encircled it. Then her glorious tongue tentatively touched the sac beneath. What he wouldn't give to forget everything that had been bothering him and stay here with his dream woman. He wouldn't care if he never awakened.

Then cruel reality pummeled him. The tenants on Chadwick land depended on him to carry out his responsibilities so they could tend to the business of feeding and raising their families. He had to arrange a visit to America to go over sales figures at the ironworks. He groaned. There would be no respite for him, save for his night time imaginings. And what grand imaginings they were…

He reached out to fondle breasts, tipped with taut nipples. His hand followed the landscape of a nipped-in waist, smooth buttocks then silken thighs. The dream woman's mouth met his in an intoxicating kiss and as her tongue delved between his lips, it seemed as though someone had poured honey into his mouth.

"So sweet," he muttered as he rolled his dream woman over and pinned her beneath him, feeling his hard phallus press against the nest of curls between the juncture of her thighs.

"Sir Maxwell…"

The voice, Max thought. *It sounds so familiar.* He searched his memory and a second later, realized where he'd heard it before.

"Miranda?"

"Yes, I'm here—make love to me now, Max. Over and over."

"Mmm, nothing could stop me."

***

This is almost too incredible to be true. The thrill of conquest laced through Miranda. Maybe getting Max to make love to her wouldn't be so difficult after all. He seemed quite willing and able to comply. Of course, what hot-blooded male wouldn't be thrilled to wake up next to a warm, willing female body? Still, she'd expected more resistance.

She enjoyed another deep, soul-searching kiss with him, during which their tongues imitated the mating act. Goddess above, she was hot. And ready. Oh, so ready for him to take her.

Then Sir Maxwell did something terrible. He opened his eyes and gave her a long, perplexed inspection. As he looked her up and down in confusion, all her hopes of an easy conquest crashed and burned.

"Miranda!" He blinked at her several times, allowing his gaze to focus. "By Jove, you can't be a dream. I can actually *feel* you." Inhaling deeply, he added, "And I can *smell* you."

"Hopefully I don't smell like burnt toast anymore, do I?"

"Of course not, but what in the devil is going on?"

Chapter Three

Upon seeing Miranda pressed beneath him in all her naked glory, Max's jaw went slack. He could hardly believe his eyes. So, he hadn't been imagining her after all.

His dream woman had turned into flesh and blood. *And she was highly desirable.* He wanted her. Hot blood coursed lustfully through his veins. It was all he could do to take her right here and now.

But as much as he wanted her, and no matter how temping it was to make love with her, it wouldn't be right. Too many questions ricocheted through his brain, for example, how she'd gotten in his house and his room. He found it difficult to choose which one to ask. And even more difficult to fight down his animal urges.

"I say, how did you enter my bedchamber?" he finally managed. "Better yet, where did you go the other night? I swear by all that's holy I saw you ride away on a…a *broom!*"

She lifted a slim brow. "So many questions."

"Yes, and I'd like an answer to all of them." A muscle ticked in his jaw as frustration wound through him. This couldn't be happening, yet it was. The unreality of it all made him question, once again, his sanity. Somehow, he had to get a grip on himself.

As he talked himself into a reasonable state of mind, he reassured himself, once again, the woman in his arms was indeed real. There was no question of that fact. Why she had come here and wound up in his bed, was another matter altogether.

Flicking her tongue across her soft pink lips, she smiled up at him. Mesmerized, Max watched as the top of the sheets teased her nipples into pebbled crests. As those rosy half-moons peered out at him, uncontrollable tremors ached in his groin.

His head began to ache, and it almost seemed as though his body craved her, he wanted to make love to her so badly. What in God's name was going on with him? He had an uncanny urge to take her here and now, which would have been most inappropriate. He suppressed the urge to groan as he struggled against the overwhelming physical urges.

She smiled, obviously aware of the effect she was having on him. "Which question do you want me to answer first, Sir Maxwell?"

Control yourself man!

"It doesn't matter," he said in a gritty voice, his rigid penis about to burst from unfulfilled desire. "Choose whichever one you wish. Just answer me please."

Animal instincts continued to hammer him, telling him to take her first, and ask questions later. Always a man able to control himself, his logical nature prevailed. Unfortunately, not without an extreme measure of difficulty. Miranda's satiny skin and her soft body added to his inability to think straight, yet he was reluctant to release her for fear she'd disappear again.

"Okay," she responded in that unusual manner of hers. "To answer your question of how I got in here, I came in through the door."

"But I locked it last night."

She seemed to consider his answer a moment then replied, "Locks can be picked."

"What about the servants?"

Again, she hesitated. "I slipped past them."

He cocked his head to the side and studied her closer, noticing that one of her lids began to flutter. "That seems highly unlikely."

She rubbed her wobbly eye. "Unlikely or not, it happened."

"Tell me, where did you go the other night?" His brows furrowed. "And what about the broom?"

Miranda swore under her breath. The spell of forgetfulness she'd cast on Sir Maxwell obviously hadn't worked. Damn this seven-year witch disease. It was really messing with her mojo. Max remembered everything so she knew she'd better come up with some good answers quickly.

She shrugged. "A simple trick. I must be getting really good at it if you actually believed what you saw."

"I definitely didn't believe it," he said in a huff. "I merely wondered where you went."

"I was…around. I had to go somewhere to get cleaned up."

"Do you have family here in London?" His dark brown eyes glimmered with curiosity.

"Actually, I'm from America."

"Ah, you're from the colonies. Cheeky lot, that."

He gave her a look of disdain, as if the fact she hailed from America explained her unusual appearance and behavior.

"Please enlighten me, why have you come to my home and invaded my bed?"

A smile tilted her lips. "You were acting as though you liked it."

"I didn't say I wasn't enjoying myself." He cleared his throat. "I'm just not accustomed to waking up with naked women in my bed. At least not unless they were there when I fell asleep."

She shifted herself in the satiny sheets, uncomfortably aware she couldn't tell him the truth. How would he react if she were to say, *Well, I was itching with horniness and just had to get back here to find you…*

Conjure up some crocodile tears! Men always hated it when women cried. It got their macho genes totally screwed up. Even though Sir Maxwell seemed taken aback by her sudden appearance, she assumed he would behave the same way as a modern man.

She quickly sorted through various ideas in her head, trying to find what would get her all choked up. Clear as a bell, it suddenly came to her. All she had to think about was how upset and disappointed her parents would be if they came home and found out she'd failed her final task and had to repeat her entire battery of witch exams.

That's the ticket.

"It's just not good at home, Sir Maxwell," she murmured softly. "Things…things aren't right there. It's d-difficult to explain. Don't make me go back." She allowed raw emotion to well deep in her chest and managed to emit several heart-rending sobs. To further dramatize the effect, she buried her face in his broad, muscled chest and held it there, enjoying the musky scent of man mingled with tobacco and whiskey.

"You've run away from America, have you?" He cleared his throat and his voice sounded strained. "That was quite a long trip."

With stiff movements, he reached up to gently smooth locks of mussed hair away from her cheeks, cupped her chin and tilted her face toward his. "What's so terrible that you're this frightened? Has someone threatened you?"

"I honestly can't talk about it. You were so kind to me when we met that's why I hoped I could come here. I thought perhaps if I offered myself to you, you'd take me in."

Max cursed inwardly when he felt his resolve crumble. Once again, an ardent attraction to her rose within him. This was such uncharacteristic behavior for him to give into her feminine wiles. Was she really telling him the truth or was this some sort of parlor trick to bilk money from him?

Once again, he felt hot and confused, either due to his inappropriate fixation on Miranda or some strange malaise. His mind had fragmented into thousands of pieces and concentration seemed impossible. Even though he was concerned about the circumstances, a part of him wouldn't allow him to turn her away.

Her beauty intrigued him—definitely part of his reasons for entertaining the idea of allowing her to stay. Confoundedly, his inclination was to help her, even though he assumed he must be losing his mind.

To be fair, perhaps his inner instincts were trying to tell him something. It was entirely possible Miranda had come upon some misfortune, which is exactly what he'd suspected when he'd initially found her in the empty field. It seemed she wasn't willing to share that with him right now, but hopefully soon she'd let him know what had frightened her so much. He couldn't leave an injured animal lying in the street without trying to help it; therefore, he certainly couldn't ignore a human being's dire predicament.

"I feel so safe with you," she added. "And I have nowhere else to go."

That did it. For some reason, her words wound their way through his brain and the effects of a bizarre intoxication came over him. It seemed as though a fine wine ebbed through his veins and he couldn't resist her magnetism. She shivered and her warm body pressed even more intimately against his, drawing him deeper into her web of desire.

The urge to protect her outweighed his concern that a controlling father or abusive husband may come looking for her. He had no doubt if that happened, he'd be able to purchase their willingness to leave Miranda alone. Either that or he'd merely have a word with Queen Victoria and have the offensive fool deported from Britain.

Anything to keep Miranda safe.

Now he knew for certain he was either losing his mind or he'd been taken over by some strange force because his next words defied all logic and common sense. "Of course, you can stay here."

"You are too good to me," she mused, looking up at him with her large blue eyes.

Holding back a needful groan, he pushed down his male urges and declared, "But I'd never force you to earn your keep in my bed. That would be unconscionable."

"I honestly wouldn't mind." She studied him through long, tear-spiked lashes. "I don't expect you to let me live here for free."

"Bah, that's nothing for you to worry about," he said, feeling as if some entity had invaded his body and used him like a puppet to speak. "I wander around in this big empty house all on my own. I can certainly allow you to stay in one of the spare bedrooms."

She rested her head against his chest and sighed deeply. "Only if you are one-hundred percent certain, Sir Maxwell."

"Rest assured. And please, call me Max." He shook his head, wondering what in hell possessed him to invite her to stay. She could be some gutter snipe out to rob him blind! And he'd just asked her to live in his home as simply as if he'd asked her to tea.

What was this confounded, unusual attachment he'd developed to her? God help him, he had behaved so rashly with her. What strange compunction had come over him and why?

To top it off, he felt nearly feverish to make love to her and he wondered how long he could remain a gentleman around her. He only had so much self-reserve. Yet, he was torn between needing her and wanting to help her. If she'd suffered some misfortune, he didn't want to add to her problems. But if she was out to dupe him out of money, he didn't want to fall into her snare. It was confusing.

Max's penis was still rock hard, so he tried to coax himself into settling down. Unfortunately, the blasted appendage would have nothing to do with his cajoling. Gritting his teeth, he decided the first order of business was to get Miranda dressed so the temptation would be removed from his grasp. With that accomplished, he hoped he could think more clearly as well.

"The one thing I insist upon is that we find you proper attire," he told her in a ragged voice. "I'm sure one of my maids can lend you spare clothing. For the time being, however, please wear this."

"Whatever you'd like," she purred.

He reached for his red silk robe hanging on the bed post and handed it to her. When she stood and compliantly slipped it on, he saw a flash of her creamy thighs, full hips, and curvaceous backside. As she turned to face him again, his gaze lowered to her breasts and he noted how her erect nipples lifted the material in the most enticing way.

Sons of perdition help me. I've got to get out of here. Quickly!

Swallowing a groan of unfulfilled desire, he swung his legs over the edge of the bed and slid on his trousers, then stood and tugged them up. Shoving his arms into his shirt, he turned toward her. As the unbuttoned edges flapped about him, he asked, "Are you hungry?"

At the sight of Max's broad chest peppered with dark curls, Miranda longed to say, "Hungry for you." As she watched the dashing duke finish dressing, she realized he wasn't about to make love with her, at least not yet. No doubt his proper gentleman's upbringing prevented him from taking her right here and now, even though she'd offered herself willingly.

And as much as she wanted to do the deed with him, another urge needed to be satisfied. A rumble issued from her stomach at the idea of food.

"I'm starved," she admitted.

"I'll send up someone with a tray. In the meantime, I've got a business meeting, and I'm not certain how long I'll be gone." Tucking his shirt in his trousers, he backed awkwardly out the door.

***

He's so prim and proper! She giggled softly as he made his hasty departure. It was obvious she'd have to play this cat and mouse game for a while before he felt comfortable doing the mattress mambo. The duke's behavior was charming, but hopefully, it wouldn't take too long for him to warm up to her. Her final, unfinished task weighed heavily on her mind.

She had a Harry Potter wanna-be to deal with. Once she'd gotten the Philosopher's Stone from the little punk, she could achieve her dream of becoming a high witch. A dream she'd entertained ever since she'd been a kid. A thrill of anticipation shot through her. Her objective was so close, she could practically taste it.

The only thing in her way was seducing Sir Maxwell so she could cure this ridiculous seven-year witch disease. *Will I be able to leave him alone after seven rolls in the hay?* She recalled Tavis and how much he'd meant to her. It hadn't been easy to leave him, even though she'd been in danger of getting burned.

Literally.

This time, she vowed not to let her emotions get involved. She'd decided after Tavis to swear off dating mortal men. It was difficult to maintain relationships with them because their world was so different from hers. Despite her convictions, she wondered, after spending time with Max, what part of her would fare worse when all of this was over.

Her heart or her pride?

A knock sounded on the door and a man's voice called out, "It's Henry, Sir Maxwell's personal butler. May I come in?"

"Yes, of course."

Wearing a dark uniform and spotless white gloves, a man entered carrying a tray stacked with silver covered dishes. A maid carrying a dress, several petticoats, and shoes stood beside him. The delicious aromas tickled Miranda's nostrils and her stomach lurched.

"His Grace, the duke, requested that I show you to your room," Henry announced.

A moment later he'd whisked her into well-appointed accommodations down the hall. He invited her to sit in a tapestry-covered chair as he set his tray on a table. The maid quickly laid out the clothing on the bed, curtseyed, and left. Miranda expected Henry to leave as well, but he remained—his expression disapproving.

"Perhaps it's bold of me to broach this subject, but I wanted you to know that the last year hasn't been easy for Sir Maxwell. It was very difficult for him when both his parents and his brother died. And losing Lady Catherine was also difficult…" He cleared his throat and straightened, as though he felt he'd said too much.

"I'm so sorry for his loss." Concern tugged at her heart, and she wondered who Lady Catherine was. Wife? Girlfriend?

She'd never considered whether the duke might be involved with someone. Which made her face, once again, the depravity of her condition. *Shame on me for pursuing him for sex.* But considering her situation, she didn't have much choice. The least she could do was to make sure that he would thoroughly enjoy himself.

What hot-blooded man wouldn't want that?

Henry narrowed his gaze at her. "After Sir Maxwell's family passed on and he was required to take over the Duke of Pellamshire's title, he inherited numerous responsibilities along with the Chadwicks' large estate. He's a good man. I hope you're not trying to take advantage of him."

Ah, so that was it. Henry probably figured she was a gold digger, determined to fleece Sir Maxwell out of his fortune. Considering the circumstances, she didn't blame him. Though caught off guard by his accusations, she realized he was just concerned for Max's interests. She decided she'd better get this squared away with him.

"Sir Maxwell is just a friend and I appreciate that he's helping me through a difficult situation."

He relaxed his stiff, severely squared shoulders but still didn't look convinced. "Very good, Miss. However, if I discover that your intentions are less than honorable, I'll immediately report you to the authorities. Have I made myself clear?"

"Crystal."

Lifting a curious brow at her, he spun on his heel and left, closing the door.

Miranda ate the eggs, toast, and bacon on the tray, deciding she'd never tasted such scrumptious food in her life. Then she poured herself a cup of tea, sat down on the four-poster bed and sighed with relief. Hopefully when Max came back, they could get down to business.

Monkey business, that is.

With an appreciative eye, she glanced at the exquisite marble fireplace, the luxurious carpets, the silken drapes, and the carved furniture decorated with intricate needlepoint cushions. There was one thing about it—she'd definitely be comfortable as she plotted the duke's seduction.

Once again, she tried to deal with her hot-to-trot emotions and realized the disease had caused her libido to go haywire. Since she wasn't her typical self these days, she considered doing the duke on the dining room table or maybe she could find a sexy bear rug somewhere in front of a fireplace.

Who am I kidding?

Right now, she didn't care if they did it in a broom closet. Scratching her elbow, she realized she simply wanted to get the deed done then leave the poor duke alone. Considering the typical attitude in this day and age that men practically owned women, she wondered how Max would like it if he knew she only wanted him for his body?

Recalling her thrilling encounter in bed with him a short while ago, she shivered with anticipation. Even now she could still feel his warmth and remembered how his musky scent teased her nostrils. Goddess above, when he touched her…it had been wonderful.

The duke must be the most handsome mortal she'd ever met, hands down. She licked her lips. Now all she wanted for dinner was Sir Maxwell, served up naked on a gleaming platter.

***

The business meeting had been an excuse to get away from Miranda so Max could have an opportunity to clear his head, which by now pounded like a drum. His first thought upon getting away from the townhouse was to find his friend Edward and see what he thought of this entire Miranda business. Maybe Dundridge could talk some sense into him about how to deal with her, since he seemed unable to do it himself.

Unfortunately, the further he got away from home, the more his heart hammered and the more his head hurt. Pinching the bridge of his nose to try and clear his vision, he drove his carriage over to Edward's townhouse, not far from his own. Max needed his advice badly.

Unfortunately, Dundridge wasn't in, but the maid explained he was at the Hightower Gentleman's Club. Frustrated, but determined, Max drove across the city and parked in front of the venerable three-story brick establishment. He stumbled inside and raked a shock of wild hair away from his forehead. Rubbing his neck, which had begun to itch like the dickens, he headed to the large parlor.

Inside the smoke-filled, mahogany paneled room full of esteemed gentlemen and their whiskey decanters, he located Edward. Relief swirled through him as he charged toward his friend who sat in a leather wing chair beside Sir Percival Wyndham, one of London's highly respected bank owners. Conversing intently, the two played chess, manipulating the ivory pieces with calculated movements.

"There you are," Max said in a raspy voice as he met Edward's surprised gaze. "I have to talk to you. It's good seeing you, Sir Percival," he added as an afterthought.

"And you," Sir Percival returned with a bemused grin.

"I say, you look terrible old man," Edward commented. A short and stocky, good-natured fellow, he narrowed his gaze at Max and a lock of unruly brown hair slanted across his forehead. "You seemed rather out of sorts last night and it appears things haven't improved."

After the incident with Miranda, Max had returned to the pub to drown his confusion. While there, he'd run into Edward. During their visit, Max had been in a rather perplexed state of mind. He'd explained all about Miranda, even down to the ridiculous part about the broom. Now he felt like a complete fool; what had possessed him to actually believe she'd flown away?

A muscle ticked in his jaw. "Actually, they're worse. I've gone from bemused to completely bewildered."

Edward lifted a curious brow. "For some reason, I sense it involves that woman you spoke about last night."

Miserable, Max nodded.

Sir Percival pushed up on the arms of his chair and stood. He pointed to his gray hair. "See this, boys? It took a lot of women trouble in my day to earn it. If you don't mind, I'll leave you two to sort out the female dilemma." Chuckling and shaking his head, he picked up his cane and walked away.

Max slumped gratefully into the chair Sir Percival had vacated and rubbed his brow. Since he and Edward had been chums since childhood, both attending the same boarding school and Oxford University, he wasn't surprised his friend could read his mind.

"What's troubling you?" Edward asked.

"Miranda turned up this morning, in my bed, no less. Somehow she slipped past the servants."

Edward's nose twitched thoughtfully. "That could be good or bad, depending."

"Depending on what?"

"Whether or not she was naked."

Warmth filled Max's face. "The latter, of course."

"You said last night she is very pretty. What seems to be the problem, my friend?" Edward laughed and patted his rounded stomach. "Since I don't seem terribly attractive to the opposite sex, I wouldn't turn down such an offer myself."

Despite his own concerns, Max chuckled. "You are too critical of yourself, Edward. Women are fools if they don't see your worth."

"I suppose my looks are my cross to bear. Now, getting back to your female problem, what is amiss?"

"Aside from the fact I thought I saw her fly off on a broom, which I definitely must attribute to fatigue and whiskey, what kind of woman simply shows up naked in a man's bed?"

Edward held up his hands and shrugged. "A woman who wants something? I assume you know what."

"Yes, she obviously wants that—something most women don't care to engage in," Max agreed. "But what else? She brought nothing with her and there's something unusual about her. In fact, I have this strange impulse to give into her on everything and do everything she asks. It's as if she's got some extraordinary hold on me. It's completely irrational."

"Ask her to leave if you're uncomfortable."

"I tried, and I can't. I'm telling you she has some strange power over me. These curious circumstances have me boggled, and I'm not quite certain what to do."

"What do you want from me?"

"I've come to you for serious advice." Max breathed a ragged sigh. "Ever since I met her last night, my mind has been so fogged up I can't think straight."

"She's really gotten to you that badly has she?" Edward instantly sobered.

Scratching his arm, which had developed a perplexing itch, Max nodded.

"All joking aside, this is a different situation than I've ever encountered. Do you think perhaps she's gaming you?"

"I know she's not telling me everything, but there's a part of me that actually feels she is sincere. In a completely bizarre fashion, however. I'm just trying to decide how to proceed. I don't want to take advantage of her, but it's extremely difficult to resist when she's offered herself. She claims she's from America. Perhaps that's why she's so—forward."

"Ah, that explains a lot. She's definitely no proper, well-bred English girl. You know how rough-mannered the colonials are. I'd say get a bit more acquainted with her and if you have the inclination, let nature take its course."

Max rubbed his neck, which seemed unreasonably warm. "I'm sorely tempted to, even with all I've got going on in my life."

"All the more reason to partake of her offerings. You work far too hard and the diversion will be good medicine for you. If things work out and you're both agreeable, make her your mistress. You can set her up in a place of her own and sneak away on forbidden trysts together."

"I don't know..."

"Relax, my friend. What could possibly happen? God knows you have the resources to afford her. And if you happen to have a little Max or Maxine during the affair, it's not the end of the world. Many a man in the history of the world has fathered one or more of those."

"I'll consider the idea." Strangely enough, weight lifted from Max's chest as he entertained the idea of getting to know Miranda better. But he still didn't trust she would tell him the truth about why she'd sought him out. "Since you've spent more time at court than me recently, could you ask around about her, Edward? See if perhaps someone's missing a wife or a daughter. I fear she's running from something and I'd like to find out what."

"I'll visit with some of my associates. If you don't hear from me, you'll know I haven't discovered anything."

After visiting with Edward, Max's headache resumed with pounding force. Irritated at this frustrating interruption, he took a break from his business errands and drove by his physician's office. He described his symptoms to Dr. Hudson, also a longtime family friend, including his embarrassing propensity to want to make love to the young woman who had shown up most unexpectedly in his bed this morning.

"You're a healthy young man," Dr. Hudson said with a chuckle after he'd examined him. "I doubt there's anything wrong with you."

"But I barely know this woman. And when we're not together, I develop splitting headaches and itching episodes." He rolled up his sleeve and showed Dr. Hudson his rash-covered forearm. "Even my skin's affected and it itches like the dickens when I'm away from her."

Dr. Hudson handed him a bottle of ointment and a package of headache powder. "I think you've worried yourself into a dither, my man. Go home and get some rest."

Still perplexed by his behavior, Max spent the rest of the day taking care of affairs pertaining to his family's properties and their estate up north, Applewood Manor. Trouble was brewing between the tenants. He'd soon have to pay the place a visit in order to settle several boundary disputes. It seemed there was always something to take care with this duke business. He suffered a pang of regret, realizing this type of nonsense would consume the rest of his life.

On his way home, he paid a brief visit to a dressmaker and a cobbler, ordering a few things in what he assumed were Miranda's size or at least close to it. It was late evening by the time he finally returned home, and lights had already been dimmed. He was hungry, but too tired to care. Sleep beckoned, especially since he hadn't gotten much rest last night.

His footsteps echoed in the quiet house as he slipped upstairs to his room. Just as he was about to enter, he thought of Miranda and realized, with a jolt, that since he'd returned home his pounding head and body aches had disappeared. *Strange indeed.* Thinking it must surely be a coincidence as Dr. Hudson had suggested, he brushed it aside.

He supposed if he'd been in his right mind earlier, he'd have arranged a hotel room for Miranda, but in the absence of his commonsense, he'd asked Henry to set her up in a room down the hall. He envisioned her sleeping there at this moment. Unable to quell his curiosity, he walked softly toward her door and tapped on it.

There was no answer, so he opened it a crack. Once his eyes adjusted to the darkness, he saw her on the bed, her hair a golden sheath across her shoulders, like a lighthouse beacon. No doubt she was weary after her incident last night. And even though she slept, her exquisiteness filled the silent room.

Her naked, voluptuous shape was outlined by the sheets, detailing the curve of her hips and the rise of her ample breasts. A jagged breath caught in his throat, and warm desire flooded him. It was all he could do to prevent himself from waking her gently and making sweet love to her.

How unconventional that she would sleep naked. His gaze feasted upon her ravenously, and he was barely able to think of anything else but being with her.

How can I want her so much, when I barely know her? What is this strange hold she has on me?

He considered her mysterious behavior and her unusual manner of speech. Since she said she came from America, that would explain her choppy English and harsh accent. What in the devil was she running from? And what happened to her belongings? How could she have arrived at his home without a stitch of clothing to her name?

Is she a criminal, hiding out from the law?

No, that couldn't be it. He hadn't heard any reports from the constables about desperate individuals on the loose, and there'd been no stories in the newspaper either. He gripped the doorframe, as if by holding it hard enough, he could extract the answers he sought. Confusion ran rampant through his soul and he wondered, once again, why she'd come to him. *Remain wary*, he told himself, so he could avoid being caught off guard if she was playing some sort of game. Despite his indecision about whether or not to become involved emotionally with her, he still found himself intrigued.

I say, she is beautiful, probably the most fetching woman I've ever met.

Immediately memories of Catherine flooded him, and he felt almost disloyal to her memory and his abiding love for her, which he'd kept buried deep within himself for so very long. After she'd married Marley, he'd still cherished her secretly in his heart.

He recalled her burnished chestnut hair, rosy cheeks, and the fetching way she smiled. Yet she'd always remained distant and detached from him, despite his affection for her. Obviously, she'd never returned his feelings, and the reality sent a sharp pain through his chest. What a fool he'd been, nursing unrequited love.

He suddenly realized that as much as he'd admired Catherine, she'd never garnered his interest the way Miranda did. Ever since the woman had shown up in his bed, he'd been completely preoccupied with her and unable to allow thoughts of her to stray far from his mind.

So, what did his feeling for Miranda really amount to?

Curiosity, my man. Mere curiosity. And the fact you've been without a woman for far too long.

Fearing to delve into his sentiments any deeper than that, Max released a heavy sigh and returned to his room. Crawling naked into bed, he found, to his dismay, he still couldn't sleep, despite the weariness sifting through his bones.

Miranda consumed his thoughts, and a sharp longing rose in him. He remembered her warm, naked curves pressed up against him this morning and the softness of her lips on his body. Just imagining her smooth curves caused his penis to grow rigid and throb as it rested on his thigh. He could still *feel* her. She'd managed to somehow bury herself permanently in his thoughts, and it perplexed him.

Punching his pillow with frustration, he rolled over and buried his face in the feather-softness. From downstairs, the sound of the grandfather clock striking midnight drifted up to him. He yawned from exhaustion, rolled over again, swore, and at last mercifully fell asleep.

Eventually he dreamed of the attractive, mysterious woman he'd allowed into his home and his heart. It was easy to conjure up the vision of her loveliness, and just as easy to recall her enchanting touch that burned through his skin like silken fire.

Miranda, who in the world are you?

Chapter Four

The next morning Max rose bright and early. Though his first thoughts were of Miranda, he forced himself to focus on the work he needed to accomplish. He didn't feel he had the strength to deal with his confusion about her, so he forced her image to the back of his mind. After dressing, he made his way downstairs to the kitchen. Snatching a few pieces of bacon from a platter, he asked Edna, the cook, to bring a pot of coffee to his study.

Shortly after he'd seated himself at a large desk in his father's book-lined room, she arrived with the hot brew and placed it before him. He barely acknowledged her as he poured a cup and he began reviewing the ledgers. It took a while, but eventually he identified the property boundaries on every parcel of Chadwick land.

A measure of relief washed over him. He'd be well prepared to stand his ground with the tenants when he paid a visit to the estate. His goal was to quickly clear up their confusion and encourage everyone to settle their differences. Now he just needed to draw up plot maps, clearly marking the farming dimensions so there should be no confusion in the future. He'd also make copies for himself and file them away.

Noting that it was approaching noon, he rose and stretched his stiff muscles. His stomach growled. Sorely needing sustenance, he made his way down the hall. Laughter drifted to his ears and he paused to listen. It had been quite a long time since happy voices rang throughout his house.

Picking up his pace, he found Miranda in the kitchen visiting with the cook. A frown touched his lips.

What an unusual place for her to go, especially if she'd been raised by a wealthy family. Titled young ladies of the upper class did not spend time in the service areas of an estate, prattling away with the hired staff.

The thought occurred to him that she most likely hadn't been raised by noble, wealthy parents. She could be of humble birth and had perhaps spent her life among the serving class. Whatever the reason for her finding her way to the kitchen, she looked completely animated and so very beautiful; his concern quickly faded.

It really didn't matter where she came from. He still wanted her. Once again, his desire for her rose like an exhilarating mist—dismissing all rational and sane thoughts from his mind. As before, he was completely lost to the unique sway she held over him and sweat beaded on his brow. He watched her, transfixed, as though in a trance.

As soon as Edna, a heavyset older woman with pudgy cheeks, noticed him standing in the door, she blushed and gave a deep curtsey. "Forgive me, my lord. I...I..."

"Please don't be upset Max." Miranda, who had been leaning against a large butcher's block, stood up straight. "I distracted her. We were only discussing herbal cures and remedies."

"It's all right." He waved his hand dismissively, taking note of the way Miranda's blue dress clung to her curvaceous figure, accentuating her ample breasts, the curve of her hips and her nipped-in waist. It also matched her eyes, making the sapphire shade stand out with vivid clarity. Hair tumbled down her back in a cascade of shining ringlets, and he envisioned himself burying his face in the glossy golden curls.

His mouth suddenly went dry as a bone and a vein began to throb in his temple. Bloody hell, it was all he could do to keep from sweeping her into his arms and hauling her up to his bedroom. Again, he reminded himself she'd obviously come here to seek refuge, not to be ravished, even though she'd offered sexual favors in exchange for her room and board. As much as his mind knew it, his traitorous body wanted other things.

"Look what Edna's made for us." Smiling brightly, Miranda held up a large basket. Before he could utter a single word, she grabbed his arm and walked with him through the drawing room. She stopped in the spacious entry hall in front of the double entry door and looked up at him.

Something about his solid gaze at the basket must have made her take pause. "It's a picnic lunch, Max. I thought you could take a break. You've been working like a dog, and you're so uptight." She switched the basket to one hand and reached up to knead the knotted muscles in his neck with the other. "You need to chill, hon."

Her peculiar words barely made a dent in his mind and he continued to stare dumbly at the basket. Her wonderful touch loosened the tightness in his shoulders, and he finally found the words to speak. "I don't know…"

"Don't tell me you've never been on a picnic. That would be terrible."

"Yes, of course I've dined outdoors. It's just been a long time." He recalled his last day trip with Catherine at the park. It was a perfect June morning with brilliant sunshine and blue skies. That's when he'd asked her to marry him. She'd never answered and had refused to see him after that. Picnics conjured up painful memories. Even now, the sting of her callous dismissal twisted through him. "I don't like picnics, Miranda. Besides, I've got a lot of work to do."

"Can't you spare a little time for me? Just an hour or so?"

Despite his desire to be with her, he didn't feel as though he could do it. "I've got mountains of paperwork to complete. Edna can take her noon lunch break and go with you."

"No," she pleaded. "I want to be with you, Max. Besides, you must eat sometime. I bet you didn't even have a decent breakfast this morning, did you?'

Damn, but the girl was right. How did she know his stomach was gnawing on his backbone at this very moment? As if to prove Miranda's point, it gave a loud rumble.

"I knew it." She grinned triumphantly and pulled back the lid on the basket. "Have a look at all the scrumptious goodies Edna put in here. You know you'd like some."

He leaned over and studied the food, the aroma of which was enticing, yet he was more affected by Miranda's warm female body pressed up against his side. When his arm brushed against one of her breasts, his knees actually went weak. He couldn't help but admit to himself that there was nothing he wanted more than to spend more time with her. How could he resist?

Realizing how easily she'd broken down all of his opposition, despite his vow to try and not be affected by her, he felt himself giving in. "All right. I'll have Henry bring round the carriage. I know a nice spot by the river where we can enjoy our meal. But after that, I need to get back to work."

"Of course! Thank you, Max." She stood on tiptoe and kissed his cheek.

Incredible!

When she laid a hand alongside his cheek, his face tingled and his spirits soared higher than birds on the wing. He barely knew this woman and he had no idea where she'd come from or what her motivations might be.

How in the world had she captured his emotions so quickly? Her attractiveness, combined with her unique personality, proved irresistible. He found himself daring to hope that with her around, the melancholy he'd suffered over the last year might finally lift. The house seemed more alive and the weight on his chest seemed lighter.

I'm behaving like a complete fool!

Even though his irrational behavior started a niggling fear, he couldn't help himself. His enjoyment of Miranda's bright smile and encouraging presence could easily disappear overnight if the truth of her circumstances turned out to be of a dark nature. Numerous possibilities clouded his mind, but the moment he looked at her again, it was as though all of his concerns were instantly banished.

As she tugged him toward the door, the present circumstances seemed to be all that mattered. Because of the remarkable pull she had on him, he had no choice but to push his worries to the back of his mind. Admittedly, after all the troubles he'd had to deal with recently, he wanted to take pleasure in her. Miranda offered a breath of fresh air.

To hell with everything else. He intended to enjoy every minute of this afternoon with her.

***

It had been a long time since Miranda had been in a horse-drawn carriage, and she found the ride quite enjoyable. Sitting beside Max in the jostling conveyance, she grew more comfortable with him as they chatted about the lush, rolling green hills, the low stone fences, the farmsteads, and the people who lived there.

She'd lived in Britain a few centuries ago and had spent quite a bit of time among the mortals. But time had a way of fading those memories. Now she recalled with vivid clarity the quaintness of this simpler way of life. It made her long for less confusion in her soul, and she realized how driven she'd been lately while on assignment from the council.

During a pause in the conversation, she lifted her head and closed her eyes, enjoying the gentle breeze caressing her cheeks. This was very relaxing. She'd been so busy lately, completing tasks to become a full-fledged high witch. There had been no time to pursue leisure activities. Now she realized what she'd been missing.

Max's large warmth pressed against her side filled her with tingling desire. Her goal to find the Philosopher's Stone now seemed unimportant. She could almost forget everything that had been on her agenda back home. It occurred to her she was attracted to the duke in a major way and she wondered if everything she felt for him could be attributed to the seven-year witch disease.

Stick to your plan, Miranda. Seduce the duke and hot foot it out of here. Don't let your emotions get involved.

Initially, the prospect of having sex with Max had consumed her every thought and she'd wanted to get it over with quickly. But as time went on, she realized she enjoyed spending time with him. A part of her wished it could remain like this forever—a man and a woman getting to know each other. Yet she knew it couldn't last.

She came from an entirely different world than his, and she had to be careful not to let him know the real nature of her visit. She had no idea how Max would react if he found out who and what she really was. It could prove extremely dangerous if he found out, especially if it happened before she got her powers back.

"You looked content for a moment, now you look worried. What's on your mind?"

Max's voice jerked Miranda out of her intense thoughts. "Many things," she returned.

"I'm still curious about why you came to me for help." His dark, questioning gaze met hers briefly. Then he glanced at the horse, grasping the reins with a white-knuckled grip. "Do you feel comfortable enough to confide in me about your troubles yet?"

Son of a monkey!

He wanted more information. She couldn't blame him for probing. She'd be wigged if some guy showed up in her bed one morning, too. The problem was she simply couldn't admit the truth.

She chewed her lower lip for a while, stewing about what to say, when she spotted a grassy spot along the river. She pointed at it, hoping to divert the direction of their conversation. "Let's stop there."

It worked. He drew the carriage over to the side of the road and parked it alongside the bank, then helped her down. Carrying their lunch and a blanket he'd taken off the seat, he walked with her toward a shady area under a grove of trees. He spread the covering on the ground and placed the basket on it.

Concerned that he'd begin questioning her again, she knelt and arranged the food on plates, slices of crusty bread, meat, cheese, and apples. After talking most of the way here, they ate in silence. When they'd finished, she poured them both glasses of wine and handed him a goblet.

"Henry told me about your family, and I'm so sorry. How did they pass?"

He drank slowly, his face clouded with emotion. When he set aside the glass, his expression was grim. "It was a fever. I'd been called off on a military duty the summer they died, and I begged them to spend the hot months at our estate in the country, but they insisted on staying in London. Both my father and brother had pressing business to attend to and scoffed at my concerns. While I was away, they were at home dying."

Seeing the pain in his eyes made Miranda's heart squeeze. "You warned them—you did all you could."

"Somehow I feel as though I should have done more to save them. I feel responsible for what happened."

"It's not your fault, Max." Realizing he suffered from survivor's guilt, Miranda set aside her glass and scooted closer to him, feeling his thigh tingle with electricity through her clothing. She took his arm and held it close, attempting to ease the ache of his loss. "I know how terrible it is to lose a person you love, and you lost several."

He looked down at her, his eyes glimmering with a strange light. "Is that what happened to you?"

She searched his gaze, recalling Tavis and the difficulty she'd had making her decision to let him go. "Yes, but he didn't die. I left him."

His brow furrowed. "Why?"

"It was too dangerous to stay, but believe me, it broke my heart to say goodbye." She felt the familiar twinge of angst at her separation from the man she'd loved. Even after several centuries, it still wasn't easy to deal with the grief. She closed her eyes, willing the tears not to come.

"Miranda, look at me."

Max's deep and commanding, yet tender, voice prompted her to let go of the ancient sorrow. When she felt his strong hands gentling cupping her face, his rough thumbs stroking her cheeks, she looked at him.

"Is that why you came to me? Are you running away from him?"

She swallowed hard, realizing she absolutely couldn't tell him the truth. Would it really hurt anything to let him believe she was fleeing from a lover? Mulling the idea briefly in her mind, she decided it would be for the best.

"Yes," she told him in an uneven voice, using the raw emotion at having to leave Tavis to her advantage.

"If he hurt you, I'll find him and make him regret it. I promised that night in the field that I would protect you and I still intend to." Anger at the man who had hurt her flashed in his eyes. And something else.

Protectiveness.

It warmed her heart to realize that even after the short amount of time they'd known each other, he wanted to help her. His old-fashioned chivalry appealed to her feminine nature, and she recognized his integrity and genuine honesty. She'd play hell ever trying to find a man like him in the 21st century.

Guilt twinged in her stomach at the idea she was misleading him. Somehow, she managed to justify her white lies by claiming it was necessary and convinced herself he surely wouldn't be hurt by it.

"He can't get to me anymore, Max. He's far away from here."

His brows furrowed. "In America?"

She nodded, going along with his assumption. Pressing a hand to his whiskered cheek, excitement rippled through her. The sound of hot, rushing blood filled her ears. She felt more alive than ever. Colors were brighter, sounds stronger. "You're a unique man, Sir Maxwell. And I admire you greatly."

He licked his sensuous lips. "Enough to allow me to kiss you?"

She traced an index finger on his shirt, right above his heart, which now seemed connected to hers. Her voice dropped to a breathy whisper as she returned, "I thought you'd never ask."

His dark, hypnotic gaze held hers, their eyes exchanging the hint of their inner desires. Whether or not her longing for the duke was due to the disease, he'd evoked a dangerous passion from the depths of her soul. An intense passion she'd never known she possessed.

Miranda tried to tell herself the disease made her feelings stronger, but somehow, she doubted it.

She tilted her head up as his mouth crushed over hers, every inch of her prickling with arousal. He drew her into the curve of his arms and pressed her against his chest, as though he never wanted to let her go. Her nipples hardened in response and her nether regions moistened in anticipation.

Dizziness threatened to overwhelm her, but she held onto the moment and to the feel of his mouth claiming hers. Beneath her snowstorm of petticoats, a tropical heat wave blossomed.

Abruptly, he pulled away and stood. "I apologize. I shouldn't have asked to kiss you. You must think I'm a beast."

"I'm no China doll, Max," she murmured, savoring the lingering sensation of his mouth on hers as she rose up beside him. She took his hand and kissed the work-roughened palm. "And I'm definitely no shy, retiring female; I'm a woman with desires."

"I appreciate your eagerness, Miranda. But I can't allow myself to take advantage. What kind of man would I be if I did?"

"A happy one?" She grinned saucily.

He chuckled. "I imagine I'd savor every minute of making love to you, but it's rather unorthodox for us to be together. You came to me for protection—not to be ravished. And what if there were...*consequences?*"

She knew exactly what he referred to. "You don't need to worry about that. I'm unable to have children." With a mortal, anyway, she thought. Only with a man of her own kind, one with magical abilities such as a male witch or a wizard, would she be able to reproduce.

***

Concern gripped Max's thoughts, and he wondered about Miranda's impatience. Well-bred young ladies did not typically allow men to take liberties. But if Edward was right, it could be she held a lighter view of sexual relations since she came from America.

If that was so, he didn't seem able to deny himself the opportunity to enjoy the pleasures she offered. However, he knew he was playing with fire—she was no woman to be toyed with and had proven that by leaving her previous lover.

Throwing caution to the wind, he gathered her into his arms and captured her mouth with his again. There was no stopping him now. Heat inside of him had churned to a dangerous point and he couldn't hold himself back any longer. The taste of her honeyed lips—the lips of an angel—encouraged him, making him want more than stolen kisses. He cupped one of her breasts, stroking the soft mound through the material of her dress.

She groaned and arched her hips against his, inviting him to explore other regions of her supple body. His cock grew hard, pressing against his trousers, begging for release. Perspiration dotted his brow as he pressed her back against a boulder, his hot mouth trailing across the hollow of her throat then down to her pale cleavage.

To his eager delight, her borrowed gown did not have numerous ruffles like other fashionable female attire, but offered a simpler, scooped neckline. He unlaced the top and lifted out one of her breasts, sucking the rosy-tipped nipple into his mouth. A nearly animalistic sound rumbled in her throat as she drew his head closer, her fingers buried in his hair.

"Miranda," he whispered roughly against the petal-soft skin of her flushed cheek. "Are you certain you want this?"

"Yes Max," she returned eagerly, her blue eyes bursting with fiery zeal. "More than you know."

As if she wanted to indicate her willingness to make love with him, she began to tug at her gown. Chuckling, he helped her shed her clothing. Once she stood before him in naked, curvaceous glory, topped off by a light fuzz of hair at the juncture of her thighs, he stripped. He never expected such eagerness from her, but found it refreshing, rather than having to teach a virginal maiden the facts of life.

As he stepped from his trousers, his penis sprang from its confines, hot and eager to seek satisfaction. He spun her around and pressed her against a boulder, which was exactly the perfect height. Leaning over it, she sucked in a breath and wriggled her backside invitingly, taunting him.

Her body language said it all—she didn't have to ask him twice. Parting her nether lips, he thrust a finger inside her and swirled it around, anxious to make sure she was ready. Her responding moan let him know she would gladly welcome him.

Guiding his cock, he slipped the tip inside her moist cavern and she reached behind to grab his hips, as if she feared he would pull away. He began to thrust, moving slowly at first then building up a rhythmic tempo. Comfortable in this position, he reached around to find her nipples, which he pulled between his thumb and forefinger and pinched softly.

The harder he plunged inside of her, the more she pushed her buttocks against his, moaning and muttering encouragement. His strokes intensified, taking him higher and higher, until he exploded with a shuddering groan.

As he spilled into her, she clamped herself around him, as if she intended never to release him. Drained and exhausted, he curled over her and rested, nibbling the soft curve of her neck. Incredibly she began to move her hips again until the friction caused him to grow hard once more. As he began to move inside of her, his girth increased as her warmth closed around his cock.

"You're a greedy little wench, aren't you?" He drew the tender flesh of her ear lobe between his teeth and began to nibble.

"Mmm, don't you like it?" She reached around to stroke his thigh.

"Hell yes!"

After he'd reached his pinnacle, he spilled himself inside of her with a final thrust. They stayed together for a while longer, caressing and exploring each other's bodies.

Max was amazed. He'd never known a female with such a sensual nature, and she intrigued him like no other.

At some point, they parted and began to hastily don their clothing. As she tucked stray hair behind her delicate ears, he noted how captivated he'd become by each of her moves.

The angle of her slender hand, the tilt of her head, the softness of her creamy shoulders as she reached to lace the top of her gown. Each gesture seemed intricately calculated to draw his eye. His mouth went dry and if it weren't for decorum's sake, he'd lay her down in the grass and take her again.

Glancing at the sun sinking in the sky, he realized how long they'd been out here. He trusted his servants not to start passing around scandalous gossip but knew they would surely be wondering about the two of them by now. And anyway, simply having her living in his home would raise eyebrows.

"Here, let me do that." He gently nudged away her fingers and tied the black silk ribbon into a bow. When he met her gaze, his insides filled with incredible warmth, and he realized he was more in danger of drowning in those limpid blue eyes of hers than the ocean.

"I've never met a woman like you Miranda. You're…insatiable."

She grinned. "Is that good or bad?"

"Definitely good." He lifted hair away from her brow. "Though you've thoroughly drained me this afternoon, I feel better than I have in a long time."

Lowering down, he kissed her deeply, amazed that a woman like her had simply shown up on his doorstep. As she clung to him, wrapping her arms around his neck, he knew one thing for certain. He and Miranda's passionate natures were well matched.

For a long time, he'd believed the only mistress he would ever need was the sea. Miranda had changed his mind.

Chapter Five

Leaning into Max's warm, muscular body, Miranda felt more relaxed than she had in a long time. His musky, spicy scent, which had become familiar by now, wound its way through her nostrils, filling her with a zing of excitement. There was something about his smell that made her breath catch in her throat.

As he drew his carriage to a stop in front of his large, shuttered red brick townhouse, she realized this must be one of London's upper-crust neighborhoods. Surrounded by emerald green lawns and lush gardens, the residence literally reeked of the Chadwick family's nobility and old money.

But it wasn't his sumptuous lifestyle that impressed her. It was Max. She'd come here intent on seducing him, not thinking about anything else but getting what she needed. So far, her ploy was working, yet she realized that with his masterful touch, he'd turned the tables on her.

Rather than her being the seductress, he'd been the one to capture her soul and her essence. Though Max was a mortal, he possessed a finer magic than any other man she'd met in her life. Delight bubbled in her chest, and she counted herself lucky that her crazy disease had chosen to bestow him with her favors.

Be careful, Miranda. Don't get too attached to him. You're only with Max for one thing.

Ignoring that small, annoying voice of reason, she allowed herself to fall further into infatuation with him. What could it possibly hurt? Once again, she ignored the voice that added, *more than you know...* She refused to listen to self-reproach. After all, she'd been around the block a few times. She knew what she was doing.

"You have a beautiful home," she murmured as she reached up to nuzzle the juncture between Max's shoulder and neck.

He kissed the top of her head. "It was my mother's pride and joy, along with the house at our country estate."

"Are you lonely, living here with no one but your servants?"

"It's not what I'm used to," he said with a nod. "I've always had people around. When I'm at sea commanding my ship, I have my crew. At home, I'm used to having my parents, Marley, and Catherine..."

When he trailed off with a pained expression on his face, she questioned him further. "Who is Catherine? Henry mentioned her to me."

He didn't answer as he handed the horse's reins over to a male servant that had come out of the livery stables. Helping her down, he took her elbow and guided her up the gravel path toward the entrance.

"Max? I asked you a question."

"I know you did. It's difficult to answer." He cleared his throat. "Catherine was my brother's wife."

As she observed him closer, she noticed a myriad of expressions flicker across his face. Many were hard to distinguish, but she eventually detected profound sadness. "What happened?"

He took her hands in his and met her gaze. "Do you really want to know?"

"I told you about my past." Well, not all of it she realized, but enough for now.

"I asked her to marry me, but she chose to walk down the aisle with my brother instead. As the oldest son, he stood to inherit all of this." He nodded toward the house. "And the duke's title."

"How did that make you feel?"

"Like a numbskull."

"I know you had feelings for her Max, but she must have been a very shallow person to behave that way."

He nodded. "It was a definite blow to find she could so easily transfer her affections."

"What happened to her?"

"She died in childbirth along with the babe. It was a boy." He lowered his gaze. "I was upset at her for throwing me over for my brother. But she didn't deserve that."

Miranda lifted a shock of dark hair away from his forehead. "Of course, she didn't. And you didn't do a thing to cause what happened."

When he looked at her again, the hollow, pained appearance his eyes held a moment ago had disappeared, and now twin fires of passion burned in their depths. Very slowly, he brought his sensuous lips down to hers, meeting them with such tenderness that a sweet ache spread through her abdomen.

He teased her mouth with his tongue, eliciting her eager response as he drew her into his arms and held her against his broad chest. Every feature of his tall body pressed into her, and she thrilled to the sensation of his very evident maleness prodding her hip.

Her clothes seemed scratchy and hot. She wanted them gone—wanted his gone, too. "Max, can we go somewhere?"

Sucking the skin on her neck into his mouth, most certainly leaving major hickies, he muttered, "You want to make love? Again?"

"I told you, I'm a woman with needs…"

"Evidently. And I'm not complaining."

Opening the front door, Max swept Miranda into his arms, thoroughly enjoying the feel of her hot, persistent body pressed against his. All thoughts of propriety had long since vanished. He wanted her and that's all that mattered. With long, eager strides, he headed toward the stairs, intending to take her up to his bedroom where they could continue their unique sexual explorations of each other.

He needed her, like a man in hell needed a drink of water to quench his thirst.

For the life of him, he couldn't quell this yearning. She understood him like no other female ever had. With Miranda, all the control he had over his emotions went out the window. He'd never thought he'd never feel this way about anyone again. Surprisingly enough, here he was, completely mesmerized by the woman in his arms; ready to open his heart to her enthralling charms.

Halfway up the staircase, as Miranda rested her head against his shoulder, a small voice warned him to beware, that this whole scenario was too good to be true. The throbbing in his groin prompted him to disregard it. His urges were too powerful, too intense. Nothing could stop him—

"Maxwell Avery Chadwick. Whatever is going on?"

Except that.

Swallowing the frustration that had lodged like a lump of clay in his throat, he turned slowly toward the landing. Aunt Winifred, his father's sister, stood down there, her hands shoved on her hips, her expression extremely disapproving. Behind wire-framed spectacles, fire and brimstone burned in her hazel eyes. In the midst of her gray hair, which had been pulled back into a severe bun, two horns seemed to sprout.

The devil in a spinster's dress.

"Oops," Miranda whispered. "I think you'd better put me down."

Feeling as though he was eight and still wore knickers, Max allowed Miranda to slip from his arms and stand. The heat in his groin dispensed, leaving him with an emptiness he knew only Miranda could fill.

"Bloody hell, Aunt Winifred. Why do you insist on these surprise visits? I didn't know you were coming today."

She snorted. "Obviously. What kind of nonsense are you carrying on in my brother's house?"

Max grasped Miranda's hand and led her back down to the landing. He lifted a stern brow at his bossy aunt. "It's my house now," he reminded her, though he realized for propriety's sake, this did look bad. "And it's my business what goes on here."

"Hmmph." She squared her shoulders and lifted her sharp, pointed nose into the air. "I suppose you've paraded your little trollop all over London, besmirching the Chadwick name. You and your scandals will be the death of us all."

He winced at the word *death.* They'd experienced enough of that the last year and he didn't even want to hear the word spoken aloud. He was tired of death and dying. And even though his behavior with Miranda was questionable, he was unable to stop it. Again, it was almost as though he'd been possessed, and his actions weren't his own. But he couldn't explain all of that to Aunt Winifred. Hell, he couldn't even explain it to himself.

Weary of his Aunt's constant histrionics, he glared at her. Ever since his parents had died, she'd decided it was her job to keep an eye on him. The problem was she stirred up more trouble than she settled.

Paying no heed to her outburst, he told her sternly, "You should have let me know you were coming so I could be more prepared."

"Yes, I suppose I should have. You could have swept the rubbish out of the house before I arrived." With a sniff, she glowered at Miranda.

"It's so nice to meet you Winifred." Amazingly, Miranda smiled at his haughty aunt. She didn't seem to be bothered one iota by the woman's cold reception.

"*Lady* Winifred," his aunt responded haughtily.

"Ah, yes of course. *Lady* Winifred." Miranda gave a lovely curtsey. "I'm sure the two of you have a lot to catch up on. I believe I'll go up to my room and take a nap. I'm very tired." She shot Max a meaningful glance and warmth rose in his face.

"I'll have Henry fetch you when supper is served," he told her.

As she walked around him, her breasts brushed against his arm, leaving a trail of sizzling delight before she climbed the stairs and disappeared.

Disappointed at not being able to properly douse the fire consuming his loins, he tried to decide what to do with his interfering relative. He was in a quandary—go to Miranda or pay his aunt the proper respect? Gadzooks, why did she have to show up now? Her timing was most inconvenient.

"I appreciate you stopping by to visit, Aunt Winifred. How long do you plan to stay?"

"Just for the night. I'm on my way to Somerset and I thought I'd stop to see how you are getting on. Thank goodness I did." After a deep sigh, she launched into one of her typical rampages. "Maxwell, I simply will not tolerate you having *that* woman in this house. It's unseemly. I know men typically keep mistresses tucked away but have some decorum and set her up in a place away from here."

He folded his arms across his chest. "I'll choose where Miranda lives. Remember, I am the man of the house."

"Hmmph, you're not showing very good judgment in my opinion."

"I didn't ask for your opinion." He met his aunt's disapproving gaze straight on. "And she's not leaving."

***

Miranda practically floated on air as she entered her bedroom and flopped on the sumptuous four-poster. She stared up at the white tray ceiling, decorated with carved frescoes of flowers and cherubs. Things were working out splendidly so far. How many times had she and Max made love now?

She held up a hand, recalling the hours they'd spent together, and ticked off two fingers. "Five to go," she said, feeling completely wanton. Never in her life had she pursued a man for the sole purpose of having sex. Now, she couldn't get enough of it—she was addicted. It was practically all she thought about.

It was wrong to treat sex like a game, yet deep down, she couldn't help but admit how fun it was with Max. She could get used to having him around. When bright color caught her eye, she rolled to face the tall mahogany wardrobe in the corner. Earlier today, it had been empty. Now it was bursting with fashionable long gowns and frothy negligees.

Max must have taken the time to pick out clothing for her in between his business meetings this morning. Warming inside at the idea, she muttered, "What the heck have you done, sweetie?"

It didn't take long for her to hot foot it over to the wardrobe. Each of the brocade gowns was richly appointed with frills, ruffles, and bows. A row of shoes peered from beneath the skirts, the pointed toes reminding her of days gone by when she'd actually lived during this era. The clothing had been glorious.

Despite her enthusiasm at Max's kindness, her insides leapt at the idea of wearing the lovely items. He had exquisite taste and the clothing was gorgeous, even though she'd rather have worn jeans and a T-shirt. Nevertheless, since he'd gone to all this trouble, she decided she'd enjoy his generosity. She reached for one of the gowns then guilt stabbed her middle, sharp as a knife.

Liar, liar, pants on fire...

Poor Max thought she'd suffered some sort of calamity, and she'd managed to be so evasive. Shame on her, she allowed him to believe she needed his protection. He was spending good money on her and showering her with affection.

If he only knew her motives. But it wasn't forever. After they made love five more times, she'd zip herself back to Wysteria to concoct another plan to catch the wizard. Max would become ancient history. Literally.

How would he feel when she disappeared on him again? How would *she* feel?

"Son of a monkey," she mumbled. Catherine had broken his heart once. How could she live with herself if she hurt him again? Warning bells clanged in her head as the intensity of her feelings for Max pitched into overdrive. She was quickly approaching the danger zone—getting involved with him, even though she'd warned herself not to.

Desperate at where her emotions were heading, she tried to convince herself that maybe she was worried about nothing. She didn't know for certain what he thought about her. He was a man, after all. What healthy male, historically or in modern day, wouldn't take a woman up on an offer of sex? It didn't mean anything. Just because they'd spent several hours of ecstasy and bliss together, it didn't mean he'd be upset when she left.

There, now I feel better. I got myself worked up over nothing.

Having managed to justify her dogged chase of the man, she decided to put the whole incident into perspective. After it was all over, she'd go on to successfully complete her final task and become a high witch. Max would continue with his duke business, and someday when he was old and gray, he'd reminisce about their brief interlude with a smile on his face. Anyway, by the time their affair ended, her powers would be restored, and she should be able to wipe his memory. That way he wouldn't suffer any after effects of their time together. If she really concentrated on what she was doing, the spell should take this time.

She took a deep, cleansing breath, clearing away the bad aura that had settled about her. Feeling ridiculous for getting so sappy about the whole episode, she pawed through the gowns until she found one to her liking. The least she could do was dress to the hilt and give him some eye candy to take to dinner. Wouldn't that put a bee in old Aunt Winifred's bonnet?

Giggling, she slipped out of the plain blue dress.

***

"You really don't need to leave, Aunt Winifred." Frustrated, Max leaned against a wall and folded his arms over his chest. He'd tried for the last two hours to convince her to stay, but she refused. Stubborn, stubborn woman.

She picked up her small black bag and shot a meaningful glance up the staircase. "One of us has to go. And since you refuse to put that chit of a girl back on the street where she belongs, it'll have to be me."

"You've gotten yourself worked up over nothing."

She rolled her eyes. "Maxwell. Don't tell me you've been hoodwinked by that little trollop. She's only after you for your money, can't you see that? Why, if your parents knew how you've been carrying on, they'd roll over in their graves. And poor Marley, too."

"I'm not *carrying on* with her. I like her. You'd like her too, if you would simply allow yourself to get acquainted."

"Well, that's certainly not going to happen. I can only hope and pray you'll soon come to your senses before it's too late, young man."

With that, she stormed out into the gathering darkness toward her waiting carriage. Following on her heels, Max helped her inside and shut the door securely. As the coach rocked down the drive, he shook his head at his aunt's obstinacy. It wouldn't have hurt her to stay a while longer and get acquainted with Miranda. But he realized in her world, things had to be done with proper decorum. And neither of those words fit into his new relationship with Miranda.

But he couldn't begin to explain to Aunt Winifred what Miranda did to him. He had no idea how it would all end, but he intended to enjoy it while it lasted.

Contrary to what Aunt Winifred and other society matrons may think, he didn't give a whit about Miranda's background. If he wanted her in his life, he'd have her, and nothing would stand in his way. Edward was right. He had the financial stability and influence to set Miranda up as his mistress in any fashion he desired.

Hurrying back inside, he took the stairs two at a time, intent on finding the woman who'd been on his mind day and night. Eagerly, he rapped on her bedroom door. When she didn't answer, he opened it and peered inside. She was gone.

Fearful that his aunt had scared her away with her nonsense, he hurried back downstairs. He'd take out a carriage and hunt her down if necessary. When his butler approached, he asked breathlessly, "Henry, have you seen Miranda?"

Cool and respectful as usual, Henry lifted a curious brow. "She's in the dining room, sir, where you instructed me to take her at supper time. Is something amiss, sir?"

"No, no. Everything's fine…" Feeling like an idiot, Max hurried into the dining room, lined with sideboards and glass-fronted cupboards filled with fine china dishes and the glass figurines his mother had collected. Thinking of his mother, his heart squeezed. Damn, he missed her.

She would have understood why he liked Miranda, even though she may not have approved of the strange circumstances surrounding their relationship.

His gaze swept the area, searching for the woman who currently consumed his attentions. She sat at one end of the long, mahogany table, but she looked very different. The young lady in the simple blue dress had been transformed into a vision of extraordinary feminine magnificence that bedazzled his eyes.

A shimmering green gown hugged her voluptuous curves like a glove, while her hair had been swept to the side in a simple style that allowed her hair to fall in a cascade of ringlets across one of her bare shoulders. The gown's lowcut top revealed her creamy breasts, cradled perfectly into the snug bodice.

When she smiled, the chandelier light paled in comparison to the illumination in her heart-shaped face. God, she was beautiful—more beautiful that any woman he'd ever known.

"You look wonderful," he managed, though his tongue had gone slack and the ache in his loins, which had become all too familiar of late, flared again. He sounded like a blubbering idiot and felt like one, too.

"You think?" She patted her head. "The hair isn't anything fancy, but the gowns you chose are fantastic. I really like this green one."

He wet his lips. "So do I."

"Thank you so much for getting those things for me. You really are a sweet man, you know that?"

"Sweet?" He chuckled. "I've been called many things in my lifetime. But never sweet."

Grinning, she nodded at the seat next to her. "Come sit down."

He slid into the chair, seriously considering skipping dinner and taking her straight to bed. Aunt Winifred's surprise visit had halted his earlier plans and he longed to sweep her into his arms and carry her up to his room. Unfortunately, it looked like his sexual needs would have to wait to be sated because the servants were already carrying out platters full of steaming food.

Miranda lifted a pale brow. "Where's your aunt?"

"She was called away unexpectedly."

"She doesn't like me, does she?"

"Aunt Winifred doesn't make friends easily."

"That's okay." She shrugged. "I'm just sorry I made her so uncomfortable."

"Don't worry. She'll be back again to haunt me another day. She means well. Unfortunately, her eccentric nature often drives me to distraction."

"Relatives." Rolling her eyes, she added, "Can't live with 'em, can't live without 'em."

Max laughed, astonished, once again, at how comfortable he felt around Miranda. Her attitude about everything carried a certain devil-may-care ring, which always improved his mood. By Jove, but the girl was refreshing and unique. She brightened this dark old house like a lighted Christmas tree.

Directing her comments to the kitchen staff, she rubbed her stomach and said, "You guys, this looks awesome. Thank you so much!"

She continued to speak freely with the servants, and didn't display an ounce of disdain toward them, like a spoiled society chit born with a silver spoon in her mouth. Before long, she'd engaged every one of the servants in conversation.

They sent hesitant glances at Max, apparently concerned with acting overly friendly toward her. But his smile must have let them know it was all right, and as they carried in trays and plates, placing them on the table, they began to visibly relax.

For the first time in his life, Max realized what nice people they were, and he felt ashamed at never bothering to get to know them better. Before long, Miranda had drawn out various tidbits about their lives such as the names of their wives, husbands, or their children, and where they lived.

It was incredible. Her behavior intrigued Max so much that he sat, chin in hand, completely amused by what was transpiring before his very eyes. The fact that he leaned an elbow on the table—very bad manners indeed— didn't even occur to him.

As he did every night, Henry presided over the kitchen staff as they served the various dishes. A savory soup started the meal, followed by the main course of roast mutton and spinach pie, and finally a sweet vanilla pudding Max had ordered especially for tonight.

No matter how he tried, he couldn't keep his gaze off Miranda. He observed, spellbound, as she ate the food off her fork, her pearly white teeth nipping at the tender morsels. She licked her lips enticingly, watching him with those luminous blue eyes of hers, taunting and teasing.

He knew exactly what she wanted him to be thinking—of that mouth of hers on his manhood. Even now the very idea of it made him grow hard, and he shifted in the chair, trying to get comfortable. *Impossible.*

"Do you find the meal to your liking?"

"Absolutely." She winked then flicked her pink tongue across a tidbit of mashed potato that still lingered on her fork. Setting aside her utensil, she sank lower in her seat, sipping from her goblet filled with sparkling ruby claret. Her gaze rested only on him, devouring him with its intensity.

When he felt something softly kneading his cock, he glanced in surprise down at his lap. Miranda's stocking-covered toes peeked out from beneath the white table cloth as they prodded his bulging crotch. To his complete amazement and immense pleasure, she continued to tease his rigid flesh.

By George, what a talented girl! Does she have any idea what she's doing to me?

Considering the sheepish smile on her face, she obviously did. Feeling as though his cock was ready to burst, he clenched his jaw and suppressed a groan. Though he was eager to go somewhere private with her, he also realized an overabundance of food remained. He glanced at Henry, stationed across the room with a prim expression. Thank God he couldn't see what she was doing to him.

"The meal was most excellent," Max told him. Noting that his voice held a strange tightness, no doubt to Miranda's persistent manipulations, he cleared his throat. "Please divide up the leftover food between yourself and the kitchen staff."

Henry blinked. "Sir?"

Max nodded. "As a matter of fact, please do that after every meal from now on."

"Very good, sir. I'll see that it's done straightaway."

"Thank you." As Max picked up a spoon and prepared to at least taste the pudding, Miranda held up a hand.

"Stop!"

He slowly lowered his utensil and stared at her. "Is something wrong?"

"No, something's right." Gripping her dessert bowl, she met Henry's stoic gaze. "Is everything ready?"

"Yes, Miss."

"Henry, you're a doll." After blowing him a kiss, she turned to Max. "Come with me. And bring your pudding."

Pushing back his chair, he rose beside her, brimming with curiosity. "I say, what's happening?"

"It's a surprise. Bet you can't catch me!" Grinning saucily, she ran from the dining room.

Feeling foolishly frisky himself, he followed her at a vigorous pace, wondering what in the world she was up to.

Chapter Six

The seduction chamber awaits...

Hands on her hips, Miranda took quick stock of everything she'd prepared in Max's bedroom. Since she wasn't able to use magic to attract him, she'd been relying upon feminine wiles. They may be a bit rusty, but so far everything she'd done had worked out well, and she was pleased with the results.

Nevertheless, her greedy seven-year witch disease existed like a living entity and it demanded more sexual encounters—five to be exact. Practically a slave to the lust coursing through her blood, she felt the need to conquer Max sexually and she envisioned him on his knees, begging her to make love with him. Though she doubted a lusty man like him needed much coaxing, she decided she'd give him some incentive by setting the proper mood.

While Max had been occupied visiting with his Aunt Winifred, she'd slipped downstairs and collected a basket of petals from the expansive rose gardens out back. After spreading them on his large bed in a velvety red carpet, she'd opened his veranda door to catch the light evening breeze.

True to his word, Henry had orchestrated the delivery of a large bathing tub filled with hot, steaming water. Though he'd been a loveable old grump about it, the butler had also agreed, with much cajoling, to bring her a collection of fat candles which she'd placed on the fireplace's marble hearth. All she needed now was some soft music, and she wished she had her iPod, but the gentle night sounds drifting through the window would have to suffice.

Quickly, she stripped out of her stiff dress, leaving on only the lacy, lavender-colored negligee that had been amongst the clothing in her wardrobe. She was lighting the last candle when Max finally burst into the room and stood in the doorway.

Breathing heavily, he leaned over and gripped his knee caps. A moment later, he straightened and said, "By Jove woman…I could barely…keep up with you."

"I work out a lot," she replied.

"Work out?" He gave her a puzzled look. "What does that mean?"

"It's not really important." She held out her arms, slowly spun around and faced him again. "So, what do you think? Nice, huh?"

He kicked the door shut, placed the pudding on a table next to hers, and raked his fingers through his dark hair. His chocolate brown gaze flared with a hunger that had nothing to do with food. Need—raw and consuming—smoldered in their depths.

"You look much more than nice," he said in a deep, raspy voice. "You look ravishing."

He wants me. Again. Miranda's heart flip-flopped and her insides trembled with warmth. She smiled. "I need you, Max."

"And I need you." How amazing, he thought, realizing her very presence made his cock spring to life. She commanded the appendage like a conductor led an orchestra. "Even if you are the most brazen, shameless woman I've ever known."

She wet her lips with the tip of her tongue. "Does that bother you?"

"On the contrary, my lady. I'm quite intrigued." Her silken flesh beneath the wispy negligee fabric taunted his ravenous gaze. He drank in the sight of her milky cleavage thrusting from beneath lace that barely concealed the rosy tips of her nipples. The cleft between those two tantalizing objects drew his gaze and held it, while the smell of female, raw and sensual, teased his nostrils.

Once again, he entertained the titillating idea of making love with her. He'd been thrilled with the time they'd spent together at the picnic. But this—this was more than he could ask for. Most women he knew, except for those who plied the flesh trade, shied away from sex. Miranda amazed him—she obviously enjoyed it. He could hardly believe she'd prepared all of this just to seduce him.

It was bold; it was audacious.

And he loved it.

He briefly considered what the servants may think about all the questionable activities happening between himself and Miranda. Now he realized there would be no stopping it. The hot rumors would spread rampantly all over London about Sir Maxwell Chadwick and his new woman. For once, he didn't care about them and he threw caution to the wind.

To hell with the gossips.

"Take me again," she murmured as she edged up to him. Reaching up, she pulled off her negligee, then she began to unbutton his shirt. "I need you."

Perspiration sprang to his brow as he studied her naked beauty. His mouth watered. "This is most unexpected, Miranda. I really should retire to my study and get some more work accomplished—"

Her persimmon mouth closed over his, silencing his protests. She took his face between her hands and kissed him deeply, thrusting her tongue into his mouth and allowing it to mate with his own, mimicking the lovemaking act.

It occurred to Max that upper class women saved themselves for marriage, giving away their virginity over only their husbands. What had happened to Miranda that she behaved so wantonly? A wave of desire washed away his questions and they disappeared from his mind. Right now, he didn't care. He liked being with her and he liked what she was doing to him. For once, he wasn't the pursuer. He was being pursued, and he found it invigorating.

Groaning with desire, he gathered her warm shape into his arms. She remained there only briefly, then pulled away and reached for a bowl of pudding. "Strip and lay down on the bed. And whatever happens, you can't touch me."

A muscle ticked in his whiskered cheek. "You're giving me orders now, eh?"

"I think you're going to like this."

"Indeed. We shall see."

Once Max had removed every stitch of his clothing and shucked it aside, Miranda watched as his thick penis bounced free of its confines. With a mischievous grin, he hopped onto the rose petal-covered bed and leaned on one elbow. His large, muscled physique in repose on the flowers created a very interesting picture. Miranda wished like hell she had a camera.

"What now, mistress?" He lifted a dark brow.

"I'm going to blow your mind."

"You're going to *what?*"

He gave her a strange look, as though she'd lost every one of her marbles. With a giggle, she added, "Relax and enjoy this, Max. Forget all your troubles—just let them fade…"

Crawling on the massive bed beside him, she dabbed pudding on his penis which sprang insistently against her touch, bouncing off his hair-swirled groin. Then she lowered down and licked the tip of the hard, velvety appendage, tasting the vanilla flavor mixed with his musky essence. A thrill of excitement pulsed through her as he groaned and gripped the bed covers in his large fists.

"Miranda…you little minx…"

Electrified by his response to her gentle assault, she now began to lap at the vanilla pudding coating his shaft. Slowly, she lowered her mouth up and down then reached underneath his scrotum to tickle the soft, wrinkled flesh.

"Ahhh," he cried raggedly. Spreading his legs, he thrust himself into her mouth, his hips arching in an erotic frenzy as she began to suck harder.

"You're killing me woman," he finally growled. Then he wrapped her in his large arms and flipped her onto her back. His lips captured hers possessively, and his tongue delved into her mouth, swirling and claiming all that was his. With calloused fingers, he stroked the length of her, feeling her tremble. His hard penis rested on her thigh, hot and ready to seek her core.

Miranda finally broke free and murmured, "Max, you should have let me finish."

"No, now I'm giving the orders and I say it's your turn." Retrieving a bowl of pudding, he dabbed the creamy white substance onto her nipples. He licked and laved it off slowly then closed his sensuous lips around her nipples and began to suckle.

Miranda moaned and watched, in a haze of passion, as he dribbled a trail of pudding down her abdomen and stomach. Licking it off, he kissed a blazing trail down her torso, down her abdomen, and finally, across her mound. Parting her legs, he positioned his dark, shaggy head between her thighs. With his large hand, he tenderly separated her nether lips until the found the small nub that brought her pleasure.

Licking flames threatened to consume her as his hot breath raced across her quivering center. His eager fingers prodded her moist folds until they opened easily to his touch. Burying her fingers in his hair, she drew him closer, bracing herself for his sweet onslaught.

"Hurry, Max. Take me before I die…" A moan rose in her throat, low and needy as his tongue sought and found her clitoris, teasing and licking until her thighs quaked in anticipation.

He alternately nipped and sucked the flesh as he probed first one then two fingers into her molten core. A rhapsody of pleasure wove its way through her, driving her to higher and higher pinnacles until at last she burst into a million pieces. A shuddering sigh escaped her, and she grasped his shoulders, hauling him up so that his cock dangled against her nether lips.

"You must take me," she insisted, the hot-cold sweat of lovemaking coating her body in a fine sheen, causing her to shiver. "Now!"

"Such a demanding wench," he murmured huskily, her intimate honey glistening on his lips. "But I'll happily comply."

With that said, he drove himself inside her, thrusting mightily until he came in a great wave. In and out he pulsed, grunting with exertion. Finally, his breathing settled to harsh rasps and he relaxed inside her.

"By George, that was one dessert I won't soon forget." He kissed her forehead. "Stay the night with me Miranda, my sweet."

"Don't worry; I won't leave your side."

Leaning back on an elbow, he played with one of her nipples, watching with amusement as it pebbled in the pale starlight streaming through the window. "You won't be uncomfortable if the servants realize you've warmed my bed all evening?"

"No."

He grinned. "You truly are a shameless woman! I find you completely without compunction."

"I know what I want when I see it. And I want you, pure and simple." She winked at him. "Does that bother you?"

"Hell no."

"Good. Then never stop what you're doing to me."

"Are you this insatiable with everything in your life?"

"Not always. You're a special exception."

"Lucky for me."

Max began to tickle her sides until she squealed with delight then tickled him back. Their muffled laughter filled the chamber, until their play turned into serious lovemaking once again. By the time they were ready to bathe, the water was tepid, but that didn't stop Miranda from enjoying the silken feel of the depths against her skin as they made love yet again.

Activity in the room did not cease until the early hours of morning, when the stars began to fade into the canvas of pale lavender sky.

***

Even though he and Miranda had been up until the wee hours, Max awakened early, just as he did each morning. In order to maintain his busy schedule, it was a necessity. He quickly slid on his trousers, a shirt and boots, then walked over to Miranda. She looked so comfortable and completely at home in his bed.

Her hair splayed in a golden waterfall across her shoulders and the pillow. Her sweet face glowed with a radiance that he dared hope he'd put there, and the roses in her cheeks made the flowers in his mother's garden pale in comparison.

Hunkering down, he gently lifted hair away from her forehead, considering her loveliness to be finer than any work of art. As he concentrated on her soft breathing, he noted her clear, creamy skin tone rivaled that of a goddess, and he had no doubt Venus would envy the matchless curve of her hips, the faultless contour of her breasts, and the smooth lines of her graceful limbs.

A powerful beauty resided within her, and he'd discovered that her qualities sparkled uniquely, like facets of the finest gemstone. She made him laugh; she made him cry. She reached within the depths of his soul and brought out the best in him. With her, the world seemed to be a much better place than it had been before she'd come into his life.

Who are you Miranda, and why did you come to me?

Rubbing his forehead between a thumb and forefinger, he questioned the providence that had brought her here. Thankful for whatever event had caused her to cross his path, a slow smile spread across his lips. He still ached for what he'd lost—his parents, his brother, and Catherine. However, since he'd met Miranda, the sting of his sadness had lifted. Incredibly, he envisioned being able to live the rest of his life carrying the memory of his loved ones in his heart, rather than pining his life away for what could have been.

Max glanced at Miranda in a new light. Despite her optimism, she seemed preoccupied by some worry. He often saw a distant look in her eyes and a furrow would form between her brows.

He made a solid vow that he'd do everything in his power to help her find her way again. It was the least he could do since she'd brightened his life. He wondered about the chap she'd mentioned, the one she'd left. No doubt the foolish brute had abused or insulted her in some way.

A surge of protectiveness washed over him. Confident he could knock the knucklehead over with as single blow, he itched to do exactly that. Yet it appeared Miranda wished to handle matters herself. She was indeed a most unique young lady and his admiration for her ratcheted up several notches.

What will I do if she decides to leave me before I can ask her to be my mistress?

A muscle ticked in his jaw. That idea was difficult to consider, yet he knew there would come a time when she may want to go. As much as he wanted her in his life, he couldn't hold her against her will. Hopefully, she liked this arrangement as much as he did, but he may be hoping for too much.

Leaning over, he kissed Miranda's soft cheek and watched her snuggle deeper into the sheets and blankets, which were still littered with rose petals. He liked her unusual approach to love making. Her techniques may be most unorthodox, and in most circles considered unladylike. Nevertheless, he'd bypass all high born, well-trained women of nobility in order to be with her.

You're dawdling, my man. You've got hours of work waiting for you.

Sighing with reluctance at leaving the side of such a vision, Max pushed to his feet and stepped into the hallway. He plucked a long-stemmed rose from a vase and brought it into his bedroom, placing it on the pillow next to Miranda. A slight chill had crept into the area overnight, so he tucked the covers around her shoulders.

Making his way downstairs, he ordered breakfast and a pot of coffee to be brought to his study once again. Gathering papers and his quill pen, he sat down at his desk to begin the day. To his dismay, no matter how hard he tried to concentrate, he couldn't entirely shake the mental image of Miranda, writhing in ecstasy beneath him as they'd made love last night.

"You're one devil of a distraction, woman," he muttered as a grin touched his lips. "A distraction I could easily become accustomed to."

***

Sleep slowly released Miranda from its grip and as she became aware of her surroundings, a smile came to her lips. She wriggled beneath the sheets in delight, recalling how incredible last night had been. Max was, hands down, the most skilled lover she'd ever been with. Of course, considering this was the nineteenth century, he seemed surprised by her forwardness and had seemed hesitant by her eagerness at first.

Most women in this day and age weren't quite as obvious about their sexual needs. Typically, the things she'd done with Max last night would be left to brothel women. Though it had been a long time since she'd lived during this time period, she still recalled the popular opinion of the day. It was so sad how repressed women were.

Nevertheless, Max had seemed completely pleased with her performance. And, to her credit, she'd scored three more touchdowns. Soon, she'd be on her way to deal with the punk wizard. After getting the Philosopher's Stone from him, she'd hot foot it back to the witch's council to present them with her prize.

Then a strange disappointment wound through her—disappointment that her time with Max would soon end. Also, disappointment that she'd met him under these circumstances, and not at a time when she could have relaxed and enjoyed getting to know him better.

Another emotion gripped her heart, and she recognized it as longing. A large part of her wanted to simply forget about everything back home and stay here with Max. If he wanted her to, that was. Nevertheless, she sensed he wouldn't object if she made her wishes known.

Yet she had a problem. Her high-achieving parents would frown upon her decision to throw away all she'd worked for to live her life with a mere mortal. Following their parents' example, her six sisters had all achieved such goals as becoming nuclear physicists, neurosurgeons, geologists, psychologists, financial strategists…and the list went on.

Here she was, simply trying to become a high witch of the coven, and she wanted to toss it all aside for a man?

Oh, my word. They would give her grief if she ever admitted to what she was thinking right now. Besides, she couldn't hide the fact that she was a witch. Eventually, Max would find out that and no doubt be upset. People in this century held many incorrect notions about her kind, and she assumed Max did as well. In fact, she feared he may even be afraid of her.

It really wasn't meant for them to be together, just because the seven-year witch disease dictated they had to make love seven times. Their affection for each other had been manufactured by this physical condition, nothing more. Again, she reiterated to herself that once she got what she needed, she should move on. Her stomach clenched, realizing that since she was afflicted with this condition for life, as Ursula had told her, every seven years she'd have to deal with a similar situation.

It could be worse.

"Right," she muttered facetiously, wondering what that would be. Focusing on what she needed to finish up with Max—two more lovemaking sessions to be exact, she rolled over, intending to give him a unique breakfast in bed. She blinked, realizing he was gone.

However, a red rose rested on the pillow at her side. Picking it up, she inhaled deeply of its sweet fragrance. Max was so thoughtful. He'd make some lucky girl a great husband someday. Her heart squeezed, realizing it wouldn't be her.

Hoping Max hadn't gone too far, she donned his robe and hurried to her room. She dressed in one of the new gowns he'd purchased—a simple, dove gray affair that fell away from her shoulders with a soft ruffled collar and nipped in at her waist. She drew her hair up into a simple bun and secured it with hair pins she found in a dresser drawer, then hurried downstairs to the dining room. A tall, grandfather clock let her know most of the morning had passed, and it was fast approaching noon.

She smiled, realizing she and Max had stayed up into the witching hours last night. It's no wonder she'd slept so late—she'd been exhausted. He must have been just as tired, yet he'd obviously risen early. There must have been a good reason for him to start cracking as soon as the rooster crowed.

"I assume you're looking for Sir Maxwell," Henry said as he came around a corner, his hands tucked behind his back. His dark uniform impeccable as usual, he added, "He's in his study. It's down the hall, third door on the right."

"Thank you, Henry." Miranda started to leave, but Henry's voice made her stop.

"I haven't seen Sir Maxwell this happy in a long time. And I never thought I'd hear myself say this, but I think we all have you to thank for that."

Miranda smiled at the unexpected compliment. "Why, thank you Henry. You have a good day." As Henry smiled and resumed walking toward the kitchen, she hurried toward the study and knocked on the door. "Max?"

"Miranda, please come in."

When she entered, he looked up from a desk piled high with parchment paper. He clutched one in an ink-stained hand. "Did you sleep well?"

"Incredibly. Except for the fact you left me. I missed you when I woke up."

He colored slightly and his expression took on a mischievous appearance. "I'd have liked to stay, but duty calls."

"What kind of duty?" She came up behind him and massaged his shoulders.

Sighing, he sat back in his chair and tapped the desk papers. "I've been poring over boundary maps of our estate property. Some of the tenants are bickering and I've drawn up duplicates for them so I can settle their dispute once and for all."

The fleeting thought of Xerox copy machines and the like crossed Miranda's mind and she realized how far mankind had advanced since 1877. But Max was a man of his time and he copied things longhand. No wonder his duties were consuming.

"Will the land owners come here to pick them up?"

"No, they're too busy tending to their crops and livestock. I'll need to travel north to meet with them. Our family's country estate, Applewood Manor, is up there. I'll stay a few days and settle the affair."

The blood drained from Miranda's face. Feeling faint, she sat on his desk and took his hand in hers. "When are you going?"

"This afternoon."

Her breath caught and she chewed her lower lip, aware what would happen if they were apart. "You c-can't go. I w-won't let you."

His brows arched. "I appreciate your eagerness to be with me, Miranda. Believe me I don't really care to go either. However, I must attend to this—it's very important."

She rose and began to pace, feeling unusually sensitive. Every fiber of her being pinged with anxiety and her head had begun to ache. Just thinking about Max being gone caused her ridiculous disease to wreak havoc. A silent curse rocketed through her mind.

"Why do you have to leave me?"

He tapped the desk impatiently. "Come now Miranda, you must be reasonable. It's only for a few days. You're more than welcome to stay here until I return. Or if you prefer, I'll arrange a hotel for you."

"Can't I go with you? Please?" The desperate note in her voice made her wince. She wasn't used to begging, and it struck a weird note in her.

"I'm afraid it will be terribly boring for you at Applewood Manor as there's not much to do. I'll be occupied most of the time with business. I'll have to meet with the farmers quite a bit. I'm certain that even though I'm providing them with maps, they'll want me to actually walk the boundaries so they can use stone markers to set them off."

"Max, it's important to me. It's hard to explain, but I can't be away from you."

"Honestly, I believe you'll be happier staying in London, even though I'd enjoy having you with me. Wouldn't you rather to do some shopping in the city? I can even have Henry escort you to the theatre—"

"I don't want to do any of that," she interjected. "You see, I...I'm afraid. Afraid of what might happen." She scratched her upper arm, just thinking about how she'd be ravaged by patches of itchy skin, a hairy chin, and a tongue the size of Manhattan if he got very far away. The thought of lapsing into that tormented creature again made her shiver, and a sob caught in her throat.

Max pushed aside his paperwork and stood. He gripped her shoulders gently. "Bloody hell, Miranda, are you afraid this fellow you told me about might show up and cause trouble?"

Chewing her lower lip to quell its trembling, she nodded. Inside, she castigated herself for her weakness. Shame on her for allowing Max to think she was being stalked by some madman in order to elicit his sympathy. *What else can I do, considering the circumstances?*

He drew her into the warm comfort of his arms and patted her back. "Of course, you can come with me. How thoughtless of me not to consider your circumstances. I'll have Henry send a trunk up to your room so you can pack your things."

"You don't know how much this means to me," she managed, filled with relief.

He pressed his lips to hers in a reassuring gesture, chasing away the demons that had threatened just a few moments ago to devour her. His arms, wrapped so possessively around her, tamed her heart's wild beating. When he finally pulled his mouth away, both of them were breathless.

"You are such a brilliant presence in my life, Miranda." He smiled. "Even this dreary trip will be delightful with you along."

"Believe me, I'll make it worth your while."

He lifted a brow. "Indeed?"

"You won't be disappointed." She smiled, concentrating on her need to be cured of the seven-year witch disease. A familiar twinge at the idea of eventually having to leave Max caught in her chest but she did her best to ignore it. There were more important things to concentrate on.

Like how to ramp up her seduction of the duke a notch or two. Goddess forbid that he should ever grow tired of being with her before they'd hit the magic number seven.

Chapter Seven

Max watched Miranda leave his study, mesmerized by the sway of her hips beneath her gown. His mouth went dry and his ardor rose, hardening his groin. Bloody hell, what that woman did to him was nearly a crime!

As the door shut behind her, he closed his eyes, his nostrils tingling with her lingering feminine scent. His mind immediately filled with questions about the mystery woman who had walked into his life. They swirled with such intensity it was difficult to pluck one from the air and concentrate properly on it.

He sat back in his seat and raked a hand through his hair. In such an incredibly short time, she'd become quite attached to him, and he to her. What would cause him to become so easily captivated?

In the year since his family had passed away, he hadn't been with a woman, and had been totally preoccupied learning the Duke of Pellamshire's duties. Duties so mind-numbing and dull he'd had little time to socialize. Perhaps the novelty of breaking his chaste lifestyle caused him to be so damnably infatuated. Or it could be the highly unusual circumstances of Miranda's appearance in his life.

Either way, the woman had provided a sweet distraction to his ordinary, tedious existence. The fact that she wanted to be with him day and night might be flattering, but he knew it more than likely indicated a serious problem from her past.

He entertained, once again, the very real possibility that a cruel husband or a controlling father may be distraught at her absence and would absolutely not be pleased to know she'd found a safe haven in his home. No doubt her fear of being discovered, without him there to protect her, prompted her to insist upon riding along with him up to Applewood Manor. While he welcomed her company, it also struck a note of serious concern in his gut.

Someday soon he would probably have to face reality and deal with the truth. He wasn't terribly worried about it, however. He had enough influence to thwart any jaded fellow from the lower classes or otherwise. Foul individuals like that had appeared more than once in his life, and he assumed the dirty sot could easily be paid off to leave her alone.

He *was* worried about Miranda's reaction afterward, though. Once she realized he'd banished the hounds of hell that pursued her, once she realized she was truly safe, she wouldn't need him anymore. Would she leave him then? His throat became unusually tight, and he told himself to quit being such a fool about her.

He'd been used by a woman before and tossed aside like a piece of rubbish. Catherine's betrayal still burned in his chest, and just thinking about it brought the entire painful incident back, as if it had happened yesterday. He'd told himself at the time that he'd never put himself in the position of being vulnerable with a woman again. Ever since then, he'd been careful not to allow it to occur.

What am I risking by being with Miranda?

A frown touched his lips as he toyed with the idea of whether she would hurt him. By growing as close to her as he had, he knew it was a real possibility. She was a sweet girl and he was thoroughly entertained by her. He felt drawn to her gregarious personality and she made him laugh—something he hadn't done in quite a while.

Nevertheless, as easily as she had flitted into his life, she could flit away. He would be saddened by her absence, but until that happened, he couldn't help himself from wanting to be around her. She was the one bright thing in his life, like the stars that guide sailors through the dark seas. Gritting his teeth, he stood and looked out the window at carriages clattering through the street.

As he gripped the wooden frame, he examined the true nature of his feelings for Miranda. He admired her greatly and thoroughly enjoyed making love with her. He sympathized with her plight. Groomed to be a gentleman from the time he was young, he couldn't idly stand by and see her abused by anyone. If that was indeed the case.

It wasn't necessary to let his feelings for her go any deeper than that, but he knew it would be a struggle to prevent them from expanding. A sigh escaped him as he thought about his request of Edward to seek information about her. Since his friend hadn't contacted him, obviously he hadn't discovered anything. Her background still remained a black slate of questions.

"Bah, this is stuff and nonsense that I don't have time for," he growled to the empty study. Attempting to shake off his dark mood, he gathered up his maps and put them in a leather case. He had work to do, and it wouldn't do any good to spend the day brooding. When the time came, he'd deal with whatever the future had in store for him. Meanwhile, he'd do his best to protect Miranda from harm, and protect his heart from being stolen.

***

Leaning forward in the rumbling carriage, Miranda watched the passing English countryside with its gentle green rolling hills and ridges of trees. A dome of blue, cloudy sky arched over the landscape, and a bright sun showered the area with bright, cheerful rays.

She could barely wait to reach Max's estate. She wanted him now as she felt his large, warm body sitting so close to hers. A shiver of excitement shot up her spine and she realized she was becoming far too attached to him for her own good.

Her time with him would soon come to an end. She only had to make love with him a couple more times before her powers would be restored. Then her search for Balthazar the Wizard and the Philosopher's Stone could resume. As a numb reality spread through her, her hands and fingers went cold.

Son of a monkey!

Somehow that quest didn't seem as exciting as it used to. A part of her wished she could stay here with Max, forget all about becoming a high witch and competing with her families' numerous accomplishments. But it just wasn't practical. He was a mortal and she was a magical being— the two simply didn't mix well. She could never have children with him, he would die long before she went onto her next plane of existence. Besides, the fact that she was a witch might not sit well with him.

He'll never understand my powers or appreciate my abilities.

It occurred to her that she'd never even tried to explain what she was. He'd never been able to make up his own mind, but it was probably for the best. He'd been able to rationalize her riding away on a broom by believing he'd imagined it all. How in the world would he deal with the truth—that what he'd seen *was* real and that she was an actual witch?

If all that wasn't enough, there was the problem of their differing life spans. She would live on for many more centuries, while he would eventually pass away. Sooner or later, she would have to learn to live without him. She decided it might as well be sooner so that she didn't delay the inevitability of their parting.

"I say, you're terribly quiet, Miranda. Do you feel well?"

Max's deep voice cut through the fog of her ponderings. Trying to quash the growing anxiety in her soul, she attempted to find something that would take her mind off unpleasant matters.

"I'm fine," she finally said. "I've just forgotten how lovely it is around here."

"Has it been a while since you've been out?" Max's serene expression faded.

"Actually, it has been. You could say I've been cooped up far too long."

He drew her chin between his thumb and forefinger and turned her face toward his. Alarm flared in his chocolate brown eyes, and he bristled with male protectiveness. "Has some brute had you locked away? Just tell me his name. I'll find him and deal with the scoundrel in an appropriate manner."

A thrill shot through her at his sensual touch and at the concern filling his voice. It may be quaint and rather old-fashioned, but it was also appealing. For the first time in her life, it made her feel wanted and totally cared for by a man. Something she'd always longed for but had never actually found. Not even with Tavis.

Max was *sooo* damn cute. Her very own hottie Mc-hottie. *How am I going to be able to leave him when the time comes?*

Refusing to dwell on unpleasant thoughts, she pushed away her concerns and focused only on the man seated next to her. For now, anyway, she had him exclusively to herself—even if it was only for a little while longer. She needed to make the most of it because after she'd gone, the memories of their time together would have to suffice.

He eyed her closely, as if he peered into her very soul. "Tell me, Miranda. Don't be afraid."

"It's nothing as dramatic as that, Max," she replied, appreciating his concern but not wanting him to worry needlessly. "I've just been busy lately."

His stiff shoulders relaxed. "I see. I've had the same problem myself. My duties seem to consume most of my time."

"I think we both work too hard. We're so stressed out. It's a shame." Weariness seeped into her bones and as she yawned, she leaned her head against his broad chest and snuggled closer.

Softly stroking her hair, he lifted an inquisitive brow. "Stressed out? Whatever does that mean?"

"It's like we're frazzled and uptight by everything going on in our lives." Lulled into sleepiness by the swaying of the carriage, she drifted off, her nostrils filled with Max's musky scent. Her dreams were filled with him.

***

Though Max didn't much like traveling in a cramped carriage, this ride gave him much pleasure. Miranda's head was pillowed on his chest, and she slept contentedly as she leaned against him. No doubt her fatigue stemmed from the bedroom pursuits that had kept the both of them up past any decent bedtime the last couple of nights. A wry grin touched his lips, and he decided their passions were well matched.

When the carriage slowed down, he glanced through the window at the fertile meadowland littered with cattle, horses, and sheep. Beyond that, the village of Pellamshire rested on a chalky, limestone hillside overlooking the sea. Rooftops of Saint Mary's Church, the town hall, the jail, the King's Inn, and numerous thatch-roofed cottages crowded the small burg, which was surrounded by a boat-filled harbor. Residents enjoyed a rich fishing industry in addition to their farming pursuits. It was a good place to make a living.

Miranda yawned, rubbed her eyes and sat up. "Where are we?"

"Not far from Applewood Manor."

She blinked and looked outside. "It looks so peaceful."

"I spent a lot of time here as a youth. We usually visited during the warm months of summer and early fall when illness typically ravages London…"

He trailed off, thinking of his family and how he'd lost them. When he felt Miranda squeeze his hand, he met her soft blue gaze. He knew she understood what he was feeling right now.

"I'm sorry for your loss," she murmured.

He squeezed her hand in return, his heart filled with the knowledge that she was all his, at least for now. Somehow that lessened his pain. "Though I'm not a religious man, I believe my family's in a better place."

"I have to agree with you." She cast a glance toward a grassy ridge where a large, red brick residence sprawled like a giant crab. "What is that?"

"Applewood Manor. My family's country estate."

"It's huge. And it looks really old." She continued to examine it curiously as the carriage drew closer.

"It was built in 1548, but the surrounding property has been in our family's possession for more than four hundred years. It was awarded to one of my ancestors by royal charter for his uncommon valor in battle."

"And the people who live around here are Chadwick tenants?"

He nodded.

"I see you truly care about them. You've been working day and night, slaving like a dog to sort out their troubles."

Surprised once again by her unusual wording, he smiled. By now, he should have become accustomed to her manner of speech, but it still caught him off guard. "Their welfare is my responsibility."

"I admire your dedication."

"I do my best, especially considering I'm new to all of this. I never planned to inherit the duke's title."

"Really?"

He nodded. "I trained to become a naval officer. Settling disputes among tenants is much different than whipping a crew into shape aboard a ship."

Her pale brows lifted inquisitively. "How so?"

"Aboard ship, the men have to follow orders. They're not allowed to speak back to a superior officer. If they do, it's considered insubordination and they can be court-martialed. Even though I'm the steward of the Chadwick's land, there's less discipline involved. Men are free to argue their points."

"That's what happens when men aren't enslaved."

"True, but it can be trying at times."

"Speak softly but carry a big stick."

He studied her with amusement. "I say, that's good advice. Did you just make that up?"

"No." She smiled. "Someone much wiser than me said it once."

They pulled into the estate's wide gravel drive, which was surrounded by large trees, lawns, and hedges. When the carriage finally rolled to a stop, Max opened the door, jumped out and helped Miranda step down.

She whistled in a most unladylike manner and said, "This is totally awesome."

He lifted a brow. "I take it you approve."

"Absolutely. Show me around, okay? I definitely want the royal tour. It's not every day that you get to see digs like this."

Chuckling, he held out an elbow. When she placed her hand on his arm, he walked with her toward the ivy-draped, double door entrance held open by servants.

"When I was a child, I used to play with my toy boats over in the pond there." He pointed to the sparkling blue water surrounded by oak trees and bushes. "I was an unruly boy, and I gave my parents much grief. All I ever wanted was to sail the world."

Miranda tried to imagine Max as a little boy. He must have been a cute kid. "And have you done all the sailing you wanted?"

"After I finished college at Oxford, I joined the Royal Navy and I've been a lot of places. But I still feel like something's missing—as though there's one final adventure left for me."

"What's holding you back?"

"I'm in charge of the family's holdings. I can't be at sea and take care of the home front, too." He sighed. "There's nothing like standing on the deck and feeling the trade winds in my face."

She patted his arm. "I'm sure you'll still get to travel again."

"I'm afraid it won't quite be the same as captaining my own ship." He kissed the top of her head. "But let's not discuss this anymore, it's far too depressing."

Lips tilted with a smile, he ushered her up the broad steps and inside the sumptuously appointed hallway of Applewood Manor.

***

Two days had passed since Max brought Miranda to the country. Practically every moment of his time had been occupied with business. He'd had numerous meetings with his tenants, and he'd spent hours riding across Chadwick's rental properties to mark off boundaries. He came home late each night, and despite Miranda's attempts to get him in the mood for some hankie pankie, he usually tumbled exhausted into bed.

As he held her close in bed, thrilling her with his large warmth, he would tell her everything that had gone on that day, and his frustration at getting the tenants to trust him. They were accustomed to either his father or brother making decisions on their behalf and seemed very reluctant to accept him.

Miranda wished she could treat him to a relaxation spell to ease his concerns. Since her powers were on the fritz, she decided to try something else. When they were together, she would massage his shoulders and broad back. He always thanked her afterward, but it didn't completely do the trick to help him relax.

Even though Max was under a lot of pressure, being with him felt great to Miranda. A part of her never wanted their time together to end, yet she knew it eventually had to. It was important to keep in mind the only reason she'd hooked up with Max was because of this absurd seven-year witch disease. As much as she'd come to appreciate him, and desire him, their relationship couldn't last.

He was a nineteenth century duke, for Pete's sake. And she was a modern-day witch. They would never work out as a couple. He had a duty to his people, and she had a duty to the witch's council. End of statement.

The dilemma always gave her a terrible headache. To keep her mind off it, she passed most of her time roaming throughout the huge three-story structure, awed by her surroundings. The intricate details, rich furnishings, thick Oriental carpets, and richly flocked wallpaper fascinated her. Of course, she'd lived through this period of history. But that had been a long time ago, and she'd forgotten a lot.

On the third day after they arrived, she discovered a wide hallway filled with portraits of stern-faced Chadwick ancestors. She moved through the gallery, observing all the paintings, finally locating one with a man that looked very much like Max. His dark brown eyes and square chin were almost identical. She decided it must be his father because it hung next to a woman who also had similar features to Max, obviously his mother. Beneath their portraits were those of two small boys, who she assumed were Max and his brother Marley.

Even though there appeared to be about a five-year difference between Max and his older brother, they looked very much alike. They could almost have passed as twins. The next space on the wall had been filled with a portrait of a woman in a wedding gown standing next to a tall man who also looked very much like Max.

Miranda assumed this must be Marley on his wedding day with Catherine—a ravishing beauty with burnished red hair tucked beneath a wedding veil. This is the woman Max had loved. This is the woman he had wanted in his life forever.

The woman who had betrayed him.

Jealousy niggled at her, and she pushed it away. How ridiculous. Catherine was gone from this earth. She couldn't compete for Max's affections any longer. Why that would bother her, she didn't have the slightest idea. She and Max didn't have a future together, therefore she had no right to feel so possessive.

The colors on the portrait suddenly began to melt and swirl around, then Ursula's face appeared where the bride's had been. Amazed, Miranda watched as the old witch took Catherine's place beside the groom. Placing her hands on Catherine's slim hips, she cackled outrageously, then glared at Miranda.

"I shouldn't have had to come here, Blondie."

Miranda folded her arms across her chest, annoyed by Ursula's interruption. "Then why did you?"

"You still haven't returned with the Philosopher's Stone, and the council is getting impatient."

"I'm doing my best. This seven-year witch disease has really put a crimp in my plans."

Ursula rolled her eyes. "You mean you still haven't done the duke seven times?"

"It's not that easy. He had to come up to this country estate to handle family business. That's got him preoccupied."

"Excuses, excuses. You're just delaying, I can tell."

"No, I'm not—"

"You've fallen for him, haven't you?"

Miranda thought about that for a moment. Yes, she really liked Max. But was her hesitation to prolong her time with him due to her reluctance to leave him? That could be a problem.

"Well?" Ursula glared at her.

"This isn't easy." She hated how whiny her voice sounded.

"Oh, give me a break, Blondie. What is difficult about hitting the sheets with a guy like Maxwell Chadwick? Did you piss him off or something?"

"Well, no…"

"Then get the deed done. Or else."

"Or else what?" Miranda didn't like the tone in Ursula's voice. It sounded like a threat. "I haven't run out of time."

"No, but the council knows you're dawdling. You're using this disease as an excuse not to get out and find the stone. You want to stay with the duke, don't you?"

Miranda had no response. Even though it was difficult to admit, she knew she was guilty of the accusation.

"Think about this," Ursula continued. "If you don't get a move on, the council will take your aunt Aggie and hold her prisoner. They'll lock her in the Tower of Destiny until you've fulfilled your obligation."

"No, they can't!" The Tower of Destiny was a place where condemned witches were imprisoned. It was dark and dank and filled with terrible spirits that haunted the inmates day and night. "Aunt Aggie hasn't broken any of our laws!"

"No, but you are in danger of doing it. You know the rules about consorting with mortals for too long. We are only tasked with helping them, not actually living amongst them or interfering in their progression."

Miranda studied her feet. Her insides squeezed with remorse, simply imagining what her aunt might have to suffer because of her inability to control her passions. "I promise I'll finish up with the duke as soon as I can."

"Good girl." Ursula smiled, causing the paint in the portrait to lift and bubble.

"I just want to know why the council is in such a heated rush to have this stupid stone," Miranda said. "What's the big deal?"

"Many of the mortal governments are in trouble. If negotiations continue to spiral downward with their leaders, there will be a widespread war, such as the world has never known. Only the stone, with its exceptional magical powers, can assist the council in helping to set things straight."

The significance of her mission was not lost on Miranda. In fact, it was sobering. "Why didn't you tell me this in the first place?"

"The council prefers only to assign orders to novices, not explain the details. It's easier that way in case someone decides to babble about our secrets. However, in this instance, since Aggie is a relative..." Ursula flicked a piece of lint off Catherine's bodice "...I think you need to know."

"Ah, there you are."

Miranda turned to see Max enter the room. She glanced back at the portrait, fearful he'd see Ursula's face distorting it, but she'd disappeared. Everything had returned to normal and nothing looked out of place. Thank the stars.

Max moved closer, and she could feel his warmth sizzling into her skin. It never failed; even the mere sight of him filled her with urgent need. She swallowed hard and tried to quell the welling desire. Did he know how crazy he was making her?

He lifted one of her curls and rubbed it between his thumb and forefinger. "I've been trying to find you for the last half hour."

"Sorry, Max. I've been in here looking around." She glanced back at all of the stern faces lining the walls. "The portraits are all quite fascinating."

His expression turned grim. "They make me sad. Let's get out of here."

With his arm around her waist, he guided her toward the door. They walked down the hallway, then he led her outside into a small garden. A variety of vines, flowers, and shrubs made the area into a brilliant display.

Pulling her against his broad chest, Max kissed her. When he drew back, she noted the hunger gleaming in his dark gaze. She could tell he wanted her. One thing was certain, it wouldn't be difficult to make love with him two more times so she could get on with her task of finding the Philosopher's Stone. She looked forward to it and knew it would have been too easy to forget her desire to become a high witch. But now that Aunt Aggie's freedom might be taken away if she didn't produce the Philosopher's Stone, the stakes were higher.

I'll have to start chasing that punk wizard again...

Damn the witch's council for putting her in this predicament. Those old biddies sure knew how to stick it to a person. With difficulty, she pushed all of her frustration to the back of her mind so she could try to enjoy Max's sweet onslaught.

For the moment, that's all that mattered.

***

Max had only come looking for Miranda to tell her about the dinner party he had planned for this evening. For some reason, seeing her filled him with an exceptional madness. He wanted to take her right here. A rather foolish notion since tenants would be arriving at any moment now for another meeting in his library.

Yet Miranda was a difficult woman to resist. Her lips offered soul-soothing nectar, and her soft, pliant body invited him to plunder its warmth. As he rubbed her taut nipples through her gown, she moaned with desire, filling him with a reckless need to rip away every stitch she wore.

He wanted nothing between them but air.

She met his tender assault with wild abandon, and he sensed her eagerness. She was so sweet, so desirable. He wanted more of her. Funny how his need to make love to this woman had quickly become habit. Day and night, she was on his mind. Each hour they spent together elevated her importance in his life. He admired her sensitivity and her charming ways. He appreciated her passionate nature and her willingness to admit to her own sexual needs. Rather than shy away from intimacy, she embraced it. She freely allowed herself to reach the heights of ecstasy with him, never ashamed to voice her desires.

She offered a temptation akin to fine whiskey and exotic tobacco. He found her stimulating and refreshing, a woman who matched his appetite in bed stroke for stroke. Never had he wanted anyone as much as he wanted her, not even Catherine, whom he had believed at one time to be his soul mate. Now he knew better, yet he realized it wasn't only lust that drove him to possess Miranda.

His regard for her went so much deeper, he hesitated to put a name to the sentiment. How could she so easily strip him bare and leave his heart free for the taking?

It confused him. He had no idea who Miranda really was or where she came from. Her entire life posed a great mystery. Yet, as soon as he had the opportunity, he planned to ask her to be his mistress. If she agreed, he'd set her up in a proper flat near his home, but far enough away from prying eyes. Then she could hopefully avoid the hurtful gossip that might come her way through his loose-lipped servants.

He wished he could just keep her with him. Damn it all, he wished he could make her his wife. But he couldn't wed a commoner. Because of his family's reputation, he would have to marry someone of the proper social class. Miranda wouldn't fit the bill. Nevertheless, he wanted to take care of her; protect her and keep her safe.

With their lips fused as one and their bodies closely entwined, he made up his mind he would ask her tonight to become his mistress. He didn't want to wait any longer.

Chapter Eight

"Ah, hem."

Max and Miranda pulled apart and looked over at Henry, who was staring off into space, anywhere but right at their lovers' tryst.

"The gentlemen have begun arriving for your meeting, sir," the butler stated firmly. "Shall I assemble them in the drawing room?"

Max quickly moved behind a wrought-iron chair, attempting to conceal the bulge in his trousers. "Yes and offer them tea. I'll be there shortly."

"Very good, sir." A muscle ticked in Henry's jaw, and lines of disapproval filled his face as he spun on his heel and went back inside.

"I've got to go." With his smoldering gaze still trained on her, Max pressed his lips to the back of her hand, sending sizzling tremors through her body. "Dinner will be served at six o'clock this evening. I'm inviting my tenants as a celebration. I'll see you there, correct? It should be a lovely meal, considering the small fortune I've dropped for it."

"Of course." Miranda wasn't terribly interested in the food. She wanted the dessert afterward that would be served in bed with Max. Of course, it bothered her that after two more mattress mambos she would have to leave. Ursula's visit had reminded her of her responsibilities. Sighing wistfully, she headed up to her room to get ready for dinner. She wanted to look especially nice for Max tonight.

***

Fathers, mothers, and children milled around on Applewood Manor's front lawn visiting with one another. These were Chadwick tenants, and their families had worked the duke's ancestral land for centuries. They were good, hard-working people, and Miranda understood why Max wanted to reassure them by extending his generosity.

Tables had been artfully arranged and covered with white cloths. Centerpieces consisted of flowers gathered from the surrounding gardens. A small group of musicians sat on a patio area providing soft music. Champagne flowed freely from a fountain. Sideboards offered rich cheese, crackers, and fruit. It appeared that no expense had been spared.

Max and Miranda, in a sky-blue gown that matched her eyes, had posted themselves under an oak tree near the gravel drive. As people arrived, they greeted the new guests, shaking hands and making polite conversation. It would have been boring to Miranda, except that she had such a handsome dinner companion at her side.

When Henry came out of the house to announce dinner would be served, Max took Miranda's elbow and steered her toward the head table. He pulled out her chair so she could sit, then he pulled out his own and lowered down next to her. Servants now began to bring out silver platters heaped with steaming food.

Courses included hearty soup, choices of mutton, chicken, or fish, roast vegetables, flaky biscuits and preserves, rich vanilla pudding, and fruit pies. Max had even raided his wine cellar, and adults were treated to fine vintages, while children were offered milk or water.

From the snippets of conversation Miranda overheard, people seemed genuinely impressed with the Duke of Pellamshire's generosity. Holding the dinner had been a good move on Max's part. With his keen senses, she had no doubt he would be celebrating many business successes in the future. A twinge of regret hit her. She would have liked to share it with him, but it wasn't to be.

As everyone began to eat, Max's glance often strayed toward her. At first, they were only quick, assessing looks. Eventually, they turned to sudden smiles and an occasional wink in her direction. Her insides stirred with warmth. He was such a fine man. Why couldn't she have met him at a different time under different circumstances? It didn't seem fair.

When the meal seemed to be winding to a close, Max stood and addressed the crowd. "I appreciate your presence here," he told them in his deep, rumbling voice. "I realize we've had our differences, but I'd like to reassure you that I intend to deal fairly with each one of you. My father and my brother always did, and I will continue in that vein." He walked toward a table that had been piled with cloth-wrapped bundles. "As you leave this evening, please pick up a smoked ham for your families."

"Here, here," someone shouted jovially.

Other rousing cheers rose from the assemblage as the guests began to file toward the table to receive their gifts. Once Max had given out all the hams, and the guests had wandered off to their carriages, Max strode confidently toward Miranda. When she rose, he took her hands in his, giving them an affectionate squeeze.

"I feel this was a rousing success," he said. "I'm glad this has worked out so well."

Miranda couldn't take her gaze off him. He was so handsome... Hot flames of need licked at her insides, filling her with urgency. Goddess above, she wanted him. She knew it wasn't only the need to cure her disease that spurred her longing. What she felt for him went beyond lust.

It was deeper and more meaningful.

She knew it could develop into something more, given enough time. But that wasn't going to happen. The idea of leaving him filled her with an aching, bereft sensation. A powerful trembling erupted within her. Clenching her teeth, she tried to quell it.

Max frowned. "Miranda, are you all right?"

"Yes, I think I'm just tired—"

"Sir Maxwell, it's been ages since I saw you last."

Both Miranda and Max turned toward the high-pitched, feminine voice. It came from a woman with dark, burnished curls. She wore a frilly yellow gown, her décolletage draped with strands of pearls and a golden locket. Her gaze followed Max steadily, as if she wanted to devour him.

Max straightened his shoulders. "Beatrice, this is a surprise. What are you doing in this part of the country?"

"I'm visiting my cousin. You remember Harriet Langdon, don't you? I'm certain Catherine told you about her. She just lives down the lane."

Max nodded. "Yes, Catherine spoke of her a time or two."

She giggled, a high-pitched silly sound. "When I saw all the activity going on at Applewood Manor, I thought I'd come have a look." She removed a fan and began to wave it slowly in front of her face. "Now, is that any civil greeting for your sister-in-law's kin? And what about your guest?" She nodded at Miranda, assessing her with narrowed, catty eyes. "Aren't you going to introduce us?"

"My apologies." A muscle ticked in his jaw and lines appeared on his forehead. "Catherine, this is Miranda. Miranda, this is Lady Beatrice Fettiplace, my brother's wife's sister."

"Pleased to meet you." Miranda gave a slight curtsey, as did Beatrice. All the while, she wondered what this little snipe had up her sleeve. She obviously had the hots for Max and behaved as though he belonged to her.

She couldn't help but notice the sparks of flirtatious green flaring from Beatrice's eyes and wondered what had transpired between her and Max. He'd only mentioned his relationship with Catherine, never anything about her sister.

What hasn't he told me?

Beatrice was a desirable woman, and Max was a healthy male with needs. She couldn't blame him if he'd had an affair with her, yet something strange began to happen as she envisioned the two of them together. Her stomach clenched and a tug of alarm pulled at her heart. Unconsciously, she scooted closer to Max as if defending her territory.

Am I jealous?

Crapola, she hadn't experienced that emotion in centuries. It felt strange, and she didn't like it much. But there it was, sinking its claws into her and making her feel like an idiot.

A part of her hinted that she should be happy—once she'd left Max, she could be assured there would still be plenty of women willing to help him through the lonely nights. Nevertheless, disappointment still cut her in two.

Even though the disease had forced her to do this, she couldn't deny she had feelings for him. In the end, she wondered who would be hurt worse, her or Max?

Darn it, she wanted to spend more time with him, but it wasn't possible. Not with Aunt Aggie's freedom hanging in the balance. And this war between the mortals that Ursula had mentioned—she certainly didn't want to be responsible for it happening, especially if she could help prevent it.

"Maxwell, I'd like to speak with you in private, if I may." Beatrice smirked at Miranda. "You don't mind, do you my dear?"

Cold infused her insides as she looked at Max, willing him to tell this twit to take a hike. "Excuse me?"

"Honestly, Bea. I'm quite busy here, as you can tell." He waved his hand toward remaining guests. "Can't talking about old times wait until we can arrange another visit?"

Beatrice lifted a finely arched brow and tilted her head toward Miranda. "Oh, I assure you, I don't intend to discuss that. What I have to say is very much about the present and people you are currently spending your time with."

A slow burn started deep within Miranda and flushed her face. Clenching her fists, she felt the heat of humiliation burning fiercely. There was no way she could stand here any longer and allow this hoochie mama to talk about her like that.

If only I had my powers. I'd turn her into a giant wart on a pig's snout!

Since she didn't have magic at her disposal, she'd just have to settle this situation in the old-fashioned mortal way—*with fists.* Little Miss High and Mighty had probably never had to duke it out with anyone in her life. In comparison, she'd grown up with six older sisters and had to fight for everything, including a spot in the bathroom line.

"I wasn't born yesterday, Beatrice," Miranda growled. "I assume you're talking about me."

"My, my, you're very astute, aren't you?" Beatrice daintily clasped her hands. "Considering where you've probably come from, it's quite surprising."

"What is your problem?" Miranda stepped closer to her and stared her straight in the eye. "Do you want a piece of me? Huh?"

Beatrice laughed. The sound dripped like poison. "I have no idea what you're referring to. But you're highly amusing."

"If you've got something to say about me, say it to my face."

"I have no idea what rubbish heap Sir Maxwell found you in, but it's about time he sent you back."

Miranda swung a fist at Beatrice's well-coifed head, but Max caught her arm in his and drew her against his broad chest. The more she struggled to break free, the tighter he held her. She could feel the muscles tense in his abdomen. His familiar, musky scent filled her nostrils. His arm brushed against one of her breasts and the nipple tightened, despite her combative pose.

"Let me go, Max," she growled. "I need to teach your friend here about the facts of life."

"Enough, I say," he said in a firm voice. He treated each of the women to a lingering frown. "Ladies, I think you both need to calm down. Nothing is worth exchanging insults of this nature."

"You seriously need to reconsider your association with this…this *harlot*," Beatrice spat, sniffing with disdain.

Miranda squirmed even harder in Max's arms. "How dare you talk to me that way—"

"You're the Duke of Pellamshire and you have a reputation to maintain," Beatrice continued, completely ignoring Miranda's outburst. "Taking her into your home and parading her around is shameful. Everyone's talking about your outrageous display of poor taste. Why, what do you suppose Queen Victoria thinks of your behavior? And the people you've invited to your party, what do you suppose they are saying about your arrangement?"

Max's face lined with anger. "You've been talking with my Aunt Winifred, haven't you?"

Beatrice shrugged.

"Let me go, Max. I'll give her a knuckle sandwich. I'll rearrange her face!" Miranda swung at Beatrice, but the woman merely stepped back.

"Your aunt is merely concerned about you, Maxwell." Beatrice gestured toward Miranda. "Look at her.

She's such a pitiful, ill-mannered guttersnipe. Having her in your home is most inappropriate."

Anger sparked from his brown eyes. "How I live my life is none of my aunt's business and definitely none of yours."

"It's distressing that you've lowered yourself to this level." Beatrice shook her head slowly. "What woman of good breeding would want to be your wife after you've made it so clear that you prefer to openly spend time with street walkers? Just think of the diseases she has probably exposed you to—"

"That's it! Now I've really had it!" Miranda broke free of Max's arms. Fuming with outrage, she charged toward Beatrice.

Chapter Nine

Max watched Miranda and Beatrice fall onto the lawn and roll across the ground in a hair-pulling, nail-scratching heap. He'd never seen two women embroiled in fisticuffs. It was difficult to grasp the concept, but it was indeed happening.

He couldn't help but be amused. He honestly didn't know whether they fought over him or the insults they'd tossed each other's way. Right now, it didn't matter. The servants and his guests had all stopped what they were doing to watch the nonsense. He needed to break them up before someone became seriously injured.

"Slut!" Miranda yelled as she raised a hand to slap a cheek.

"Je-ze-bel!" Beatrice called back, grabbing a handful of her golden hair.

Max walked over to the two, took one of Beatrice's arms and one of Miranda's, and yanked them out of their huddle. Their hair had become a tangled mess, their faces were scratched, their dresses torn and covered in grass stains.

"Enough!" he barked as he dragged Miranda a safe distance from Beatrice. Bloody hell, but she was strong. He'd never have been able to judge her strength simply by looking at her. "By Jove, the both of you need to calm down. You've made a laughingstock of yourselves."

"She started it," Miranda complained, shoving a waterfall of golden hair off her forehead.

"No, *she's* completely at fault," Beatrice shot back, wincing as she rubbed her red cheek. "Little tart."

"I say, if I didn't know better, I'd think the two of you were small children," he growled. "In fact, the children I know have better manners. This is no proper way for ladies to deport themselves."

"She's no lady," Beatrice snarled, pushing tousled hair away from her face.

"Why you little—"

Max held up a silencing hand and the words died on Miranda's sputtering lips. He turned to Beatrice and lifted a brow. "After your behavior today, I can say with certainty that you're no lady either. Since you weren't invited to this party, I'll forgive your bad manners if you'll take your leave."

Beatrice's mottled and bruised face fell. "But Maxwell—"

"Unless you have difficulty hearing, Bea, I suggest you do as I say. Or perhaps I shall let loose of Miranda and allow her to finish what she started."

Defiant to the end, Beatrice lifted her arrogant nose in the air, picked up her tattered skirts, and limped across the lawn toward the driveway.

"By the way, when you see my aunt again, tell her I would appreciate if she kept her opinions to herself," Max called to her.

Beatrice ignored him as she limped down the lane toward another large estate.

Muffled laughter drifted toward Max as he turned to his guests. He decided a Shakespearean comedy couldn't have provided more entertainment than what had transpired this evening.

"I apologize for the unseemly display, ladies and gentlemen," he told them.

As people drifted away, still whispering about the incident, he took Miranda's arm and walked her toward the gardens where they would be out of earshot. He couldn't be angry at her for long. She'd only been defending her honor from Bea's sharp tongue.

And defending her right to be with him? *Perhaps.*

Her forlorn expression touched him, so he held her dirty, scratched face in his hands, noting that her gown was probably beyond repair. But he didn't care about that—he cared about her. Relief sifted through him as he looked her over thoroughly, determining there were no broken bones or cuts that needed medical attention.

"Are you all right?"

She gave a hesitant nod.

"What were you thinking, sweetheart? Are you mad?"

"What does Bea mean to you?" Her chest rose and fell unevenly as if asking the question had come from a deeply emotional place.

He suppressed a chuckle, not caring to enjoy humor at her expense. It seemed she could be jealous, and he found the idea strangely intoxicating.

"As I said before, she is merely Catherine's sister. There was never anything between us. However, after today, I sense that since my financial circumstances have changed, she entertains the idea of something romantic developing between us."

"She deserved to get her butt whipped, Max. She's a snake in the grass."

He frowned. "A what?"

She sighed with frustration. "You *know* what I mean. She's not a very nice person. I can't believe how bossy she is."

"Bea can be a trying individual. Nevertheless, you never fail to confuse me, Miranda. Why do you care what she is to me?"

Lowering her head, she scuffed her shoes on the paving stones, as if frustrated. "It's hard to explain."

"Would you please humor me by trying?"

Finally, she met his gaze. "I care about you Max. I care about you like I've never cared about another man in my life."

Her revelation thrilled him. Of course, he'd sensed they both had deep feelings for one another. Having her say it outright was wonderful.

"Miranda, I sense someone has hurt you. I told the truth when I said I'd defend your honor. Who is this chap?"

She crossed her arms over her chest, deep in thought, then met his gaze. "You wouldn't believe me if I told you."

"I think it's time you told me. I can't stand to see you hurt like this." He held out his hands in supplication. "I even asked my friend Edward to uncover any information he could about you in case you'd had a temporary loss of memory."

She tossed an icy blue glance his way. "Are you trying to dig up something about my past?"

"Edward merely asked around at court if anyone's heard of you." At her nervous expression, he added, "I apologize, but I merely want to know who you are."

"I guarantee, you won't find out anything."

"Why?"

"Again, it's complicated."

"Consider the situation from my perspective." Max began to pace, trying to work off his irritation. "You could have escaped from an insane asylum, you could be a thief hiding out from the law—it could a million other things I haven't thought of. You can't blame me for wondering."

Miranda realized she needed to satisfy his curiosity. Otherwise he might not want to make love with her again. And she needed to hit the hay a couple more times so she could get back to finding the Philosopher's Stone. As fond as she'd grown of Max, and as much as it pained her to think of leaving, she needed to do it.

Max was already in trouble with his aunt, and now all of London would be gossiping about his affair with her. Even though Bea was a snot bag, the woman had made some valid points. Max wasn't just some schmoe off the street she could toy with. He was a duke—he had serious responsibilities and a reputation to maintain.

While she was aware that powerful men in this century nearly always kept mistresses, they typically had them stuffed away in discreet love nests. They didn't install them in their homes and parade them around genteel society. She cared enough about Max not to want to ruin his future.

The longer she hung around, the longer she might jeopardize his ability to marry a good woman from a decent family who could give birth to the future Duke of Pellamshire. That thought evoked a pang of anguish, and it felt like someone had shot an arrow through her heart.

It was time to blow this Popsicle stand and get back to real life. That punk wizard had something she needed, and she was bound and determined to get it. Her love life would have to take a back seat.

"Miranda?"

She'd been so immersed in her own thoughts, she'd practically forgotten Max stood beside her, watching her with a critical eye. "I'm sorry. I've got a lot on my mind."

"Indeed?"

Though it had happened centuries ago, she decided to tell him about Tavis. She sensed it would ease Max's mind, even though it would reopen raw wounds in hers. "I was married to a man named Tavis McClarren in America. I had to leave him because he…he betrayed me."

Max lifted a dark brow and a look of concern filled his eyes. "What did he do?"

Emotion welled up and her shoulders began to shake with sobs. Even though she'd made light of it all these centuries, the truth still hurt like a son of a gun.

Max drew her against his broad, warm chest and rubbed her back reassuringly. Goddess above, it felt so wonderful to be in his arms. She wished she could stay like this forever with him.

"I swear, I'll go after the fool," he growled protectively. "Any man who would hurt a woman in such a manner deserves to be punished."

"You can't, it's too dangerous and I can't let anyone know where I am. You see, a storekeeper accused me of being a thief, which was a complete lie. Instead of Tavis defending my honor, he turned me over to the authorities and would have let me hang. I believe he never really loved me…"

Actually, she'd been accused of being a witch and the people in Tavis' Scottish village had nearly burned her at the stake. Through her own quick thinking of bribing a jailor, she had escaped. Hoping the version of the truth she'd told Max would satisfy his curiosity she buried her face in his broad shoulder and sobbed with authentic misery.

It had been devastating when Tavis betrayed her, and just as devastating to bare her soul about it now with Max. No matter how she'd tried to pretend that it wasn't a big deal, it really had been. She'd truly loved Tavis.

Max wisely remained silent but held her even tighter as she released centuries of pent-up emotion. Finally, when no more tears would come, he produced a handkerchief and tenderly wiped away her tears.

"I'm sorry for being such a boob, Max."

"No need for apologies. I know how terrible it is to lose someone you love."

She sniffed back another sob, remembering Max had also suffered a loss. "Catherine betrayed you, too. Aren't we a pair?"

A slow smile spread across his face. "But we found one another, didn't we?

His words struck her like a bolt of lightning. She had no choice but to break his heart. Again. It would be difficult, but she knew it was for the best. At least once her powers were restored, she could cast a spell of forgetfulness to wipe his memory.

I'll never forget him, though.

Lowering his face toward hers, he gave her a tender kiss that spoke volumes with its intensity. As his lips sizzled against hers, a melting sensation came over her, like an ice cube on a hot sidewalk. She felt positively giddy, yet bittersweet emotion erupted with a hollow ache.

When Max finally pulled away, she drank in a gulp of sweet air. Son of a monkey, that man always left her breathless. She traced her hand on his chest and looked up at him with undisclosed longing. "I want you Max."

"As I want you sweetheart. Why don't you retire, and I'll join you shortly." Taking her elbow, he walked her toward the front doors of the estate.

"I am very sorry about what happened earlier." She released a heavy sigh. "I really messed things up, didn't I? Your tenants didn't exactly come here to watch a catfight."

"Actually, I believe they now realize I'm a real human being, and not some stiff, unfeeling brute."

Max walked with her inside. When a maid in a white ruffled apron came rushing forward, her black skirts swishing, he told her, "Please prepare bath water for Miranda, and arrange for it to be carried up to our room."

"Yes, sir," the maid said as she hurried away.

"I'll find you as soon as everyone's gone home," he told her, kissing the top of her disarrayed golden locks.

"I'm looking forward to it." She winked saucily at him, silently sending him the message that he was in for a treat when they were together again. As she climbed the stairs, she moved her hips in a provocative manner.

Max's mouth watered as he watched Miranda walking away. *The little minx!* Even in her current state of disarray, she drew him like a bee to honey, and his loins ached with yearning.

Now he understood why she'd hesitated to tell him about her past. Being accused of a crime that heinous would ruin a woman's life. No wonder she'd come to him in such a deplorable state. He imagined that in order to avoid prison, she had fled America with very little to her name.

He assumed her husband had treated her so poorly because the blackheart had his eye on another woman. As a matter of fact, it seemed likely he had started the rumor of Miranda's thievery himself.

The bastard.

Righteous indignation boiled over in his gut. Now that Miranda was under his protection, he would see to it that no one ever hurt her again. She belonged to him—it was as simple as that. He hurried back outside into the gathering dusk, knowing he'd move heaven and earth to keep her at his side.

***

Aching after her fight with Beatrice, Miranda limped into the bedroom and shut the door, leaning against it and thinking about what it would be like to make love with Max for the last time. She planned to savor every single moment of their time together. As she anticipated his arrival, warmth prickled her spine. Would he amuse her with the same sweet torture that always held her spellbound?

The idea excited her beyond belief. By the time she'd pulled the covers down on the bed and coaxed a blazing fire to life on the hearth, servants arrived with a tub of hot, steaming water and left. Miranda decided the bath was still too warm to get in, so she dangled her fingers in the luxuriant warmth.

Fascinated, she watched as the surface broke and rippled with gentle waves. She wished she could stare through those depths and predict the future, but with her powers completely wiped out, she saw nothing.

It wasn't much longer before Max entered the room with a bottle of wine in one hand and two goblets clutched in the other. He tossed a grin at her as he sat everything down on a small table near the bed. Due to his rigorous military training, he moved with precision and confidence. Muscles rippled in his biceps and thighs and she decided she'd never seen such a powerful build on a man before.

And to think he was all hers—for a night, anyway. She planned to leave in the morning, after one last night in paradise.

He sat on the bed and patted the sheets. "Come here, sweetheart."

She moved over beside him, noting his gaze was filled with heated desire. A shiver slid up her spine as she imagined his hot, eager lips trailing across her skin. There could be no denying the man possessed great talent in the lovemaking department.

After pouring two goblets of wine, he handed one to her. "This is one of my finest vintages."

She sniffed the aromatic ruby liquid. "Are you sure you want to waste it on me?"

"It's no waste, I can assure you. After your brawl with Beatrice, you could use something to ease your joints." He smoothed hair away from her brow. "You have earned yourself a few bruises, you know."

"I'll be fine." Miranda sipped at the liquor, pleased to feel a relaxing tingle. After she'd drained her cup, he took it from her and placed it on the bedside table along with his own.

He nodded toward the wooden tub. "Your bath awaits. Do you mind if I join you?"

"I'd be disappointed if you didn't."

With exquisite precision, he peeled away her clothing, piece by piece. As cool air caressed her body, her skin prickled. Without taking his gaze off her, Max undressed as well, his erect penis springing free of his trousers when he tossed them aside.

Hot blood throbbing in her veins, she took his hand and led him toward the tub. Together, they sank into the warm, silken depths. His brown eyes smoldered with hunger as he picked up a cake of soap and began rubbing it gently across her limbs. Lowering down, he moved it slowly across her breasts in circles, lingering extra-long over her nipples until they crested into rosy buds.

Her breath caught in her throat as he sank his hands beneath the water's surface and sought the juncture between her thighs. There he began another dance with his fingers, stroking her slick, sensitive folds and exploring her thoroughly. Sliding a finger inside her, he mimicked what she knew he wanted to do with his penis.

In and out he thrust, ever so gently, until she bit her lower lip to keep from moaning with pleasure. His fingers found her tiny nub and with circular motions, brought it alive with tingling. She pressed against his touch, wanting more.

Abruptly, he removed his hands leaving her with a wicked desire. Shoving to his feet, he reached for the towel on a chair. "Let me dry you off."

Attempting to control her breathing, she stepped from the tub, enjoying that he was taking the lead tonight. It allowed her to savor every inch of him for this last time.

He wrapped her in the fire-warmed cloth, rubbing and massaging her limbs. "Lay on the bed, sweetheart," he instructed in a husky voice.

Without comment, she did as he told her. The sheets felt like the softest silk against her skin. He rubbed her feet with his large hands then her legs, working loose the kinks and soreness. Like a balm, his touch soothed. She sank deeper and deeper into a state of blessed contentment.

Naked and shameless before him, she watched, mesmerized as he massaged her hands and arms.

"Roll over."

Flipping onto her stomach, she felt him climb onto the bed next to her, his weight sagging the mattress. She thrilled to his touch as he massaged her buttocks, her lower back, then her shoulders and neck. He moved carefully past her bruises, careful not to re-injure her, but kissing her eager flesh instead. Soon, his fingertips were replaced entirely with his lips as he blazed a trail of molten kisses across her skin.

A shiver of delight rippled through her. How could such a large, powerful man be so gentle? This was a side of him that she found endearing and delightful. Breathing became harder, escaping from her chest in short gasps. Time became irrelevant. Nothing mattered but this moment.

After such a sensual rubdown, every nerve ending sang of how much she wanted him. This slow seduction heightened the excitement, especially since she had decided to savor every second.

When his touch lifted, she rolled over to look at him. He had begun drawing the coverlet up, tucking it around her.

"What are you doing?"

"You need your rest. Beatrice really pummeled you, and you're bruised badly. I don't want to hurt you."

"But—"

"But what?" He raised a dark brow, his lips upturned slightly. His penis had grown large and bobbed insistently.

"You can't leave me like this. You're in no condition to." She nodded at his swollen groin.

"I appreciate your concern. But I'll be fine." Leaning down, he kissed the top of her head. He slid on his robe and strode toward the door.

She searched for words to explain what she felt right now but failed. She wanted Max, here and now. His touch was irresistible, her need undeniable. Once she'd fulfilled the lovemaking requirement, her disease would be cured, and she would have to leave. As much as she hated the idea, it had to be done.

She grabbed his pillow and threw it at the wall near Max. As it fell to the floor with a soft thump he pivoted toward her, dark brows raised.

"Don't go, Max. The bruises are nothing. Believe me I'll hurt more if you leave."

He grinned. "Are you certain?"

"Come here, you big lug." She held out her arms. Without further prompting, he walked toward her.

Chapter Ten

As quickly as he'd put it on, Max shed his robe and crawled into bed with Miranda. When she lifted his hand and nuzzled his calloused palm, a curl of warmth spread throughout her belly. Apparently emboldened by her gesture, he cupped one of her breasts. He drew the nipple into his mouth and teased it with his tongue until it crested into a taut little peak. Transferring his attention to her other breast, he did the same, licking and laving the nipple until she moaned with pleasure.

He drew her close and said huskily into her ear, "I promise, I'll make your heart sing and your body soar."

She recognized the burning need in his eyes, and her body practically shouted for his intimate caresses. "Kiss me, Max," she whispered, melting into his comforting embrace. "Make love to me now."

Blood rushed through her veins like warm honey as he drew her close, his lips pressed against hers. As the hairy expanse of his broad chest pressed against her sensitive nipples, they tightened in response.

She wrapped her arms around his neck, drawing him closer, unwilling to let him go. Her lower body throbbed with desire. Wild thoughts flew through her mind as she felt the beat of his heart against hers.

A fire ignited deep in her soul. The need to feel him inside of her coursed raw and uncontrollably through her blood. At first, she attributed it to the seven-year witch disease. Then another idea occurred to her.

Do I love him?

As their kiss deepened, she considered that possibility, but realized she hadn't known him long enough to be certain. She'd believed herself in love with Tavis but realized what she felt for Max was much different from what she'd felt for the Scotsman. While the Highlander had been her lover, and she'd enjoyed being with him, her emotions didn't even begin to compare to those she had for Max.

He fulfilled not only her sexual needs, but it seemed he understood her inner self. She had become unexplainably attached to him. She had no illusions, though. In her heart, she realized Max's affection for her would fade in a heartbeat if he knew she was a witch.

Don't think about that right now. Think about Max, and what he's doing to you....

"By Jove, you are beautiful," he murmured as he combed his fingers slowly through her long hair.

He said nothing else. He didn't need to. His eyes spoke of his raw need.

She shivered with delight, her limbs tingled, and her heart fluttered as though filled with a million tiny butterflies. Breathing grew difficult, concentration impossible.

"Are you sure you're all right?" He pressed his lips to the palm on one of her hands, nuzzling the soft flesh.

"Yes," she responded in an uneven voice and licked her dry lips.

"Why are you trembling?"

"I'm chilly for some reason."

"I can take care of that. Let me warm you." His lips found hers again. His hot, thrusting tongue delved into her mouth where he explored every inch of the soft cavern.

She wound her fingers in his thick hair, pulling him closer. Her thoughts flew recklessly, but her body responded enthusiastically. Primal urges overcame her senses; she became a willing slave to his captive touch.

With nothing existing between them but the warm air, he softly kissed the juncture between her neck and shoulder, sending shivers up her spine. In response, her body swelled with yearning and a sharp, pleasurable ache developed in the sensitive spot between her thighs.

As he showered her skin with hot, urgent kisses, she clung to him like a woman possessed. His hot member bounced heavily along her thigh, seeking her inner core. A whirlwind of sensation nearly carried her away. She could wait no longer.

"Take me," she begged. "Now—before I burst."

His eyes flashed with heated urgency and she knew he felt the same. He nudged her legs open with one of his knees and mounted her. When he entered her in one swift movement, she arched her back and received him completely.

His large girth filled her, and she gasped when he began to move in and out with mighty strokes. As his chest brushed against her nipples, they grew taut and firmly crested with the friction created by their bodies. Instinctively, she wrapped her legs around his waist so he could enter her more deeply. He burrowed himself in her moistness, holding her buttocks. His thrusts came faster and faster, his brow glistening with sweat until he exploded. Arching his neck, he groaned and shuddered, spilling his seed with spreading warmth. Afterward, he collapsed atop her, drawing in ragged breaths.

The idea that he rested inside of her sent a thrill of delight through her. Despite the weight of his large, muscled form, she felt no discomfort. Her mind still reeled with his sweet lovemaking.

He smiled down at her. "You intend to kill me with your insatiable sexual appetite, don't you woman?"

"You have ways of pleasuring me that—" *I'm going to miss*, she nearly said aloud. Instead, she finished the sentence with, "—are incredible."

He slid off her, leaned on one elbow and fondled her nipples one at a time, teasing them into erect little crests. When she moaned, he lowered down and ran his hand along her inner thigh. He touched the nub at the juncture of her legs, sending waves of exquisite pleasure through her.

He began to stroke her eager flesh. "Are you hungry, sweetheart?"

"Yes," she said with a gasp, "but not for food."

"I see I shall have to feed you. Are you ready?"

Once again, she felt ready to burst. "Yes!"

His touch increased in intensity until she reached a rapturous peak then burst into a million sparkling pieces. The pinnacle of sensation was powerful, blinding and all consuming.

They talked late into the night of their hopes and their fears. During that sacred time, only the two of them mattered and nothing else. Miranda ached knowing she was cured now and would soon have to leave.

***

Max awakened several hours after he and Miranda had fallen asleep. He looked over to see the stars and moon shining brightly outside the window. Amusing, how the heavenly bodies cast a blanket of soft light across their nakedness. The feel of Miranda's warm sleeping body pressed closely against his, her leg thrown casually between his knees, thrilled him.

He drank in her unique scent—roses and a spicy aroma. It filled his senses with poignant memory as he recalled how eagerly she'd made love with him. He kissed her forehead. She made soft noises and squirmed at his touch, a smile curving her berry-colored lips. Her even-paced breathing and her very presence comforted him.

She shifted her backside and it rubbed against his penis. The friction brought him to an instant state of arousal, and he grew hard. He gritted his teeth, longing to make love to her again. But she slept so soundly, and he didn't want to disturb her. Instead, he endured the agonizing, wonderful torture of waiting.

His blood raged hotly as he simply watched her sleep. This was a woman made for the bed chamber. The image of her writhing naked beneath him in bed held him spellbound. He reveled in the fact that Miranda belonged to him now, and hopefully, forever.

Satisfaction consumed him like a slow burning fire. He drew her closer, knowing he could never let her go. Considering the fact the Chadwick family held great influence in America, he felt confident he could clear up any legal situations with the authorities regarding her supposed crime.

Then he'd help Miranda obtain a divorce through the church after which she would be free to be his mistress. He realized, of course, he would need to convince her to agree to this plan, but after last night, he didn't think there would be any problem. He fell asleep, his dreams filled with her.

An insistent knocking awakened him. "It's Henry, sir. There's a messenger from the ironworks downstairs who insists upon seeing you straightaway."

Max yawned and looked out the window, noting dawn stretched ribbons of rosy color across the horizon, signaling the beginning of a new day. As much as he disliked the idea of crawling from beneath the warm covers, he knew he needed to find out what was going on. Whatever it was, it didn't bode well that John Weaver, the ironworks supervisor, had felt the need to send him such an urgent communication.

"I'll be down shortly," he called out.

"Very good, sir."

Reluctantly, he shifted Miranda's sleeping body from his embrace and rolled out of bed. He poured a pitcher of water into a bowl and splashed his face. Reaching for a towel, he rubbed it across his chin. His whiskers rasped, and he realized he wouldn't even have time to shave.

Quickly, he pulled on his trousers, shirt, and boots. After casting one final longing glance at Miranda, he jaunted downstairs into the wood-paneled receiving hall.

Max met the gaze of the lanky young man standing there. He immediately recognized John Weaver's son. "Richard, it's good to see you, but what brings you here?"

Richard handed him an envelope, stamped with the ironworks' wax seal. He nervously cleared his throat and said, "There's been a fire. My father wants you to come as soon as possible to help him settle affairs."

Max's jaw nearly dropped to the floor. "Bloody hell. How bad was it?"

"A large majority of the facility burned. Fortunately, none of the workers were injured."

"I'm relieved no one was hurt, but this is terrible news." Max ran a hand through his mussed hair. "I'll pack as quickly as I can."

"Very good, sir. Our ship, *Sea Majesty*, is docked in the Thames River harbor. We need to return to Boston as soon as possible."

Max took the stairs two at a time. He stopped to have a word with Henry and explained what was going on. He also discussed arrangements with the butler to take care of Miranda, then he headed to his room.

He thought of the fire. Damnation. Who would have imagined this would happen now? It was fate's cruel way of telling him he could never be in control of his own life.

***

Miranda yawned and stretched, her toes curling against the soft sheets. The memory of last night flashed in her mind, and a pleasant sensation filled her. It didn't last long. She knew she needed to leave.

ASAP.

Facets of sunlight sparkled through the windows, but the warmth didn't reach her soul. Last night had been special, but her fascination of Maxwell Chadwick had to be put to rest. As much as she liked him, she needed to get on with her life and allow him to get on with his.

Goddess above, why did she want him so badly? With Aunt Aggie's freedom hanging in the balance, she knew there was no choice about whether to stay here or return to her world. Yet this was still difficult.

You're a witch, Miranda. You're not the type of woman Max needs at his side.

So true. But that didn't stop her from wanting what she couldn't have. The door opened and Max strode inside, his expression stormy. "Good, you're awake. I need to talk to you."

She sat up, wondering what in the world had happened. Max's face held lines of distress. Had he discovered who she really was?

He sat down on the bed beside her, and she tensed. Was he going to kick her out? Drag her off to the pokey?

He did none of those things. Taking her small hands in his large ones, he brushed his sensual lips against her palms. "I need to leave for America straightaway," he explained, his voice edged with alarm. "There's been a fire at my family's ironworks factory in Boston."

Instant concern replaced Miranda's worry for herself. "I'm so sorry. Was anyone hurt?"

"No, but there was a tremendous amount of damage. I don't have much time before I have to leave."

She sucked in a ragged breath, waiting for what would come next.

"Wait for me to return. You can move into a comfortable hotel in London or perhaps a flat. Whatever you'd like is yours—just charge it to my account."

He looked so hopeful, as though he truly wanted her here when she returned. Goddess above, she hated to ruin his mood. "Max—"

"I know this is short notice, but I'm asking you to be my mistress, Miranda. I promise you'll lack for nothing."

Her heart soared, then it came crashing down like a bird falling from the sky. She'd anticipated he was going to ask her to marry him. Why would she even think such a thing? It was ludicrous. In his eyes, and in the eyes of polite English society, she wasn't the right class of woman. Of course, the crown would never accept her—a nobody—as his duchess. And while she understood the realities of it, it still hurt.

The pain she felt confused her. A moment ago, she'd hoped to be able to slip away. She knew they couldn't stay together. Now she was upset because he only wanted her to be his mistress. Her wounded pride made absolutely no sense. One thing she was certain of. She didn't *want* to be Max's mistress—that wasn't the type of life she'd ever envisioned. Being told by a man what to do, when to do it, and how to do it, would never suit her.

"I can't…" she managed.

"I realize you're still married to Tavis," he quickly interjected. "I have a fair amount of influence in America since my family holds business interests there. After I've handled the trouble at the ironworks factory, I can look up a few of my associates and arrange for your divorce."

She chewed her lower lip, her heart pounding. An explanation was in order, but she had a hard time coming up with one. "Max, it's not that simple."

"I'm sure it will take some time, but it can be done."

Lowering her gaze, she tried to find the right words. "There's something you need to understand."

He rose and began to scrounge around in a tall mahogany wardrobe, tossing items into a black leather bag. "Talk to me while I pack, sweetheart. I don't have much time."

Watching him pull luggage from his wardrobe, and then begin rifling through drawers, she realized she really didn't need to tell him anything. When he returned from America, she'd simply be gone. To tell the truth, his journey couldn't have come at a more convenient time.

Mixed emotions drifted through her. Relief and trepidation.

She drew her knees up to her chest and hugged them. This was it. Her time with Max was over. She should be excited about getting on with her task, but for some reason, she wasn't.

Max spun around to look at her once more, lifting a dark brow. "By the way, I've left orders with Henry to make sure my wishes are carried out. In my absence, he'll arrange for anything you need."

"Fine," she replied.

Fine, indeed. She'd be out chasing a punk wizard that might wind up tossing on her can again. Dealing with that little sawed-off shotgun was something she definitely didn't look forward to.

When Max finally closed the lid on his leather suitcase, he came over and swept her into his arms. He kissed her deeply, and they held each other for a few moments. Then he drew back.

"This is not my idea of how a gentleman treats a lady. Leaving like this, and all."

She touched his cheek. "I understand."

"Do you?"

"Of course." She smiled, though inside her heart squeezed with bittersweet emotion. "You must attend to your business."

"Yes, of course. There's always that dastardly business of mine to attend to. Blast it all, I have forgotten one thing." Rising, he crossed the room to remove a pistol from the top drawer of his dresser. He examined it briefly, then shoved it into his waistband.

"I'll write as soon as I can," he added.

I won't be here to receive your letters. She willed her lower lip not to tremble as she said, "Take care of yourself, Max."

After sending her one of his lopsided grins, he left. She hurried to the window in time to see his carriage as it was brought around. Watched as he climbed inside. Watched as he rode away.

Then the tears came. In order to make them stop, she stretched out on the bed and buried her head into his pillow. It still held his musky scent, and she inhaled deeply. By everything that witches held sacred—nature, life, and the world itself, she would miss him. Miss his face, his voice, his touch.

Why had this ridiculous disease sought her out and marked her for this type of heartbreak?

She didn't know how long she laid there, her mind filled with thoughts of Max. At last merciful sleep dulled her unease. It was not pleasant to have to give up her lover. And such an expert lover at that.

It's for the best, she finally told herself. Yet no matter how she tried to lift her mood with that knowledge, it didn't work.

Deep down, she knew she would never be the same without him.

Chapter Eleven

Max stood aboard *Sea Majesty* gazing at the harbor, which teamed with tall-masted sailing ships, boats, and vessels of all shapes and sizes. His father had purchased this ship a decade ago to haul supplies for the ironworks business. She was a beauty with her gold and black carvings, her bronze cast guns, her firm riggings, tall white sails, and solid oak masts.

He stroked the smooth wooden railing, drinking in the sights. Seagulls wheeled overhead, calling to each other. Sluggish green-brown river water rhythmically slapped against the hull, calling to him with an ancient mariner's melody. He inhaled deeply. Even at port, the air held briny, exotic scents. This was his world. Where he felt the most comfortable, and where he had always imagined spending the rest of his life.

Until Miranda appeared in his life, he'd been more than anxious to get away from the stuffy confines of London and sail the high seas again. Of course, under very different circumstances than this. He hated knowing there had been a fire at the ironworks. The men who worked there were loyal employees with families, and he knew the incident must have caused them much trouble. He'd do everything in his power to help them—from providing medical supplies to food and shelter so that they could get their lives in order again.

His jaw tensed as thoughts of Miranda rose to the surface of his consciousness again. He didn't like leaving her so abruptly. He trusted Henry to attend to her welfare until he returned, but long-term affairs between himself and his lover still needed to be arranged. He would do his best to finish up with his business and hurry back home. Yet he feared the damage to the ironworks would delay his return. By his estimation, extensive repairs would have to be completed, which may take several weeks, if not months.

An urge to hold Miranda once more surged through him. His mind wandered back to the woman with her long golden curls and sapphire-blue eyes. Her beauty amazed him. He'd never had a better lover, and the time they'd spent together still brought a smile to his lips.

On occasion he'd considered setting himself up with a mistress. However, affairs of the heart could be complicated, and he'd always decided to break it off in the end. Miranda had caused him to feel differently. She'd chased away his fears of commitment and had taught him to care. In the short time they'd been together she'd touched not only his heart, but his soul. Day and night, he wanted to be with her. The idea that she would be waiting when he returned filled him with contentment. Simply remembering what she did to him in bed made his groin harden in anticipation, imagining how she would fill his future with her enthusiastic presence gave him joy.

An image of her lovely face rose up to tease him. He focused on her moist, shining lips, which he knew were as sweet as honey. Her blue eyes were as deep and fathomless as the sea. Her body was beyond compare. Memories of last night's lovemaking sent heated warmth through his veins, filling him with mysterious desire.

His mouth went dry, and the crotch of his trousers became uncomfortably tight. He shifted his feet to alleviate his discomfort. His neck began to itch, so he scratched. When a headache started throbbing in his temples, and his heart began to palpitate, he frowned. What in the world had come over him? During a fit of sneezing, he whipped out a handkerchief from his pocket and blew his nose.

Even his throat had become constricted and felt raw. Is this what loving a woman did to a man? No, surely, he was only coming down with some minor illness.

Get your mind on business, my man.

Narrowing his gaze, he turned to watch the scruffy workers bustling up and down the gangplank. Some of the men shouted out orders while others cursed as they hefted crates of food supplies, barrels of fresh water, and other supplies into the cargo hold.

Dawn couldn't come soon enough. Tomorrow, once it illuminated the horizon with ribbons of color, they would set sail for Boston. The sooner they began the journey, the sooner he could get to work. Taking off his jacket and rolling up his sleeves, he strode down the gangplank.

On the dock, he headed toward a stack of crates next to the wharf office. Hefting a crate up to his shoulder, he hauled it aboard ship. The crewmates gave him strange looks, as if they hadn't expected him to help with the heavy lifting. They were in for a surprise.

Max worked alongside the men all afternoon. Not until the last of the supplies had been loaded did he collect his jacket and head toward his cabin. He ached all over, and basically felt like he'd been dragged underneath a carriage. When a cabin boy knocked on his door to see if he needed anything, he ordered hot tea from the galley kitchen.

Lowering onto on his cot, he scratched his arm, which had developed unusual raised, inflamed bumps. Good Lord, this was a hell of a time to be sick. But since it seemed he was coming down with something, he decided he'd better barricade himself in his room and stay away from the crew.

***

By the time Miranda awakened, late afternoon shadows draped the room. Astounded she'd slept that long, she rolled over and sat up. When she yawned, her face ached as though someone had given her a good pummeling. Reaching up, she patted her cheeks. *Oww.* They were swollen and tender. No wonder. She didn't know how long she'd cried over Max.

Enough is enough.

She was making a fool of herself over this guy. She had things to do—namely finding Balthazar, getting the Philosopher's Stone, and giving it to the council. She absolutely didn't want the old biddies to put Aunt Aggie in the Tower of Destiny because she was dragging her feet about completing her final task. And she also didn't want mankind involved in some cataclysmic war that could have been prevented if she'd turned over the stone.

Without warning, a dizzy spell swept over her. It was powerful and startling. Clutching the sheets, she braced herself.

Come on, Miranda. Get yourself together. You've got work to do.

She closed her eyes and envisioned her promotion ceremony, which would be performed beneath the light of the full moon with a leaping bonfire in the background. All her Hedge Haven friends, along with her family, would be there to see the council's head priestess bestow upon her the status of high witch.

Achieving this rank meant she had passed all magical tests and had been declared proficient at the craft. For once in her life, other clan members would give her the respect she had worked so hard to attain.

She shivered, just thinking about it. Yet for some reason, the typical excitement she experienced when envisioning her high witch ceremony didn't surface. What was going on? She'd looked forward to this for centuries.

It's Max. He's gotten to me. Could the idea of spending her life with a mortal man have overshadowed her goals?

She didn't know, and she simply couldn't worry about it. Though it pained her to toss aside the warm covers, permeated with his enticing scent, she did it anyway. Only by putting one foot in front of the other would she be able to leave this place.

Swinging her legs over the side of the bed, she stood. Once again, her skin felt as though a nest of fire ants marched over it. Just the way it had when she'd returned to Wysteria and discovered she'd contracted the seven-year witch disease. She scratched an itchy spot on her forehead then another on the inside of her arm.

That's weird, she thought, perspiration breaking out on her brow. This shouldn't be happening.

Spotting a water pitcher and a cake of soap on a wash stand, she headed toward it, intending to rinse her face. Maybe that would make her feel better. When another wave of dizziness surged over her, she staggered backward.

Slumping onto the bed, she struggled to catch her breath. Pain lanced through her head, and her vision blurred. Her heart hammered like a freight train, her stomach tossed with queasiness. Chests, wardrobes, and chairs faded in and out of focus. Her tongue felt like a wad of cotton. Her mouth tasted like a sand pit.

Alarm rocketed through her, and she pushed to her feet again, stumbling toward the dresser. Gripping the edge, she stared into the mirror.

Oh, my goddess!

A patchwork quilt of angry red boils and patches of purplish, raw-looking areas covered her skin. She stuck out her swollen tongue, only to see gross fuzzy brown patches.

Disgusted that her symptoms had returned, she wobbled toward the bed and grabbed the wooden post to steady herself. Tears stung the back of her eyes as she realized she must have miscalculated. She and Max obviously hadn't achieved the magical number seven during their love making sessions; otherwise she wouldn't be in this awful predicament.

Painfully, she dressed, knowing she needed to try and catch up to Max. She attempted to run a brush through her wild hair, but her scalp felt like it was on fire too, so she gave it up. Stumbling into the hallway, she managed to make unsteady progress down the stairs. After looking in several rooms for Henry, she staggered into the parlor where she finally found him running a feather duster across a tall grandfather clock.

When he spotted her, his eyes went wide. "I apologize for being so forthright Miss, but you look dreadful." He frowned. "Is there something you require?"

"I need Max-th," she blurted miserably.

"He's not here. He told me the two of you had discussed his orders to sail."

She nodded. "We did, but I sh-till need him."

His brows knitted in confusion.

"It's difficult to exp-wain, Hen-wy. Help me, pw-ease?"

His mouth formed a stern line. "I think perhaps it would be better if I fetched the family physician so he can give you something for that nasty rash. You must be terribly uncomfortable."

Scratching her elbow, Miranda said, "No! I need to get to Max-th!"

"Sir Maxwell asked me to watch over you while he's gone. I know he wouldn't want you going anywhere while you're this ill—"

"But I have to th-peak wif him!" She smacked her lips, irritated at how thick her mouth felt, as though it had been filled with mush. "It's a matter of wif-th and deaf-th."

"What if your rash is contagious?" He backed away, as if he didn't want to catch anything from her. "You don't want to spread it all over London."

Considering all the diseases that wreaked havoc on the people in this century, and the lack of proper medical treatments, no wonder Henry looked concerned.

"I always bw-eak out when I'm nervous. Honest-wy."

Both of her eyelids began to twitch. She felt terrible for lying to Maxwell's butler. She wasn't even good at it, but this seven-year witch crap had forced her to do things she'd never imagined herself capable of.

Her expression must have been desperate enough that Henry finally decided to help her. "I don't agree with your decision, but since you insist..." He smiled, his expression sympathetic. "I'll summon a driver and bring round a carriage to take you to the docks. the *Sea Majesty* doesn't set sail until tomorrow morning."

"Thank you, Hen-wy."

With a grave expression, he hurried from the room. His voice echoed in the hallway as he barked orders to the servants.

Relieved, she leaned against a wall, trying to catch her breath. She'd have to convince Max he couldn't go away. She could tell him...

Her heart began to race. *Tell him what?*

***

The English countryside blurred into a jigsaw puzzle of trees and gentle hills outside of Miranda's carriage. Feeling wretched, she watched it all pass by. Goddess above, she ached and itched all over. She wanted to scratch herself raw but had managed to prevent herself from doing it by wrapping herself in a shawl. Otherwise by the time she found Max, it'd look like she'd gone several rounds in the ring with Mike Tyson.

Attempting to quell her trembling, she focused her thoughts on the fact every bouncing mile brought her closer to Max. *Hurry, hurry, hurry,* her mind chanted.

As she drew closer to the man who could cure her, she began to feel more and more like her old self. Max must not be too far away now.

Shifting her aching backside on the uncomfortable leather seat, she rested her head against the carriage wall. She thought back to this morning to when he had asked her to be his mistress. He had seemed so hopeful she would take him up on the offer.

For a brief moment, she allowed herself to dwell on the possibility of them being together, realizing the impossibility of it. He lived in a time when witches were believed to be hateful creatures. She highly doubted that if he knew the truth about her, he'd want to have a witch hanging around him for long.

In her present-day world, wicca and the magical arts weren't so frightening to humans. In fact, most people found the metaphysical interesting. However, the nineteenth century was a whole different ball game.

She sighed, once again stewing over how she was going to explain her unexpected visit to Max. It was going to be difficult. To top it off, how in the world was she going to get him to make love to her one more time? He was on a ship full of boisterous men, for Pete's sake. He wasn't going to want to get horizontal with her.

Just thinking about him released butterflies in her stomach. It was apparent her attraction had gone far beyond the need to cure her illness. Even though she'd tried to prevent herself from becoming infatuated with him, she'd done exactly that.

Every quirk of his smile sent ripples of anticipation up her spine. The man filled her heart with a giddy expectation unlike anything she'd experienced. She found herself hanging on every word he uttered from his gorgeous, sensitive mouth.

She'd toyed with mortal men before, but never for long. The few affairs she'd had over the centuries left her drained. These overgrown boys and their shallow promises left her wanting more—what, she'd never known for sure. Their antics made her regret the time she wasted with them.

After the fiasco with Tavis, she'd decided mortal men weren't worth the bother. They were too full of themselves, and their egos were as big as the universe. Every one of them seemed convinced the sun rose and set on their command.

So many of them were selfish and manipulative— not at all like Max. They knew nothing of honor and selflessness, whereas those personality traits seemed ingrained in the duke. She supposed that's why she hadn't spent time with a mortal man in centuries. She'd never met anyone worth the effort. And honestly, male witches weren't much better than the mortal variety.

Closing her eyes, the vision of Max's naked, eager flesh rose before her eyes. His amazing kisses and sizzling touch always caused her soul to soar with a whirlwind of energy. Even though she had only conjured up his image, it still did practically the same thing to her.

When she felt the carriage slowing down, she glanced out the window to see it had traveled through the outskirts of the city and now approached the river. Stomach churning with anticipation, she looked past the wharf buildings, and finally sighted the harbor where a cluster of ships thrust tall masts into the azure sky. She leaned forward, eagerly clutching the frame. Max was out there somewhere. When an electrical charge pulsed through her nerve endings, she nearly fell off her seat.

Whatever had caused the zapping sensation, it was a good thing. The torturous itching had stopped, her head felt clear. Looking at her arms, she saw the patches of red had completely disappeared and had been replaced by a healthy glow. She touched her face, grateful it no longer hurt.

Feeling one-hundred percent better, she loosened her shawl and let it drop to the seat. Max would probably be livid when he saw her. Would he think she was stalking him? Hopefully not. But even modern men didn't like it when women ventured into their man caves. The docks were definitely a man's domain, and she doubted he would welcome her with open arms.

She tapped her fingers on her knee, eager to reach Max. Finally, the carriage stopped near a huge ship with gigantic white sails snapping in the breeze. A buxom, carved wooden woman holding a black sign—'Chadwick & Weaver Ironworks'— jutted from the prow.

Without waiting for the footman to help her, she let herself out of the coach. Lifting her skirts, she quickly strode up the gangplank, ignoring the stares and catcalls from the motley assortment of men on deck. A burly fellow in a striped shirt blocked her progress before she'd gone very far. A snarl of tattoos pulsed on his muscled biceps, which were about the size of tree trunks. She suppressed a giggle. He looked like Popeye.

"Where do you think you're going, missy?" His curled lips revealed dirty, rotting teeth.

She met his gaze head on. "I'd like to speak with Sir Maxwell Chadwick."

"He's sick," Popeye growled, looking her up and down appreciatively, making her skin shrivel with disgust. When he licked his lips, it was apparent what he had on his mind.

Gag me!

She quelled her irritation at Popeye, focusing only on Max. Popeye said he was sick. That wasn't good. "Please, tell him Miranda is here. It's urgent I speak to him."

After spitting a wad of tobacco into the water, he wiped his mouth on the back of his dirty hand and said, "Sure m'lady. But he won't be none too happy if I disturb him."

As he made his way up the gangplank, cussing all the way, she began to follow. He rounded on her with a terrible glare.

"Wait here. There's no wimmin allowed on board. It's bad luck."

She spent a few anxious minutes ignoring the ogles of the crew and their lewd comments. To try and forget them, she did her best to try and enjoy the harbor view. At last, Max appeared on deck. As he walked toward her, his brow furrowed. His expression was far from welcoming, but at least he looked hale and hearty.

"I heard you were sick," she said, concerned.

He nodded. "I thought I was coming down with something earlier today, but I'm feeling much better now that you're here."

"I'm so glad."

She flushed with the compliment, then realized that Max may possibly have been affected by her disease as well. She'd been sick, he'd been sick. It made sense. Ursula had described the seven-year witch disease to her pretty quickly. It was entirely possible the old witch hadn't explained all of the symptoms that could occur. Another reason why she and Max needed to be intimate one more time.

He folded his arms across his chest. "Is there a problem?"

"Well, sort of."

"This is a dangerous place for a woman, Miranda."

Again, she tried to think of a good way to broach the subject. It wasn't easy. She didn't want to appear desperate, but she was unwilling to let him get away from her again. The idea of breaking out in another horrendous rash made her stomach clench. She didn't want the same to happen to him.

"I, um, ah...I don't think you should leave right now." She winced, realizing how lame she sounded.

His mouth twitched. "I don't have a choice."

"It's just that—"

"I told you about the fire at the ironworks. I have to go."

"But…"

"But what?" His brows furrowed. "You haven't changed your mind about waiting for me, have you?"

She didn't answer him because she didn't want to lie. And she was worried. How could she tell him what she needed? If she blurted it out, he'd think she had lost her mind. He'd probably haul her off to the loony bin or worse. And how could she blame him?

He cast an anxious glance toward the men bustling around on deck. They kept looking over, but the baiting remarks had fallen off. Probably because they knew the Duke of Pellamshire wouldn't appreciate their language.

"We can talk more when I return," he told her.

"This can't wait." Her heart hammered in her ears, and it seemed as though her head had been swallowed by a drum. Everything hung in the balance. If Max wouldn't cooperate with her, she was in big trouble. Actually, they both were, now that she knew he'd been afflicted by the disease, too. If he left her here and sailed off for America, he'd be overcome by horrible symptoms.

She twisted her hands together, willing the right words to come out. The words that would magically make him understand. But they didn't.

Chapter Twelve

As much as Max wished he could stay with Miranda, he knew he couldn't. He thought she understood why he had to leave, and he was very annoyed she'd followed him here. It seemed the air had somehow been sucked from his lungs as he struggled to come up with a response that wasn't exceptionally harsh. But he had to deal with the situation.

"It's imperative that I get to Boston. The sooner we get the factory repaired, the sooner the workers can resume production," he told her.

"I know, Max. But something awful will happen if you leave me. I just know it."

He frowned. "What's this? Have you had some sort of premonition?"

"It's hard to explain."

A vein began throbbing in his forehead. Miranda was the type of woman who could hold a man's attention captive, like an insect caught in a spider's silken web. As much as he had enjoyed their time together, and looked forward to more of it, he also didn't want to become her puppet.

If he began knuckling under to her demands, he'd lose his independence. Not a very manly prospect. He stiffened his shoulders, realizing that under no circumstances could he allow her to interfere with his business or let her attempt to control his life.

He clenched his jaw. Perhaps he'd been hasty in asking her to be his mistress. Perhaps she really didn't understand him as much as he'd thought she did. Maybe it had been hasty on his part to think they might have a future together.

"Will you at least kiss me goodbye again?" She looked up at him, her blue eyes inviting.

He cleared his throat. "Certainly."

Leaning over, he gave her a light peck on the lips, his motions stiff and jerky. The men, unable to contain their enthusiasm, whistled and hooted. He felt embarrassed at first, then something unusual happened. The kiss deepened, became more intense. Despite his irritation, the icy ball of his heart began to thaw. His nostrils twitched with the fresh rose scent wafting from her golden tresses. She was so damn lovely and difficult to resist. A needful groan rose in his throat and he reached out to pull her against his chest, buried his hands in her hair.

By Jove, she felt wonderful. His mind exploded with sensual need. He wanted nothing more than to haul her up into his cabin and make passionate love to her. Even though the men continued to jeer, he ignored them.

Fool, an urgent voice in his head taunted. But he couldn't help himself.

She was like the most wonderful confection ever invented, sweet and tasty, and he found her completely irresistible. When he finally did break the kiss and pull back, the tears spiking her long dark lashes chased away the angry words he intended to speak next. Her lovely countenance drew him like Odysseus' sirens. He tried not to let her affect him, but it was useless.

Like a fish on a line, he was hooked. She had worked an intoxicating magic on him. He couldn't be upset with her any longer. His heart wouldn't let him.

God help me, I've gone soft in the head.

"Tell me, sweetheart. What did you see?"

Her breasts rose and fell unevenly as she began to speak. "Even as a child, I've been able to see things in the future. I know it sounds...unusual. But I sense danger for you on this voyage. If you hold off for just a couple of days and spend the time with me, you'll be all right."

He took her hands and cupped them in his. "I don't believe in foresight and portents. It must have simply been a nightmare."

"Max, you've got to believe me."

"You worry too much. I'll be fine."

***

Miranda's hopes sank. Even more than his words, the stubborn set of Max's jaw told her he wouldn't budge. Why should he? He had no clue what was really going on.

She tried one last time to appeal to him. "Are you sure you won't reconsider?"

He nodded. "As much as I've enjoyed seeing you one last time, it isn't right for you to be here. Remember what I told you—set yourself up in a nice hotel or a flat and wait for me to return."

Max walked her back to the carriage. When he opened the door, she crawled back inside and took a seat. She felt cold and numb, as if a blizzard had frozen her soul. Feeling his gentle touch on her arm, she glanced up at him.

"I promise I'll sail back to England as soon as I can."

She watched as he turned and walked away from her. Up the deck he went. A second later, he disappeared below deck. This was bad. Really bad. Silently she railed at the goddess, and whoever or whatever had cursed her with this disease. A raw ache shot through her breast, slicing it as though a knife had grazed her tender skin. She wouldn't be able to rid herself of this illness and she would not be able to continue searching for Balthazar and the Philosopher's Stone.

Aunt Aggie would be imprisoned in the Tower of Destiny.

Mankind would be embroiled in a cataclysmic war.

You've lost this battle, Miranda.

Sighing with frustration, she slumped back against the seat.

"If only I were a man." She glanced wistfully back at Max's ship. "Then I could go aboard with the rest of the crew."

That's the ticket!

An idea formulated in her head, and she smiled. Leaning out the window, she called up to the driver, requesting that he take her over to a pub located across the street. When he dropped her off, she gave him instructions to return home. At first, he didn't want to leave her, but she insisted.

When she entered the drinking establishment titled, 'The Bucket of Blood,' she stood still for a moment, allowing her eyes to adjust to the darkened room. With clearer vision, she saw it was full of roughly hewn tables and chairs, along with rowdy drinking men and tawdry women. People looked strangely at her, but she ignored them as she walked up to the bar. One of the waitresses was about her size, so she caught her attention.

"Would you like to have my dress and shoes?" She twirled around to model the attire, which happened to be some of the latest fashions from Paris, according to the servant who had brought everything to her room.

The girl's eyes opened wide. "Yes, m'lady. But I'm afraid I couldn't pay you for such fineries—"

"I don't want money."

Miranda explained to the girl she only needed some men's work clothing—the more worn out, the better.

"Aye, me brother over there's got plenty of tattered clothes in me mending basket." She called out to the proprietor—a rotund, jolly fellow behind the bar—that she was going to take a short break. Then she led Miranda into a back room. The girl wasted no time locating the men's clothing.

Miranda quickly dressed in brown trousers, a red plaid work shirt, and scruffy boots. Everything was large on her, but that was a good thing. If it had been tight, it would have easily revealed her sex. That would have ruined everything.

The girl also gave her a blue woolen stocking cap. She pulled it on, stuffing her long hair underneath and pulling it over her ears.

"Blimy," the girl said as she looked Miranda up and down. "You look just like a boy."

Feeling pretty cocky about her strategy, Miranda went back outside and headed toward Max's ship. She did her best to try and walk like men often did. Head lowered, she took long, swaggering strides, her arms held at her sides, fists clenched. It occurred to her that her clean hands and face didn't match the dirty ones of the dock workers. In an alley, she located a mud puddle and smeared the brown substance randomly on her cheeks, chin and forehead. She rubbed her hands on her shirt and pants.

There, that was more like it. Emerging from the alley, she resumed her march toward Max's ship. When it seemed to be the right moment, she slipped in amongst the crew and joined the activity.

A wooden box labeled 'soap' sat beside a pile of items that were being loaded aboard the ship. Picking it up, she made her way up the *Sea Majesty*'s gangplank. It wasn't terribly heavy, but it also wasn't light. Her arms strained with the weight. Perspiration dotted her forehead. Her heart hammered. She glanced around, hoping she didn't seem out of place.

No one pointed fingers at her. No one raised an alarm.

Could it really be possible her sudden appearance didn't catch anyone's attention? It seemed that way. Men continued to shoulder past her, completely unaware she wasn't one of their own.

A relieved sigh caught in her chest as she stood there, amazed and relieved. Stars above, this was easy.

Almost *too* easy.

"Hurry and put that over there with the rest of 'em boy," a grubby old man with grime rimming his eyes snarled at her. His beard looked dirty and snarled enough to hold a nest of mice. And his battered clothing looked like it had been buried in a garbage pit for ages. He pointed toward a stack of supplies. "The cap'n is payin' us extra to get things loaded quick-like. Get a move on."

With a grunt, she did as he instructed.

Dusting off her hands after she put the crate down, she studied the crisp white sails flapping in the breeze, and the mighty masts thrusting skyward. It had been a long time since she'd lived during the time of great sailing ships.

Then she saw Max.

He stood nearby, calling orders to the men. His dark hair ruffled in the breeze, and he often lifted his face to study the sky. No doubt, he was judging the weather as he thought about setting sail tomorrow. Her heart gave a giant lurch.

He seemed so alive, so vibrant. His eyes flickered with a fiery zeal and self-assurance literally exuded from his every pore. He seemed so alive, so vibrant.

I need him to be as passionate about me. Just one more time.

That was all fine and dandy. But she still needed to find a way into Max's bed again. He'd be angry beyond belief when he found out she'd sneaked aboard. A million thoughts ricocheted in her mind as she tried to decide what to do next.

One thing's for sure, I can't stand here ogling the man.

Hefting another box, she resumed the chore of loading provisions. By the time the sun sank in a blaze of fire on the horizon, the last of the supplies had been tucked away. After congratulating each other on a job well done and slapping each other on the back, the crew straggled below deck. Careful to stay a short distance behind them with her shoulders slumped, she followed. She took a seat on a long bench, far away from the others. When she was passed a tin plate with stew and biscuits, she ate it like the rest of the men, which was none too pretty. Finished, she wiped her mouth with the back of her hand, just as they did. No one could accuse them of being too prissy. Their manners were atrocious.

Once she'd finished her meal, she wanted nothing more than to lay down somewhere and rest. Every muscle in her body screamed from exhaustion. It was everything she could do to keep her eyes open. Not wanting to arouse suspicions, she remained with the men, pretending to drink from the bottle of rotgut ale they passed around the room and listening to their bawdy tales.

Eventually the salty fellows began to filter down to steerage where serviceable bunks lined the walls. As each of the crew claimed beds, she found one of her own in a corner against a wall. Burrowing beneath her rough woolen blanket, she closed her eyes and did her best to try and sleep. The quarters were small and cramped. Her back began to ache. Something warm crawled over her. When she kicked it off, it squealed.

Goddess above. *A rat.*

If the vermin weren't enough, as the night went on, the men soon began to snore. And fart. And cough, spit, and hack. When she couldn't stand it any longer, Miranda slipped out of bed and made her way through the shadowy confines up to the fresh air on the quarter deck. Gathering some discarded canvas bags, she created a makeshift sleeping area in a corner and stretched out. As her stiff body sank into the comfort, she studied the wash of stars twinkling above in the inky sky.

All was right with her world. For the moment, anyway.

She knew Max wouldn't be happy when she finally revealed herself, but she didn't plan to do that for a few days. By then the ship would be too far away from land for him to consider turning around.

He'd have to let her stay.

***

Seated at the desk in his cabin, Max swiped his quill pen across parchment, sketching rudimentary drawings of the ironworks factory. He lined out what he remembered from his last visit, intending to make revisions once he'd assessed the damage. He knew fire had ravaged an extensive amount of property, but he wouldn't know for certain how much until he arrived. Then, as soon as he could hire craftsmen and purchase materials, repairs could get underway.

He rocked back in his chair, placed his hands behind his head and allowed his eyes to rest. Damnation, but this was tedious work. He might as well do it now, though. There was no getting around it.

They'd only been at sea for several days, but he wanted to get a jump on the numerous details that needed to be done. It also kept his mind off Miranda. Her strange behavior on the docks had been confusing. He couldn't imagine what had gotten into her, but if she was this unstable, perhaps he needed to reconsider keeping her as his mistress.

Irritation came over him, but he quickly brushed it away. He didn't have time to worry about the woman's vagaries. Not right now, anyway. Once he returned, he could deal with the situation.

He really shouldn't be surprised by her curious behavior. She obviously wasn't a demure, genteel young lady of good breeding. He hadn't liked her any less for her lack of pedigree, but she had rough edges he probably wouldn't ever be able to erase. And anyway, he rather liked her as she was.

An unpolished gem, a diamond in the rough.

Yes, that was a good way to put it. Setting his jaw, he attempted to concentrate on his drawings once again. As the day wore on, the wind picked up. He grew more and more concerned as it began to howl. The ship became unsteady, pitching to and fro. He had to hang onto his pen and inkwell lest they be tossed from his work table onto the floor. Finally, he gave up and put them away.

Glancing out a porthole, he watched as massive waves slammed into the ship. A dark mood descended over him. A storm this intense didn't bode well. When a loud knock sounded at his door, he frowned.

"I told you I didn't want to be disturbed," he called out.

"Sir Maxwell, we have a problem that needs your immediate attention."

The interruptions to his work had been endless the entire trip. He supposed one more wouldn't matter. Especially since the ship's tossing prevented him from doing much anyway.

"Enter."

Captain Jim O'Reilly, a grizzled elderly man with a solid sea-faring history, swaggered into the room. He grabbed hold of a chair to keep steady.

"The men are goin' off halfcocked, sir. I can't get them settled down."

"What's the problem? I've seen worse storms than this."

O'Reilly shook his head. "It ain't just the weather, sir. They're all up in arms about a woman who stowed away, and they've descended upon her like a pack o' dogs. But she said she knows you. Since I couldn't talk any sense into the men, I thought perhaps you could."

It felt as though someone had punched Max in the stomach. He only knew of one woman who would be so bold as to stow away on a ship.

"She said she knows me?"

"Aye, sir."

A muscle ticked in his jaw. "Where is she?"

"I'll show you."

As Max followed the captain from his cabin, he decided it had to be Miranda. But how? He'd personally escorted her to the carriage. He'd stood on deck and watched as the blasted thing drove away. This didn't make any sense. Attempting to keep his temper at bay, he climbed the ladder. On deck, gusts of wind tore through his hair and tugged at his clothing. Rain whipped across the deck. Wiping water from his face, he saw the group of men standing beside the main mast, their loud voices punctuating the air. They stood in a circle, staring at something, their taunting voices loud.

He shoved his way through the crowd and made his way up to the front. A small figure in men's clothing stood there lashed to the post, flowing golden hair flattened by rain water.

Miranda.

"Bloody hell," he muttered angrily, wondering why the devil she'd come on ship. The woman must be mad.

"Max," she cried. Her face was red and mottled with bruises, her eyes and cheeks swollen. Her clothing was ripped nearly to shreds. Ropes bit into her shoulders and arms. It looked as though she'd been beaten.

"I'll have Captain O'Reilly flog every last one of you and dock your wages," he roared. Whipping out his pocket knife, he began cutting Miranda loose.

"I had to follow you," she sobbed.

"You're out of your mind," he told her between gritted teeth. "You could have been killed."

A brawny man named Jock swaggered forward, his face a mask of rage. A flash of lightning illuminated his terrible expression. "Ain't no wimmin allowed aboard ship, Sir Maxwell. It's bad luck. Right boys?"

The crew shouted in agreement, pumping their fists into the air.

"It's my ship and I'm telling you to stand down," Max growled.

"But she caused this storm." Jock pointed at Miranda. "She's brewing up trouble for all of us, skulking around in places she shouldn't. I feel it in me bones!"

"Aye," another fellow snarled. "We'll wind up rotting in Davy Jones' locker if we let her stay aboard."

Another bolt of lightning shot through the dark purple sky, and jagged thunder rolled with deadly precision above the ocean swells.

"This needs to stop," Max told them, trying to speak over the roaring wind. "Resume your positions."

"Death to the witch!" Jock spat as a spray of frothy sea water curled over the rail and lapped across the weathered deck. "Throw the wench overboard!"

"You'll have to go through me first." Max moved in front of Miranda, shielding her with his body.

"He's defending the witch!" Jock shouted. "Throw him overboard too."

"I demand you stop this madness!" The blustery weather practically ripped the words from his mouth. Consumed by a superstitious frenzy, the crew wasn't listening to him. When Captain O'Reilly spoke up, trying to talk some sense into them, one of the crew pulled out a pistol and shot him.

His body thumped to the deck.

Max stared at O'Reilly's lifeless body, stunned. As the mob surged forward, Miranda pressed herself against him. Her trembling body told him how frightened she was.

He turned around and swung her cold, chilled body into his arms, and she wrapped her arms around his neck.

He tried to step around the men, but they blocked every possibility for escape. With nowhere else to go, he carried Miranda up onto the quarter deck.

Torrents of rain pelted his face, blurring his vision. Above the howling wind, he heard Miranda's sobs. If it hadn't been for her sneaking aboard, none of this would have happened. Yet, it wasn't entirely her fault. It seemed the crew had gone insane.

As the ship tossed and pitched like an unbroken horse, he lost his footing, sprawled backward into the railing. The impact of his body cracked the wood, and he tumbled toward the black ocean. Bitter cold waves swallowed him. Liquid filled his lungs, sucked away his breath.

All he could think was to try and hold onto Miranda. *Impossible.* She slipped through his arms like sand in an hourglass. At the sound of her body splashing into the dark water, he called out.

She didn't answer.

He closed his eyes as the ocean dragged him into a watery tomb. Fingers of icy death embraced him.

Chapter Thirteen

Aggie loved her garden—she loved her entire home. She would rather be here than anywhere on earth.

Puffing on a clove cigar, she gazed out at the colorful autumn display with its deep green leaves and blossoms of blue, yellow, orange, and pink. Several light October frosts had faded the blooms, but the plants still retained a haunting beauty. The flowers and shrubbery greatly enhanced the Rose Mansion's handsome architecture. A large, white-shingled edifice with a generous wraparound porch, it rested on gentle brown bluffs that angled down toward the misty blue Columbia River. The broad waterway meandered far into the distance, eventually feeding into the Pacific Ocean shimmering to the west.

Fertile acres surrounded the mansion, filled with fruit and nut trees, berry bushes, vegetables, and herbs such as basil, celandine, dragon's blood, and rosemary. She and her nieces used them to concoct their soaps and scents for the shop in downtown Wysteria, and for their magical midnight rites of healing and empowerment.

She headed toward the lavender bushes. Leaning over, she clipped off some of the long shaggy stems, dropping them into an old basket. When the tiny purple buds dried, they would add spicy fragrance to her sachet mixes. Customers loved her sachets. They had become one of the shop's top sellers.

When a rush of panic swirled through her, she stood up straight. The basket tumbled from her hand, and lavender stalks spilled onto the ground. She placed her hands on her forehead, clamped the cigar between her teeth and allowed her intuition to take over.

Someone's in danger.

In her mind's eye, she saw two people in waves of darkness. A sense of horror and overwhelming loss came over her. She knew instinctively Miranda was one of the individuals but didn't recognize the other person. It soon became clear they would both die if she didn't do something. Fast.

"Lizzy," she cried.

Miranda's sister opened the back door of the mansion and looked out. She wore a mauve sundress and an expression of concern. "Yes, Aunt Aggie?"

"Get your sisters together and hurry out to the pond. We need to create a spiritual circle."

Lizzie ducked back inside without asking a single question.

Good girl, Aggie thought. She never asked her nieces to gather for this purpose unless it was for a legitimate reason. Hurrying toward the small pool where she and the girls often went for divination purposes, she took her position. Shiny, fat goldfish slid silently through the shallow depths. Occasionally they swarmed at the base of a fountain featuring Artemis, the Greek goddess of the hunt, then darted off in all directions.

A few moments later, four of her sisters' daughters rushed from the house, their silken curls bouncing across their shoulders. Lizzy, Cassie, Tara, and Samantha. All were so young and had the exceptional good looks of their parents. Aggie motioned them over to her side.

"Form a circle, girls."

"What's happening?" Lizzie stared at her. Her sisters echoed with similar questions, their expressions puzzled.

"There's no time to explain," she told them.

The young women soberly positioned themselves around the statue. Aggie withdrew a small vial of magical water, which she sprinkled into the pond. After stubbing out the cigar, she raised her hands skyward and began to chant.

"Wind of spirit, inner fire—reveal the answer that I desire…"

The girls repeated her words, chanting in soft voices.

Invigorating energy charged through her. A strong wind rustled tree branches, then brushed against her skin, raising goose pimples. Images appeared in the water. A large ship, rocking on murky ocean swells, its tall sails flapping during a raging storm.

Two small figures struggled in the choppy waves next to it, struggling to stay afloat. She could tell one was Miranda, and her heart clenched.

"Closer," she whispered and her inner vision honed in on a man she didn't recognize.

"That's Miranda," Lizzy cried.

"Don't break the circle," Aggie reminded everyone before she began to chant again, "Spirit touched, I see two beings. Bring them forth and harm them not, blessed be!"

A loud rumbling issued from the earth, and the ground trembled. A second later, water splashed across the lawn and paving stones. Aggie and her nieces wiped droplets from their faces and stared at the pond where two figures had appeared.

Miranda sat at the base of the statue, a hand pressed against her chest, an expression of surprise and relief on her face as she struggled to catch her breath. She looked like a drowned dog. The man Aggie had seen in the vision lay unconscious next to her, his head in her lap, his long legs stretched out across the shiny flat stones. Schools of tiny goldfish nibbled at his boots and hands.

The girls gathered around Miranda, uttering sympathetic noises and offering assistance.

"Wow, that was something else." She coughed and wiped moisture away from her face. She shot a bemused glance Aggie's way. "Are my parents home?"

"No," Aggie told her. "They haven't returned from Egypt yet. The research trip must be taking longer than they planned."

She pressed her lips into a line of disappointment.

"It's all right, dear. I'll do everything I can to help you."

"Thanks, Aunt Aggie. I hate to be a bother, and I appreciate it."

"Let's get you out of the water," Cassie suggested.

As the sisters thrust out their hands to help Miranda, she shook her head.

"I'm kind of pinned down right now." She pointed at the partially submerged man.

Cassie whistled as her gaze roved over his manly form. "Wow, Miranda. Is that your duke? He's a real hottie!"

"After what we've just been through, gods forbid he doesn't catch pneumonia. We both would have died if you guys hadn't brought us here. But won't the witch's council be irritated?"

Aggie lit another cigar and stuffed it in her mouth, studying her youngest niece through a haze of smoke. "They'll get over it. If I hadn't done something you and your dashing duke would have drowned."

"But I'm worried—"

"Relax, sweetie. You didn't bring forth the magic. We did. This won't jinx anything. Now let's get you out of there before your skin wrinkles like a prune."

"What about him?" She patted the duke's shoulder. "What's he going to think about being here when he wakes up?"

"Which won't happen for quite a while," Aggie soothed. "I cast a sleeping spell on him the second you two arrived in this dimension."

She shook her head. "I have no idea what I'm going to tell him about all of this."

Aggie studied the duke's damp face, admiring the angle of his jaw. He was definitely a fine specimen of mortal man. "Have the two of you gone at it seven times yet?"

The sisters poked each other then began to snicker and giggle.

Staring daggers at them, Miranda said, "This is *so not* funny you guys. Knock it off."

"Well, have you?" Aggie arched a curious brow. "I'm not just being nosy, you know. It's important."

Crimson filled Miranda's face. "It's not easy playing by nineteenth century dating rules, which suck by the way. I threw myself at him like a *you-know-what*. It was ridiculous and humiliating."

"And?" Cassie asked.

"And what?" Miranda's brow furrowed.

"You know," Tara coaxed. "Did you two go for it?"

"None of you will let this be until I spill the beans, will you?"

All four sisters shook their heads.

"All right, have it your way." She cleared her throat. "The Duke of Pellamshire is a healthy, hot-blooded male with zero problems in the bedroom department and an amazing tattoo on his...well, you get the picture. Now that's the end of it."

Peals of laughter echoed in the garden.

Lizzie grinned. "Get me anywhere near a stud like him and I wouldn't be able to keep my hands off the poor boy for a minute."

"Of course, that's why we appoint you with the horniest little witch award every year. We know you're a man eater." Samantha snapped her fingers and a gold statue of a woman chasing down a desperate-looking fellow appeared in her hands. She handed it to Lizzy, who took it and stuck out her tongue.

"Do you guys even realize what a terrible predicament I'm in?" Miranda's face melted into lines of concern.

The sisters stopped laughing.

"I have to convince the duke to sleep with me one last time before I regain my powers so I can get the Philosopher's Stone from Balthazar." Her chest heaved with emotion. "He's going to be furious when he finds out where he is and what I am."

"You don't know that," Aggie told her shivering niece. "Just tell him the truth."

"He lives in 1877, Aunt Aggie. Women have a certain place in his mind, and it's not riding on a broomstick."

"You've got to give it a try," Aggie urged.

"Oh, I will, but I don't have much hope. He'll think I have green blood and gobble up little children for breakfast."

"I highly doubt that," Aggie said. "I have a feeling you'll be able to convince him to see things your way. Show him what witches are really like."

"He's hard-headed, Aunt Aggie."

"Don't sell yourself short, sweetie. If you're willing to take on a cunning wizard to get the Philosopher's Stone, I'm certain you can do this."

"A cunning wizard who is like eleven-years-old, by the way. What's up with that? The way everyone talked about him, I thought he'd be at least a hundred or more."

Aggie laughed. "Many wizards have held the stone over the centuries—all named Balthazar. Whoever takes possession of it assumes that name. Typically, the wizard winds up using the stone for evil purposes. He holds it a while, then loses it because he can't handle its powers, which is why the council has tried for so long to obtain it…"

"Believe me, I'm doing my best to get it. But this seven-year witch disease has seriously messed with my mojo." Miranda squeezed water out of her hair.

"You can do it," Aggie urged. "You're smart, and you're determined."

"You make it sound easy. Too easy. And I'm running out of time."

"Look at the bright side," Aggie said. "It could be worse."

Miranda sent her a miserable look. "How?"

"It could be All Hallows' Eve and your time would be up. As it is, you have a week before your deadline."

"What?" Miranda blinked. "I thought it was still summer."

Aggie shrugged. "Time travel is imperfect. Sometimes you land in the same month you left in. Other times, it's months later. Especially when there's trauma involved. You and the duke were on a sailing ship in the middle of a huge thunder storm. That produced great amounts of atmospheric interference which influenced the time continuum—"

Miranda held up a hand. "I get the picture."

"My advice to you is to work fast." She turned to her nieces. "Come on, girls. Let's get Miranda and her duke inside and find them some dry clothes."

An evil grin crossed Lizzie's face and she held up a hand. "I volunteer to help the duke out of his damp duds. And warm him up."

"Hah!" Miranda cradled the duke closer. "Over my dead body."

"Do I detect possessiveness?" Lizzie grinned. "Have you perhaps fallen in love with His Hotness?"

Miranda's gaze became thoughtful. "I have feelings for him. Love him? I don't know…"

Aggie frowned. This wasn't good. White witches were tasked with protecting mortals, but it would be a serious breach of protocol for one to fall in love with a human. The Supreme Witch's Council had forbidden such fraternization.

Since the girls continued to argue about who would get to undress the duke, she pulled her wand from an apron pocket and waved it at the duke. When he disappeared, Miranda stared down at her empty hands and made a surprised sound.

"Don't worry," Aggie told her. "He's out of his wet clothing and safe in your bed, sound asleep." She took her youngest niece's hand and helped her out of the pond, tapped the wand against her shoulder and clothed her in a warm lavender robe and slippers. "However difficult it may prove, you'd better rein in your feelings, my dear. The council just put a ban on witch/mortal marriages. They've proven far too perilous, as you yourself know after your brief time with Tavis McClarren."

"That's right," Cassie muttered. "You need to be careful, Miranda."

"Yes, please do," Lizzie added.

Miranda's face drained of color. "I knew the council frowned on mixed relationships, but now they've completely outlawed them?"

Aggie nodded. "They met last week and declared the new ruling. And they mean business, my dear. Any witch caught trying to maintain a long-term relationship with a mortal will be hunted down and banished to Rhemsela Point. I'm certain you don't want to mine the gold fields of Zyngarth until it's time for you to join the ancestors, do you?"

"Son of a monkey," Miranda muttered. "No, I don't."

Aggie nodded. "So, you must finish up with the duke before you arouse the council's suspicions. That's why Ursula came to warn you." Noting Miranda's crestfallen expression, she patted her back and added, "I realize you've developed an attachment for the duke."

"Unfortunately, I have," Miranda said. "I tried not to, but I can't seem to help it. Hopefully it's only the disease that's making me so crazy."

Aggie agreed. If Miranda's infatuation wasn't due to the disease, she was in hot water. "Do you remember my fiancé, Thomislan?"

Miranda gave a quiet nod.

"I lost him, too, you know. They were far different circumstances than yours; but nevertheless, a terrible experience. Yet I managed to live all these years without him."

"I know," she said.

"Promise me you'll be careful."

"I will, Aunt Aggie."

"We'd rather not see you languishing in Rhemsela Point. Right girls?"

"Right," all the sisters echoed.

Linking elbows, Aggie and her nieces walked toward the mansion.

***

A raging inferno consumed Max; the flames licked wildly at his skin.

Though he wasn't a religious man, as he fought for his life, he felt the presence of an all-knowing creator. Now he deeply regretted his lack of faith for it seemed God had deemed him an unrepentant sinner and had cast him into the fiery pits of hell. Satan touched his skin with fiery fingertips, setting him ablaze and locking him in a burning cage.

It's my fault my family died. I didn't warn them in time, and they stayed in London. They remained and perished from that damned fever...

Even though he knew deep down his guilt was unreasonable, he still cursed the fact that he had lived, and they all died. It wasn't fair. Somehow, he even felt it had been his fault that Catherine and her babe had died. Perhaps having him around as a reminder of their ill-fated relationship had weakened her. Perhaps that's why she didn't have the will to fight for her life when the childbirth had gone badly.

Moaning, he licked his dry, cracked lips. He called for help, but no one answered. That didn't surprise him. He'd always felt alone.

During his youth, his mother had remained busy training Marley—the future Duke of Pellamshire—to take his place in the social structure of the English court. His father had been mostly absent while attending to the duties of his position and hadn't spent much time with Max. Therefore, Max had lived his life as an outsider, seeing his family daily, but never truly feeling as though he belonged.

In order to quell the sting of rejection, he'd joined the Royal Navy to develop a sense of belonging and of having a place in the world. The strict regimen and harsh conditions had toughened him. Before long he'd grown armor around his heart. The thick shell didn't allow him to feel any room for emotion, and he rarely allowed anyone to penetrate his defenses.

He blinked and looked down. Blood coated his hands. Thick and gleaming red, it represented his family's suffering. A sick feeling anchored in his gut, twisting through him like a poisonous vine.

Now he would pay the horrible price for his sins. The heat intensified.

Make it stop.

Despite his internal pleas, it continued. He tossed and turned, like a haunch of venison over a kitchen fireplace, sweat dripping from his skin. Somehow, a vision of Miranda rose in his tortured mind—beautiful and golden like an angel. It nearly dispelled his anguish until he realized that because of the wrongs he'd committed, he'd lost her. During that storm aboard the *Sea Majesty*, she'd slipped from his grasp so easily, disappearing into the dark maw of the ocean.

Now he had the blood of another innocent on his hands. She wouldn't have sneaked aboard his ship if it hadn't been for him. She'd been worried about his welfare and had predicted something terrible would occur to him on the voyage. Yet he'd dismissed her fears as female histrionics and turned her away.

No doubt she'd thought she could keep him safe by coming aboard to watch over him. Instead, she'd forfeited her life to try and save his. Or had her unwarranted appearance caused the danger in the first place?

The idea confused him, and he realized it really didn't matter now. Either way, in the end, his arrogance had gotten her killed. Now, he would pay the price for his transgression.

His punishment—to burn in hell as strokes of flesh-melting fire seared his soul. His immortal soul—lost.

Chapter Fourteen

Midnight.

The grandfather clock in the hallway bonged loudly, pealing the hour. It finished, leaving a hollow echo, and the old mansion continued to hum and creak with familiar sounds. At home among familiar surroundings Miranda should have been comforted. But she wasn't.

Nearly twelve hours had elapsed since Aunt Aggie and her sisters had rescued her and Max and transported them into present day. Since then, Max had been stretched out unconscious in Miranda's bed. He seemed merely a shell of his former self as his body struggled to fight off a fever. Just as Miranda feared, he had inhaled too much sea water into his lungs, and he'd developed pneumonia-like symptoms.

She'd posted herself in a chair at his bedside, at a loss for how to relieve his discomfort. He tossed and turned, mumbling in delirium. She watched him like a hawk, frustrated. At least Aunt Aggie had cast a healing spell over him, but Miranda wished she could do more. Without her powers, she couldn't offer much. She had managed to get him to swallow some fennel tea, but Max still seemed uncomfortable. His mortal body didn't have the constitution of a witch's, and he wasn't responding quickly. It took longer to repair his fragile human system.

With each passing hour, her deadline to procure the Philosopher's Stone approached. And with each passing hour, her feelings for the duke became stronger. A frightening prospect. She tried her best to tamp down the yearning. Unfortunately, she wasn't having much success.

This must be the longest day of my life, she thought. Time stretched in slow motion, merging into one continuous experience. Meanwhile, her brain remained in high gear, processing everything that had happened. There was no use mulling things over and over. Yet she couldn't stop it.

Please wake up, be all right, she willed Max. But he remained asleep.

The bond between her and the duke, invisible and unbreakable, seemed to be growing even stronger. There was one problem, though. Before all of this, he had been strong, and self-assured. Now he lay quiet, vulnerable and weak. It pained her to see him this way.

Goddess above, she hated the idea she'd put him in this precarious position. But she hadn't had much choice, had she? When all of this started, she'd hoped making love with him seven times would be a piece of cake. Unfortunately, things had taken a much different turn.

Everything had turned into a nightmare. Worst of all, she feared she'd truly fallen for him. It wasn't like her to completely ga-ga for a man. Surely, she could blame the seven-year witch disease for making her so crazy. Once it had been cured, perhaps her infatuation for the duke would go away. Desperate for something to hope for, she clung onto that idea.

The monotonous silence seemed almost too much to bear. She crossed and re-crossed her legs. An issue of Witchcraft Today sat on a table, and she picked it up. Leafing through pages, she hummed a catchy tune she didn't remember the words to. She tossed aside the magazine, bored and anxious.

Lowering her head into her hands, she tried to get a hold of herself. Her mind was in a state of pandemonium. What would happen when Max woke up?

Surely, when he found where he was, and that he'd traveled here via witchcraft, he'd be outraged. He'd think she was a wacko. How in the world could she convince him to sleep with her one last time? If that didn't happen, they would both be in big trouble.

I'm going crazy.

Her head began to ache, and her heart thumped like a kettle drum. Between her worry about finding the Philosopher's Stone, and her growing attachment to Max, she could barely harness her wandering thoughts.

It was impossible to imagine how all of this was going to work out. No matter what she envisioned for the future, there didn't seem to be any scenario that was going to work out well. In a last-ditch attempt to do something constructive, she picked up the China cup sitting on her night stand. Dregs of chamomile brew filled the bottom. No doubt it had become cold. Oh, well, tea was tea.

After draining the last of it, she set aside the cup. She reached into a basin on the nightstand, retrieving a cool compress. Carefully, she dabbed it against Max's bruised forehead. He looked so different. The robust color of his face been replaced with an ashen cast. The absence of his energy, his vitality, left an ache inside her. Touching her pentacle necklace, she offered a silent prayer to the gods for Max's speedy recovery. Then she reached over and removed an amethyst crystal from a drawer in her nightstand. Placing it in his hand, she closed his fist around it, hoping the rock, imbued with magical powers, would also help him.

Please, heal this man, make him whole again…

"No, my family can't be gone…they simply can't be…" He clutched the sheets. The amethyst rolled from his hand and tumbled on the floor.

"Second best, I'm just second best," he went on. "It's all for Marley… he'll be the duke someday when Father has passed on…"

Her heart wrenched at the anguish in his voice. One would think he'd led a privileged life, but it didn't seem all that easy.

"I'm really a fifth wheel in this family," he muttered. "I have no prospects. Catherine fears this. I'll go to sea...forget her..."

He began thrashing around, and she pressed a hand against his brow. "Shhh, Max. It will be all right."

She began stroking his dark hair. It provided a measure of comfort. Before they parted, she needed to make it right with him. She wasn't certain what she'd do, but she knew it would eventually come to her.

"Don't tell me they're gone; they can't be," he muttered again. "God help me, it's all my fault."

She picked up his hand and held it against her cheek, wanting to take away his physical pain and his mental anguish. "You're safe, Max. You must rest now."

He continued to toss and turn.

She continued to stew.

***

Max slowly opened his eyes. An angel with a halo of glowing golden hair held his hand against her silken cheek. At first, he didn't recognize her. But he knew one thing.

No one could save him. No one except her.

Then he recalled who she was. "Miranda," he muttered. The sight of her filled him with joy, eased his discomfort.

"Thank the gods, you're awake."

He gritted his teeth. "Don't leave me."

"I won't. I'll stay by your side until you're better."

"And after?" he croaked.

"I'll still be here. That is if you still want me."

He smacked his dry lips together, wondering why he wouldn't want her to stay with him. True, she was a difficult woman and he'd often been confused by her behavior. But his feelings for her ran deep. He doubted anything would ever happen to change the way he felt.

My angel, he thought, as she continued to whisper soothingly to him. A cool cloth swiped across his fevered brow, taking away the wicked heat.

She smiled, and his heart smiled with her.

"Miranda, I—"

She pressed her fingers to his mouth, silencing him. "Save your strength, Max. You've had a rough time. Rest easy now."

Settling back against the sheets, he recalled the first time he'd seen Miranda lying in that empty field, her gown in tatters, her golden hair streaked with soot. Though he'd sensed she'd suffered some misfortune, she had never completely explained what had happened. Just that she had left her husband in America.

But under what circumstances?

When she'd found her way into his bed and asked for his help, he'd simply given it. He'd never questioned his desire to lend her assistance. Aside from the fact he'd requested Edward to inquire around town about her, he'd done nothing to discover her identity.

As he sorted through his reasons for accepting Miranda's sudden appearance, he became concerned. It seemed some strange force had come over him, and he'd never thought twice about having her in his life. He couldn't deny she brought excitement to his humdrum existence. Even though it seemed dangerous, he found himself wanting her, no matter what.

She'd entered his life during a point where he had become a stoic work machine—not thinking or feeling, just fighting for God and country. Doing his job had taken precedence over all. Miranda had changed all of that. She'd allowed him to feel again, to smile again and to even feel alive again.

He decided he would survive for his golden-haired woman who healed him with her touch and seduced him with her eyes. A giver of hope, a redeeming angel, she had become his reason for living.

She is my life.

Would she be kind with his heart if he gave it to her?

"Listen to me," he managed, searching the depths of her blue eyes. "Stay with me. Now and forever."

His angel leaned over and pressed soft lips against his forehead. "I'm here."

The flames of hell dissipated, and he felt her cool touch stroking the molten skin of his brow. A healing breeze swept across his body. He fell asleep, assured and at peace for the first time in quite a while.

***

Around noon the next day, Miranda's bedroom door opened, and Aunt Aggie brought in a tray laden with bowls of chicken soup and gooey, grilled cheese sandwiches. "How goes the nursing shift?"

She sighed. "He seems better. I just don't know how long it'll be before he completely regains consciousness."

"It takes a while for mortals to heal. Be patient." Aggie sat the tray on a dresser and handed a bowl to Miranda. "Eat this while it's warm. You need to keep up your strength."

Though her stomach recoiled at the concept of eating, she spooned the savory broth, noodles, and chunks of meat, into her mouth. Aunt Aggie was right. Starving herself wouldn't do any good.

When Max muttered something unintelligible, she set aside the bowl. Slipping one of his large, calloused hands in hers, she kissed the back of it, noting the thin white scars and tight, healed flesh.

His life at sea has taken a toll. This man had survived many things and had no doubt cheated death more than once. Surely, he could survive this.

He must have sensed her touch because when she pulled back, his eyes flickered open. His smile lit her entire world. With a sigh, he fell back asleep.

"You love him, don't you?"

She shot Aunt Aggie a look of surprise. "What?"

"The mortal." Aggie's face registered concern. "I've noticed how you look at him. You're in love."

"It has to be the disease that's making me feel this way." Miranda didn't know if she was trying to convince herself or Aunt Aggie.

"We can hope that's it. But we won't know for sure until you're cured."

"That's what's making me crazy, Aunt Aggie. Not knowing…" A strange mixture of excitement and trepidation rippled up her spine.

Is that why I have a hard time breathing around him? Is that why my heart takes flight when he touches me? Do I love Max?

She'd only had feelings for one other man—Tavis McClarren. But the Scottish warrior had always seemed so involved with himself that she'd never sensed a true commitment from him. Even after they'd become involved, even after she'd foolishly married him, her feelings for the man didn't compare in any way to what she felt for Max.

She felt a full-blown passion for the Max that reached deep inside her soul and drew out the mature woman. Yet to love him was to court danger.

"I don't really know what love is, Aunt Aggie."

"No one does, dear. It's something we feel when we're with the right person. It's magical—that feeling of being needed. You might think I don't know what it's like, but I do."

Aggie hugged herself and looked off into the distance, her eyes misty.

"You loved Thomislan that way, didn't you?"

"Yes, I did. Now he's gone from me forever, but I'll never forget what we shared." A bittersweet smile crossed Aunt Aggie's face.

"It's so sad how things turned out."

"I know, dear. When he was eaten by that giant asp, I thought I'd never be able to go on." Tears glittered in her eyes. "But I did."

"You're so strong," she said. Much stronger than her, she feared.

Aunt Aggie squeezed her shoulder. "This life we live is full of twists and turns. It bestows upon us the richness of wisdom. Our obligation is to use it well."

Miranda studied Max for a moment, trying to imagine what he would think when she told him who she really was. "I'm really worried, Aunt Aggie. When Max finds out the truth, he'll be angry." A pit grew in her stomach and settled heavily, like a chunk of lead.

Aunt Aggie ran a hand through her golden hair, so close in color to Miranda's. "I'm sure he'll be upset at first. Just be honest with him. He might surprise you."

I hope she's right.

After Aunt Aggie left, Miranda settled into keeping a watch over Max again. She pulled out her laptop and began to surf the Internet. As she flipped through her favorite clothing site, Silver Dagger Designs, she purchased a skirt and a couple of tops. Humans loved retail therapy, and so did she.

The rest of the day passed with Max resting soundly. Evening arrived and when it grew late, Miranda rose and walked to the window, opening the curtains to watch the luminous moon rise over the hills. A cool breeze ruffled her hair and cooled her warm cheeks.

Lady moon hear my prayer. Heal Max's mortal flesh, blessed be…

Incredibly weary, she slipped on a nightgown and curled up beside him on the bed, snuggling her head against his shoulder. It felt so good to be near him. Sadness swept through her when she realized she wouldn't be doing this for much longer. Like Aunt Aggie had said, life is full of twists and turns. She needed to do her best to learn from this.

While drifting off, she thought of what lay ahead. When Max woke up, he would want answers. She couldn't blame him. If she were in his place, she would want them too. When he began questioning her, would she be able to give him the answers that would help him understand?

She certainly planned on trying.

***

After having a strange dream about a pond and nibbling little goldfish, Max awakened. He sat up slowly and stared around in the darkness. The moonlight pouring through a window cast everything with a silvery glow. He was in a bedroom. The dressers and chests lining the walls gave it away. Frilly curtains and a lacy bedspread suggested it belonged to a woman. The scent of perfumes and powders told him it did.

He shifted his weight, wincing as dull pain radiated throughout his chest. Looking beneath he covers, he saw he wore a pair of flannel trousers. When he rested a hand against his forehead, cool skin met his touch. By Jove, he felt much better. He knew he'd been sick. Terribly so, but it seemed to have finally lessened its hold. Relief trickled through him.

Sensing a warm body pressed up against his, he looked down and saw Miranda, her hair spread across the pillows like an explosion of golden fire. Each time he'd faded in and out of consciousness, he saw her sitting beside him, attending to his every need. His heart gave a tiny lurch. He was more than happy to see her, but he had a lot of questions. Namely, where were they, and how had they gotten here?

He recalled being aboard the *Sea Majesty* during that terrible squall, and later, the crew's attack. Grimacing, he relived the terror of falling overboard into the ocean with Miranda. Then he'd lost his grip on her. It had nearly killed him watching her sink beneath the waves. He'd thought for certain they were both goners.

Obviously, they'd been rescued? By whom, though?

Miranda must have sensed he'd awakened. She sat up and took his hand, lacing her fingers through his. "How do you feel?"

He smacked his dry mouth together. For the moment, the need to quench his thirst overcame his curiosity. "I'm parched."

She let go of his hand. Lifting a pitcher on a nightstand, she poured water into a glass and handed it to him. He drank deeply, thankful for the cool refreshment. When he gave her back the glass, she set it aside.

"How long have we been here?" he asked, his voice ragged and worn.

"Almost two days."

"How did we survive falling overboard?" He started to rise, but she gently pressed him back down.

"You should rest more. You've been through a lot."

He leaned back against the pillows. Breathing came with difficulty, and his lungs struggled to draw in air. Even though his health had improved, he still felt as though he'd been run over by a carriage. Several times.

"Tell me what happened."

Miranda touched a small lamp on a bedside table. Pale light flooded into the room, illuminating the dark corners.

He blinked with amazement. "By George, am I seeing things? What is powering that lamp?"

"It's called electricity."

"Ah, yes of course. I've heard of this concept. But few people have it in their homes. Not even the gentry. It's far too expensive..." He forced himself to stop rambling. "Where in the devil are we?"

"In my bedroom."

"I'm really confused. We're in your bedroom where?"

"Wysteria, Oregon."

"Oregon Territory?" He frowned. "That makes absolutely no sense. We were sailing the Atlantic Ocean. We should have reached the *east* coast of America, not the west."

"It's complicated," she said. "You see, when we fell overboard, my Aunt Aggie and my sisters brought us here. We'd have both drowned if they hadn't intervened."

"They brought us here *how?*" He studied Miranda inquisitively. When dizziness threatened, he shook his head to clear it. This entire situation made him uneasy.

"By means of a time travel spell."

"Bah, I don't believe that. What gibberish are you trying to feed me? Where's my ship?" The questions poured from him like bullets dumped from a pistol chamber.

She took a deep breath and said, "The *Sea Majesty* is still back in 1877, Max. This is the year 2011."

"Impossible." He dropped his fist onto the night stand, rattling the contents. "That would mean we've traveled a hundred and thirty-four years into the future. What nonsense is this, Miranda?"

She folded her arms across her chest. "It's the truth, Max. My Aunt Aggie is a witch. And I'm a witch. My whole family practices the craft—my mother, my father, and my six sisters. We belong to the Hedge Haven clan."

His gut wrenched. There had to be a plausible explanation, one that didn't involve mythical beings. Perhaps he'd drowned and passed on. Or perhaps he was dreaming. He patted the sheets. No, he could feel their softness, and he could feel Miranda's warmth. This place was indeed real.

"I don't believe in witches," he insisted. "They're nothing but the stuff of fairytales."

"Oh, believe me, they're very real." She gave a nervous laugh and ran a hand through her tousled golden locks. "But we're not what the storybooks make us out to be. We're not cackling old hags with warts, we don't bleed green blood, and we don't go around casting evil spells. At least the witches in my clan don't. We've all sworn to do no harm and to help mankind. There are bad entities in the world—witches who practice black magic. But my clan works in the light, and we strive to accomplish only good deeds. That's why we exist; to balance the life of man with nature and see that humankind advances the way the gods want them to."

"This is preposterous." Anger bubbled within him. Miranda talked about things that couldn't possibly be real. She must be delusional.

He glanced over at the electrical lamp and a small black box sitting next to it with glowing green numbers. It read four thirty a.m. "What is that?"

"A clock," she told him. "It gives the digital time."

"What in the world is di-gi-tal?"

"I don't have time to explain how things have progressed over the centuries. Let's just say mankind has made a multitude of advances."

He glanced around, taking note of several other unusual gadgets lying around the room. It was almost too much to absorb. Lord, had he lost his mind?

Miranda got out of bed and picked up a shiny flat box. She flipped up one side, tapped on the other, then turned the object around so he could have a better look.

"Look at the time and date on my laptop screen." She pointed to a corner where he saw several numbers. "What do they say?"

Incredulous, he studied the contraption, then glanced down to where she held her finger. "Ten, twenty-six, two thousand eleven," he read aloud.

"That's the date, Max. It's October 26, 2011."

"Impossible," he said.

"It's the truth."

Attempting to get a grip on reality, he slid out of bed and moved toward the window. A hilly countryside stretched beyond the perimeter of the house's lush yard. It was beautiful and unfamiliar. Large, hulking metal objects sat out front on the gravel drive.

He pointed at them. "What are those?"

"Automobiles," she said as she came up beside him. "They would have been in the very infant stages back in your time. They are motorized carriages. Driven by engine horsepower, not the actual animals."

"I've heard of the concept. Inventors are experimenting with internal combustion to make them propel forward..." He shook his head, still in disbelief.

"I'm sorry, Max." She met his gaze. "I know all of this must seem crazy."

"Indeed." He pointed at the lamp. "If you're a witch then turn that into a toad. Reveal your magical powers to me."

A smile trembled on her lips. "I can't Max. It doesn't work that way."

"How does it work? What is happening? Why are we here?"

"It's a long story, so bear with me."

"Apparently I have nowhere else to go and no way to get there, so please, tell me."

She took a deep breath and began. "The Supreme Witch's Council assigned me to find the Philosopher's Stone as my final task. Upon completion, I'm to be promoted to high witch."

He wondered how long it had taken her to come up with this cock and bull story. He also wondered how long it would be before she finally admitted all this was a prank. But she merely continued talking.

"I've been looking for the stone for years," she explained. "I finally tracked it to a wizard named Balthazar. He's holding it in an invisible tower just outside London in 1877."

He lifted a disbelieving brow. "An invisible tower, eh?"

"Don't make fun of me." She arched a brow.

"I'm not. Not really. This is all just so difficult to believe."

"I'm sure it is, but I'm telling you the truth."

"I'm trying to believe you," Max said. "So continue. What happened next?"

"I time traveled back to 1877 to try and get the stone from him."

"Tell me, why does your witch's council want this Philosopher's Stone?"

"It can be used for good or evil. Unfortunately, for centuries, it's been held by wizards who become consumed by the stone's wicked influence. They can't control the power. The council wants the stone so they can use it to prevent a cataclysmic war between the mortals."

"A cataclysmic war, eh?"

She looked down at her hands, then back up at him. "I know you're still having trouble with all of this. I don't blame you."

He carefully considered what she'd just told him. He just didn't understand why he'd been brought into the perplexing situation. "Let's go back to the beginning, shall we? When I found you in that empty field, why was your clothing and hair singed?"

"The wizard had just zapped me out of his tower. The little butthead knocked me on my can."

He could hardly believe his ears. "So that's why you behaved in such a peculiar manner, eh? You'd been attacked by a wizard?"

"Exactly. Remember when you thought I'd flown away on my broom? You weren't seeing things."

He waved his hand dismissively. "Honestly, this can't be real. You cannot possibly be telling me the truth."

"Cross my heart, I'm not lying."

His brows drew together with consternation. "How did you convince me to allow you into my life? And into my bed? Have you hypnotized me?"

"Absolutely not. As far as why I showed up in your life, there is a good reason."

"Ah, yes, well, go on and explain. You have quite the imagination."

"Look, Max. I'm not making any of this up." Her blue eyes snapped. "I'm too old to want to play games with you."

"Really. Just how old are you?"

She rubbed the side of her nose. "I just turned seven-hundred-years old. In mortal years, that's like twenty-three or so."

He snorted with disdain and raked a hand through his hair. This was too much. She wanted him to believe she was seven centuries old? *Poppycock.* He could stand by no longer and listen to her fabrications. Perhaps if he offered to pay her, she'd go away and leave him alone. Seriously thinking about doing that, he began to pace.

"I'm having a hell of a time believing you're actually searching for a...a wizard and this magic stone. I'd like very much to put an end to all of this. Can you go away and leave me alone?"

"If I could, I would. But it's not possible. We need each other."

"Tell me why I should care about this preposterous wizard?" *And why should I care about you,* he thought. At one time, she'd taken an extremely important position in his mind. Now, he didn't trust her. She was behaving as though she'd lost her mind.

"Balthazar is just a child. I doubt he's more than twelve-years-old. To him, all of this is a game. He has no idea how badly he could be hurt. I've got to get the stone away from him. For his sake, and for all of mankind."

He chuckled. "By Jove, you actually believe this gibberish, don't you?"

She nodded.

"If what you're telling me is real, then why did you return to my home? Why weren't you out pursuing that Balthazar fellow?"

She blew a frustrated breath through her teeth. "Another monkey wrench in the plan, I'm afraid. I've been afflicted by the seven-year witch disease."

By Jove, she was either a very good actress or this delusion had become dangerously real in her mind. He hated to humor her fantasies, but he'd become curious.

"What does this disease have to do with me?"

"Basically, I've had a run on the number seven, which caused me to contract the illness. Seeing you kicked it into high gear. I began itching like crazy, my head hurt, and I couldn't think, talk, or walk straight. In order to alleviate the symptoms, I have to make love with you seven times."

How ridiculous. Then he recalled what had happened to him after Miranda disappeared, which had been most extraordinary. "I say, after you, er, flew off, I began to feel quite ill as well. I had a terrible headache and my stomach wouldn't settle. After I left you to sail to America, I also began to fall ill again."

"I'm pretty certain you've been affected by the disease, too. Until we've made love for the seventh time, we'll both be miserable. I thought we had done that already before you left for America. Apparently, I miscalculated. That's why I followed you to the docks."

"Are you saying you bewitched me?" He rubbed his neck, which had begun to ache like the dickens.

"Of course not," she shot back, her eyes flashing.

"You must understand how wild all of this sounds," he said.

"I know, and believe me, if I could rid myself of the disease, I would. But I can't. You hold the cure."

"Any man in his right mind would turn you over to the authorities, Miranda. It would seem as though you're trying to dupe me."

"If I were in your shoes, I'd feel the same way." Resting a hand on his shoulder, she looked at him, her gaze pleading. "But you've got to believe me."

Max noted the ring of sincerity in her voice. If what she'd told him was true, it also explained why he'd been so drawn to her. Recklessly so. It was a relief to know he wasn't completely out of his mind for becoming so unexplainably attached to her in such a short time. But it left him wondering about what he really felt for her.

"Our affection for each other, you're telling me none of it was real?"

"The disease has caused us both to do things we wouldn't have done otherwise."

Gadzooks, he felt like the biggest idiot in the world. He, a highly educated man, a duke of the English realm, no less, had been drawn into this intrigue like a helpless puppy. He should have realized at some point that things were amiss. Yet he'd been led to the slaughter, just like a lamb.

"I hate that this has happened," she said slowly. "I'm not sorry the disease made me want you, though. I really like you."

Her expression had faded into a pale mask. Not at all like the passionate, determined woman he'd come to appreciate. Though he had become painfully aware she'd only pursued him to cure her disease, her words touched him.

I really like you, she'd said. Well, he really liked her too—there was no denying it. He wasn't ready to admit it though, not while he was still trying to digest what had happened. If there was a way to restore things to normal, he wanted to give it a try. He could decide later what to do about his feelings for her, if any still remained.

"You're telling me all we have to do is make love again and all of this will be over?"

She nodded. "My powers will be restored, and I can send you back to your time. But we'll have to hurry so I don't miss my deadline."

"What will happen?"

"The council won't promote me to high witch, and I'll have to wait another hundred years to take my exams again. They will also imprison Aunt Aggie in the Tower of Destiny. The mortals will go to war with each other. It could mean the end of them."

"No minor consequences, eh?" Looking out of the window, he watched as the sun rose over the hills in a rosy glow. Despite the beauty, he felt cold and dead inside. "You've tricked me numerous times, Miranda. How can I know this isn't simply another ruse?"

"I never tricked you. I just let you believe what you wanted to," she replied softly.

Thinking back, he recalled the way things had gone since he'd met Miranda. As he sorted through the events, he realized she was right; she'd never completely lied to his face. Just fudged the facts. Despite his frustration, he also recalled holding her, touching her silken skin and the overpowering sensations he'd experienced when they made love.

Don't think of those things, he told himself. Her disease had affected him too, clouding his judgment. That meant he couldn't be sure about what he really felt for her. He pushed his attraction to her to the back of his mind. Right now, he had to figure out where he really was, and if Miranda's story was true.

"If I prove I'm telling the truth, will you cooperate?" Her voice was tinged with anticipation.

Blast it anyway, he might as well give it a try. There was really nothing else for him to do. "Yes."

Her expression registered relief. "The only thing I ask is that you make up your mind by sundown today."

He nodded, feeling an overwhelming urge to draw her into his arms, crush her against his chest and kiss her senseless. *Stop it*, he told himself. *Focus on reality*. He needed to get home. Back where things were familiar and normal. Back where Miranda couldn't turn his life upside down.

She doesn't really mean anything to me, a small voice taunted. Then his stomach clenched. But if that were so, then why did he feel so distressed thinking of a world without her in it? *It's the disease*, he tried to tell himself.

For some reason, he didn't believe it.

Chapter Fifteen

As Miranda led Max down the hall to the bathroom, she realized she had a big job ahead of her. She needed to convince him she'd told him the truth. No easy undertaking. The duke was tough as nails and used to running the show. He didn't like things he didn't completely understand. Time travel and witches, well, those were things he definitely didn't understand.

She'd have to work hard to prove she was telling the truth. And she needed to do it quickly, or else they'd both be in trouble. Too bad her powers were still on the fritz; it would have made things easier if she'd had them. Oh, well. She might as well dive in and do her best.

"You can clean up in here." When she leaned into the bathroom and flipped on the light switch, he stepped inside. With an inquisitive expression, he examined the toilet, the sink, then the shower head. Tapping the silver device, he raised a dark brow at her.

"What's this?"

"A shower head," she told him. "We can still take baths, but showers are much quicker. Would you like to try taking one?"

"Do you mean to say water actually comes out of this?"

"Stand back." He watched closely as she turned on the water. Hot, steamy spray exploded into the tub. After checking the temperature with her fingers, she turned to him. "It's ready."

He studied everything with a quiet reverence, tapping on the counter. "I say, this is quite incredible. I've heard of water closets, but I've never actually seen the concept so refined."

She grinned. "We've come a long way, baby. These days, indoor plumbing has reached new heights." She placed a towel, a disposable razor, shaving cream, and soap on the counter.

He rubbed his raspy chin between his thumb and forefinger. "What about my clothing?"

"It's been cleaned and pressed. I'll place it on the bed for you."

"Jolly good then."

When he started tugging at the drawstring of his pajama bottoms, she felt her jaw drop. Stars above, she'd rather have him served up on a platter instead of eggs and bacon. Noting her stare, he dropped his hands to his sides.

Face flaming with warmth, she managed to find her voice. "Uh, I'll just go down and make breakfast. I imagine you're starved."

He patted his muscular abdomen, and his stomach growled. "Surprisingly so."

She nearly tripped over her own feet as she turned to go. He caught her elbow, helping her regain her balance. Feeling like an idiot, she grinned up at him and babbled, "When you're finished, meet me in the kitchen. It's downstairs and to the right. You can't miss it."

He nodded, an amused expression on his handsome face.

Leaving Max to enjoy his shower, she returned to her room and made the bed, then laid out his underthings and his suit. Brushing fluffy pieces of lint from the dark, tweedy material, she studied the proper English gentleman's suit with its cut-away coat. His white shirt featured long sleeves and a turn-down collar. Aunt Aggie had even been able to salvage his silk, burgundy-colored tie, his shiny black shoes and socks.

He wouldn't look out of place wearing nineteenth-century clothing in the twenty-first century because honestly, mortals wore the strangest outfits imaginable. The residents of Wysteria would simply consider him a bit eccentric. And these days, eccentric was all the rage.

She used Aunt Aggie's bathroom to bathe in, then went back to her room to slide on jeans, a sweater, and a light jacket. As she bounded down the carpeted staircase, she hummed a tune. She felt pretty enthusiastic, considering. Maybe this whole situation could finally get resolved. Max hadn't been too happy when she'd tried to explain what was going on, but he also hadn't been completely put off. That was a good sign.

She didn't blame him for being mistrustful. If she'd been in the same boat, she would have felt the same way he did. Most mortals, especially those who lived in his century, were disbelieving of time travel, witches, and magic. She'd just have to prove to him, beyond a shadow of a doubt, that she told the truth.

As she contemplated the different places she could take him, she began to gather pots and pans. She retrieved everything she needed from the refrigerator and placed the items on the large butcher's block. As she made preparations to cook, she realized the house was strangely silent. Typically, her aunt and her sisters were buzzing about this time of day.

Where in the heck were they?

"Ps-s-s-t!"

She looked all around. Then she saw a pair of tiny, fluttering wings above her. Their clawed feet held a sheet of pink lined paper.

"It's from your aunt," the wings chimed. "Read it, read it, read it."

"Thank you," Miranda said. When she took the paper, the wings disappeared in a small puff of smoke.

Miranda,

Your sisters have returned to their own places, and I'm flying to Hawaii to visit a friend. Your parents aren't due home for another month, so you and the duke have the house to yourselves. Remember what we talked about. Good luck...

Darn. She'd anticipated enlisting Aunt Aggie's help in convincing Max. Apparently, her aunt thought it best she work things out herself. That was probably a good idea. Having to deal with more people would probably confuse Max further, and she surely didn't need that.

Finished preparing the coffee, she switched on the pot, then flipped on the TV and turned to a news channel. She watched, stunned, as a plethora of depressing information blared across the screen. There were reports of wars in the Middle East, conflicts in South America, riots in the streets of France, and general unrest across the entire planet. What a mess the humans had made of things. It was easy enough to believe that before long, there would indeed be a cataclysmic war between mortal civilizations. She didn't want that. It was clearly obvious the witch's council needed the Philosopher's Stone so they could put a stop to all the nonsense. She was the key to helping them get it.

If it's the last thing I do, I'll get the darn thing to them.

Bacon sizzled, the eggs cooked. Before long, savory aromas filled the kitchen. When Max appeared in the doorway, he glanced around, sniffing. "I say, it smells magnificent in here..." He trailed off, glancing inquisitively at the flat-screen TV mounted on the wall. "What type of mechanism is this?"

"It's called a television," she told him. "It runs on electricity just like all the other appliances in here. It runs twenty-four hours a day with game shows, soap operas, news programs, sitcoms, etc. It's incredible and annoying all at the same time."

"Fascinating," he said.

Making his way around the room, he studied the flat Corning ware range surface covered with pans of food. As she flipped a piece of bacon with a spatula, he shook his head.

"I see these days coal stoves have gone the way of the dinosaurs. How does this work?"

She pointed to the stove knobs. "These switch on the electricity which heats up the burners. It's quite a convenience."

"Indeed."

"If you think that's nifty, watch this." She ran a few ounces of water in a Pyrex measuring cup and set it in the microwave. A few seconds later, she pulled out the hot, bubbling liquid and held it up.

He raised a brow. "By George, that's ingenious."

"We've only touched the tip of the iceberg. You won't believe the things man has invented. But before we go exploring, let's get you fed." She loaded food onto plates and brought everything to the table. Max pulled out her chair—as always, the proper English gentleman. He made her feel so special. Too bad she had to throw him back in the pool for some other lucky gal.

He sat down next to her and began to eat. After sampling everything, he blotted his lips with his napkin and said, "Superb. It's quite miraculous you prepared everything on that electrical contrivance over there. You are indeed a good cook."

When the phone rang, Max put down his fork and glanced around. "I say, what is that incessant noise?"

"Someone's calling." Miranda walked over and picked up the receiver. "Hello, this is the Rose residence."

"Thank goodness you're home," a female voice at the other end of the line said. "This is Irene Trickleman. Is your store open today?"

"Hi, Irene. Sorry, but my aunt is out of town." Irene dabbled in the magical arts. She wore dark, gothic-style clothing, gaudy makeup, and kept her nails long and red. Apparently, she thought that's the way witches were supposed to look.

"But I need some supplies," she insisted.

"This can't wait?"

"I'm holding a séance this evening for a very special client. I need patchouli oil, a sage wand, and some colored candles. Oh yes, and some herbal hair growth tonic."

"For your client?"

"No, for me."

Miranda suppressed a chuckle. Maybe that's why Irene always wore gauzy scarfs on her head.

She didn't really want to accommodate her, but she also didn't want to turn away one of Aunt Aggie's best customers. "All right, I'll meet you at the shop in an hour. How does that sound?"

"Wonderful. Thank you so much."

When she put down the phone, she saw Max had leaned back in his chair and stretched his long legs in front of him. "That's also another contraption that's been perfected to an art, I see. I recall that Alexander Graham Bell chap discussing a similar listening device at a London exposition a few months ago."

"It gets even better, my friend. Look at this." Retrieving her purse from the counter, she withdrew her cell phone. "This little guy can travel all over with me and still get reception. I can even give it voice commands to dial. Oh, and it takes pictures, too. Watch."

Miranda held it up in front of Max, snapped his photo, then handed the phone over to him. He stared at the screen with a doubtful expression.

"By Jove, I can hardly believe my eyes. I've seen tin type photographs, but never something like this. It looks like I've actually been captured inside this miniature contraption."

As he poked and prodded the cell phone, she scooped plates, cups, and utensils and put them in the dishwasher. She filled it with soap crystals and punched the on button. As a low hum filled the room, she dried her hands on a towel. Noticing Max's stare, she said, "It's a dishwasher."

"I'm duly impressed. You don't have to employ household maids."

"Exactly. Are you starting to get the impression we're not in 1877 any longer?"

"I'll have to agree there's no other explanation for the things I've been seeing."

Good, she thought. She was making progress. "Are you ready to help me?"

"Almost, but not quite yet."

"Let's go into town," she told him, a tad bit frustrated. Seriously, how much more did he need to see before he believed?

"Town?"

"Wysteria. It's about a twenty-minute drive from here. I need to open up Aunt Aggie's shop for a customer. After I've taken care of her, I'll give you a tour of the city."

"Will we be riding in one of those automobiles I saw earlier?"

"Yes."

He grinned. "A capital idea. I would like that very much."

"If my powers were working properly though, I'd fly you on my broom."

"You're joking, right?"

"Absolutely not." She reached into the closet and pulled out Nellie. Gripping her handle, she said, "Say hello to Max. Be polite, now."

"Nice to meet you, Sir Duke," Nellie said, swishing her bristles back and forth. "Are you the guy Miranda's so hot for?"

Miranda glared at the broom.

"I say, this is incredible," Max said.

"I'd give you a test drive," Nellie continued, "but it looks like Miranda has already done that. You've been ridden hard and put up wet—"

"Nellie!"

"What a cheeky girl she is," Max said with a chuckle.

Speaking of cheeks, Miranda's were tingling with warmth as she slid Nellie back in the closet. She hadn't even considered the broom might decide this was a good occasion to tease her.

"Let's go," she told Max. Collecting her purse, she turned to leave. When he placed his hand in the small of her back, sparks of attraction flared. Their gazes met, and warmth soared through her. The momentary brush with desire was pleasant, but she did her best to tamp it down.

She had things to do right now. Later, when Max finally relented, she could enjoy his company one last time.

***

The architecture of Miranda's home seemed very familiar to Max when he got a good look at the outside of it. With its broad, wraparound porches, gables, and gingerbread trim, surrounded by lush gardens, it appeared very similar in construction to the residences lining the streets of his London neighborhood. For a second, he could believe he was still in the year 1877. Yet the things he'd recently witnessed, such as he contraption she referred to as a television, proved otherwise.

She led him down a dirt pathway toward a building that in former days would most likely have been the carriage house. Inside, however, it brimmed with large, garish vehicles. Painted in a multitude of colors, each one of them gleamed in the sunlight pouring through the windows. Max strolled over and rapped one with his knuckles.

"Quite sturdy, these automobiles," he said.

"These days, people refer to them as cars," Miranda explained. "I can't tell you where that word came from. Somewhere along the line, it just came into being."

He ran a hand across the vehicle's smooth, unbroken surfaced, amazed at the intricate detail. A fair amount of dust now covered his hand, so he wiped it onto his slacks. "We used to refer to the mere idea of a motorized carriage as horseless buggies. And now they actually exist."

She laughed. "Mortals are completely attached to them. Most of the witches I know still typically prefer traveling on brooms, but we often drive cars just for fun. This garage is filled with vehicles my family has owned over the years—although everything has been carefully restored. There's an original 1908 Model T Ford over there…" She pointed to a black, boxy automobile on spoke-like wheels. "And let's see, we also have a 1918 Austro Daimler, a 1937 Hudson Terraplane, a 1968 Chevrolet Camero…"

As he listened to her animated descriptions, he suddenly experienced a strong yearning for her. Yet he resisted the urge to pull her into his arms and claim her berry lips. He needed explanations and answers—not sex, even though his body craved it.

He did his best to dismiss his need. Though he'd seen nearly enough convincing evidence to believe she had in fact brought him to her future world through some magical means, he wanted to know more. He would be more than accommodating to make love to her again, but he also realized that to do so would mean his time with her must come to an end.

Something prevented him from letting her go that easily. He would try to delay the inevitable by stalling for more time with her.

He couldn't resist reaching up to stroke golden curls away from her soft face. She leaned her cheek against his hand, then as if realizing she'd perhaps too easily shown affection for him, she pulled back.

An awkward moment passed between them. Stiffening his spine, he said, "It's difficult for me to understand how your kind has lived for so long, and that you have watched man's progress throughout the centuries."

"It's the truth, Max. We've always intermingled with mortals, yet remained separate from their ranks, watching and assisting. How do you think the pyramids in Egypt were built? The Colossus of Rhodes or the Lighthouse of Alexandria? Witches helped man build those sites, and many others throughout the world."

"If that's so, then you have done tremendous things to help mankind. Why, then, has history perpetuated rumors about witches being evil?"

"It could be jealousy, pettiness, or greed. Most likely it's plain and simple ignorance." She shrugged. "Most humans need to have logical explanations for everything they don't understand. What they don't understand, they try to destroy. Because of that, they condemned a lot of innocent humans to die, people who had nothing to do with witchcraft."

Max studied Miranda's smooth jaw and took note of her chest rising and falling with each of her breaths. She seemed so sincere, as though she shared her innermost secrets with him. Unable to hold back any longer, he drew her against his chest. She stared at him as though he'd lost his mind, which he truly believed he had.

"Max, what are you doing?"

"Kissing you."

After moistening his lips, he lowered down and pressed his mouth against hers, savoring the sweetness of her lips mingled with his. God, how he wanted her. But he feared the idea of being with her, because it meant he would lose her forever.

When he finally pulled away, she said, "I thought you wanted answers."

"I feel this compelling need to be with you, Miranda. It's nearly uncontrollable."

A bittersweet smile crossed her face. "It's the disease—I'm sure of it. I'm having the same problem."

"Bloody hell." Max ran a hand through his hair. "I know you told me before how this disease works, but these urges, they are so compelling."

They continued to stare at each other a while longer, neither of them seemingly able to look elsewhere. At last, Miranda broke the trance.

"Whenever you're ready to end this, we can make love one last time. Then the disease will be cured, and my powers will be restored. I'll send you back to your time, and then I can finish my final task."

"What if I said I don't want to leave you?"

She chewed her lower lip, then said, "You can't mean that. Surely you want your life back."

"My life. Hah. My life has become a nightmare. I don't terribly enjoy being the Duke of Pellamshire. That was supposed to be my brother's job. Only a cruel twist of fate has turned it into mine."

He leaned against a wall and stared out the window at the rolling countryside. Things were so confusing right now. His life back in London, his arrival here. Honestly, right now, he didn't know where he truly belonged.

"Let's drive this little beauty into town." When he looked over at Miranda, she stood next to a small red automobile that sat low to the ground. "They don't make 'em like this anymore."

Walking up beside her, he ran his hand along the smooth sides and touched the rounded silver edges.

"It's a 1962 convertible Mustang, all cherried out, with enough soup under the hood to take you from zero to sixty in a heartbeat." Placing her hands on her hips, she studied the auto with obvious affection.

"Soup?"

She chuckled. "Not the kind you eat. It refers to the engine power, which is awesome."

Max couldn't help but smile along with her. She had to be the loveliest woman he'd ever been with. Of course, the disease was no doubt to blame for a majority of his attraction to her, but nevertheless, he still found her beautifully refreshing.

But she's a witch. And she's interrupted your life in a most disturbing fashion. Aren't you upset by that?

Yes, he wanted to get to the truth. But he found, to his consternation, he couldn't remain angry with her for long. Perhaps it was the disease or perhaps what he felt for her was genuine. Until the disease had been cured, he couldn't be certain.

"Wait till you ride in it," she told him excitedly as she opened the Mustang's door and ushered him inside. "You'll see why."

After he got in, she peeled back the roof of the car. Then she went around to the other side and seated herself behind a large wheel. Reaching over, she demonstrated how to work the seat belt. "Hang on to your hat," she advised as she started the engine with a metal key.

An incredible noise filled the air, then they roared out of the garage and the car practically flew down the road. Fingers of wind rippled through Max's hair. Eyes stinging, he studied the multitude of gadgets in front of Miranda, including the stick in the middle of the floor she kept moving around.

"It's called a gear shift," she said loudly. "This Mustang has five speeds."

"I believe it has only had one," he called back. "Fast."

After a hearty laugh, she focused on her driving. She navigated the automobile around several sharp corners, then the hilly land flattened out into vast fields of waving golden grass. The vehicle slowed down, and she pulled over to the side of the roadway. She switched off the Mustang's motor and the sound died away.

"You need to see this," she said.

"See what?"

She pointed toward a few buildings in the distance surrounded by rows of parked vehicles. "That's an airport over there. Early in the twentieth century, mortals invented flight. These days, they can travel long distances all over the world."

Max rubbed his chin. "I've read Leonardo da Vinci's theories about man being able to fly. Most people said he was out of his mind."

"Well, he wasn't. His ideas, and the ideas of many other inventors, have been honed to a perfect science called aviation. Look out there." She pointed at a gray, hard-topped field. "See that thing coming out of the hangar? It's called an airplane."

Facing in the direction she pointed, he watched, astounded, as the airplane emerged. "By Jove," he muttered.

"It's pretty complicated, but it works," Miranda said. "The one you see is just a small, private jet. There are huge commercial airliners that can hold many passengers."

The airplane turned and continued down the hard-topped field. It rolled along for a while, then, incredibly, it lifted up into the air and flew away into the clear blue sky. Just like a bird.

Max stared and stared, barely able to believe what he'd just seen with his own two eyes. "Astounding."

"Neat, huh?" Miranda switched on the Mustang and it roared to life once again. She wheeled it around and drove it back onto the road.

Wind lifted strands of her pale hair and swirled it around her face. What other wonders would she show him before this day ended? He thought about it long and hard, but realized, the most wondrous thing of all was the deep emotions he felt for her.

What am I going to do if I still feel this way about Miranda after the disease is supposedly cured?

Gripping the seat belt that strapped him in, he watched the countryside spin past, his sentiments just as out of control. He couldn't envision what would transpire when the time came, but he knew that before long he'd have to make up his mind.

He had responsibilities back home and he couldn't simply abandon them. Yet, if what he felt for Miranda was actually real, he knew he couldn't simply abandon her.

But did she want to be with him?

Chapter Sixteen

While driving through Wysteria with its picturesque homes, churches, and businesses, Miranda stole several quick glances at Max. He watched everything that whizzed by, his gaze resolute. Hopefully, he'd begun to accept the truth. Once that happened, they could make love one last time, and each go on their merry ways. It would be back to 1877 London for him and back to chasing Balthazar and the Philosopher's Stone for her.

What would happen after that?

She didn't want to think too much about how she would feel after he was gone, but she knew she would miss him. Would he miss her? None of that really mattered. They could never have a life together. It just wasn't meant to be. Swallowing a sigh, she focused on the road.

Wheeling the Mustang down Main Street, she turned into the city park. Trees were dressed for autumn with rust, orange, and yellow leaves. Seeing the cluster of vendor booths on the rolling lawn, she realized it must be Wysteria's annual fall celebration. It seemed the entire town had come down here. People, young and old, wandered from tent to tent, pawing through clothing, necklaces, earrings, and other handmade items. She and Max would have just enough time to have a quick look at the festival before she needed to open Aunt Aggie's store.

The second she and Max got out of the car, the aroma of roasted turkey legs, corn dogs, and popcorn drifted toward them. Music and voices filled the air, lending to the jovial atmosphere.

Max took her elbow and asked, "What is going on?"

"The autumn festival," she told him. His touch sent thrills up and down her spine. Did he realize how it made her feel? Her knees went weak and her heart flip-flopped. "Every fall local businesses and crafters get together to put this on. It's always a huge tourist draw."

They strolled past the booths, then continued on down a gentle slope toward a large blue lake. Canadian Geese and ducks floated across the sparkling surface. They passed a children's play area where little ones glided down slides and pumped swings high into the sky. Next came the botanical gardens, which sported lush foliage offering a brilliant fall display.

Around the next turn of sidewalk, they encountered Wysteria's outdoor amphitheater. The featured band, composed of drummers and guitar players, offered 'oldies but goodies' music. A large poster said they were named, 'Weeds.'

Max stopped and stared. He pointed at the black snaking wires covering the floor of the stage. "More electronic devices, I suppose?"

She nodded. "Amplifiers, woofers, and tweeters…" At his perplexed expression, she added, "Modern society has become utterly dependent upon electricity. It's almost kind of scary."

"Electricity exists in my time, of course, but in very rudimentary forms. What do people do if it fails?"

"Panic," she said with a chuckle.

He laughed along with her as they passed by more vendors in striped wagons hawking caramel apples, funnel cakes, popcorn balls, and other seasonal treats. Another cluster of booths exhibited colorful patchwork quilts, paintings, sculptures, and much more.

At one booth, Max stopped to lift up a necklace strung with blue crystal beads. He held it up to the sunlight, watching the facets dazzle with brilliance.

"These beads match your eyes perfectly. You should have it." As he held it up, a smile touched his lips.

It was pretty, Miranda thought. And it would be a pleasant reminder of their time together. She lifted her purse and pulled out enough money to pay the lady behind the table.

Max's smile intensified as he clasped the crystal beads around her neck. His touch on her collarbone made her shiver.

He stood back and nodded. "Splendid. I shall owe you the cost of this bauble."

"Please don't worry about it." She nearly became lost in his chocolate brown eyes for one magic moment. Fighting back a surge of emotion, she asked, "Would you like something to drink?"

He nodded. "I am a bit parched."

Passing a drink stand, she purchased two sodas and handed one to Max. He frowned at the paper cup, plastic lid, and straw. "This is highly improper, you know. A gentleman always pays for a lady."

"Welcome to women's lib."

He arched one dark eyebrow. "What is the women's lib?"

"All you need to know is that it's not unusual for women to pay their own way these days."

He frowned at the drink and rattled the ice in the plastic cup. "How do I drink this?"

"Like this." Miranda sipped hers. "Now you try."

After doing as she instructed, he made a face and wiped his mouth on his sleeve. "Bloody hell, it's disgustingly sweet. It's like imbibing straight syrup. And it makes my nose tingle."

She laughed. "That's the carbonation."

When her arm accidentally brushed against Max's, she pulled away as heat filled her face and her body erupted with a slow, tantalizing tingle. Son of a monkey, she wanted to rip his proper gentleman's clothing off this very instant, haul him off into the bushes and get horizontal.

Their gazes met, and for a moment, the world faded away. She nearly said something about how she felt but decided not to. It would make her sound desperate, and she doubted he'd find that very attractive. Soon enough, she felt sure he'd be ready to cooperate with her so they could both get on with what they had to do.

She turned away, watching children on another playground scrambling on slides and riding the swings. When they weren't watching their little ones, mothers lounging on wooden benches either visited with each other or checked their cell phones. A little boy tugged a dog on a leash, a scruffy brown terrier mix that wiggled and squirmed, obviously excited to be on an outing.

A little girl, probably around six-years-old, scrambled off a swing and darted toward a dark-haired woman on a bench. "Mommy, mommy!" She pointed at Max. "Why is that man dressed so funny?"

The woman looked up and adjusted her glasses. She glanced briefly at Max, smiling apologetically. Grasping her daughter's small hand, she told her, "It's not nice to point, honey."

Suddenly the boy with the dog cried out, "Grif, come back here!"

Everyone turned to look. Having broken free of his young master's grip, the little dog now chased after a squirrel. The dog sped past Max and Miranda and headed toward the street, along with the little boy. A car turned around the corner, bearing down on the two.

Everything happened so quickly, but Miranda knew this would turn into a tragedy unless she did something. Since she didn't have her powers, she implored the nature spirits to help. Then, as though in slow motion, the car began to lose speed and finally stopped—seemingly suspended in time. The boy and the dog stood in front of the vehicle as though frozen. Miranda hurried toward them, took the boy's hand and the dog's leash, and led them both back to the sidewalk. A split second later, the car continued to rush down the street.

As if he'd been in a trance, the boy looked up at her and blinked. "What happened?"

She handed him his dog's leash. "Don't worry about it. Why don't you go home now? I think your mother's calling."

"Okay, lady." The boy turned around and began walking away, tugging the leash of his squirrel-chasing dog.

Max came up behind her, his face filled with concern as he pulled her against his chest. A shiver rippled up her spine at the sensation of his large warmth pressed against hers. It felt so good to have him hold her this way.

Don't get too used to it, Miranda.

"What just happened here?" His voice held a note of concern and confusion. "One minute that automobile was motoring toward the child, then it just stopped—"

"Since my powers are on the fritz, I pleaded with the nature spirits for help," she told him softly. She realized people were staring and pointing. It was always that way when they saw things like that, which for the most part, she never liked to make public. In this instance, however, she hadn't had a choice.

Max glanced around, taking note of everyone's stares. He took her elbow and steered her away from the curious onlookers. "I thought you said you don't have any powers right now," he whispered.

"I don't. It was all due to the nature spirits."

"I don't understand," he said. "Who are these nature spirits?"

"Remember when I told you witches were put on earth to help mankind?"

He nodded.

"We have not only our powers to help us, but the forces of nature are also at our disposal. The wind, the sun, the moon, the stars, and every other living entity such as trees and animals work with us. We can even bend time, if necessary."

"Is that how you accomplish time travel? You bend time?"

"Exactly."

He ran a hand through his dark, wavy hair. "I say, that's quite an intriguing concept."

Glancing at her watch, she said, "I guess we'd better get over to my aunt's store."

As they walked back to the car, Max asked, "Where is your aunt? I should like to thank her, and your sisters, for saving my life."

"She's on vacation. But I'll let her know you appreciate her help. And I'll let my sisters know, too."

Miranda drove into the part of Wysteria referred to as 'old town.' She parked in front of a red brick, two-story building that housed the Rose Sisters' Soaps and Scents shop. This was the original part of the city, which had been founded in 1869 by fishermen and farmers. Tall trees shaded the streets, and planters still held fading petunias. People bustled in and out of the different businesses, toting bags and pushing strollers holding babies.

Inside the shop, she flipped on a light, illuminating the shelves stocked with tea tins, scarves, soaps, sachets, books, tarot cards, and other objects. An antique red velvet sofa sat in one corner along with an antique floor lamp. Oriental carpets covered the wooden floors and large-bladed fans spun overhead.

"*Ra-a-ak!* Who loves ya, baby?"

Max spun around, his hands clutched into fists. "Bloody hell, who said that?"

"Relax." She tossed her keys back into her purse and set it on the counter, then walked toward a tall, gilded cage in a corner. "Come here and meet my aunt's parrot. The old boy's mouthy, but harmless."

Chuckling, Max walked up beside her. "I say, the old boy nearly scared the sense out of me."

The colorful blue and yellow bird sitting on his wooden perch began to preen his feathers. "Jacko's freaky little comments can really catch you off guard, but he's great. You're a pretty boy, aren't you?"

When she pursed her lips and made a kissing sound, Jacko began to bob his head up and down. He held out a claw and declared, "Two little lovebirds sitting in a tree, *ra-a-a-k!*"

Embarrassed heat filled Miranda's face. Son of a monkey! How could that damn bird sense what she was feeling for Max? From the corner of her eye, she noted the duke now held his hands behind his back, grinning at the bird.

She tapped her nail on the cage. "You're incorrigible, Jacko."

"Who loves ya, baby? *Ra-a-a-k!*"

"No wonder your aunt keeps him around. He makes for a good watchdog."

Jacko bobbed his head up and down, ruffling his bright feathers.

"He's just a big ham."

"Pretty bird, pretty bird, *r-a-a-a-k!*" Jacko said.

"I'll leave you two to get acquainted while I open up the register." She left Max and the bird, slipping in place behind the counter just as Irene Trickleman burst through the front doors. She wore a paisley scarf on her head, and her long black dress swished around her ankles.

"Thank goodness you're here," she told Miranda. Moving her pear-shaped body around the store, she quickly gathered her items and plopped them on the counter. "I saw blood on the moon last night. Something awful is going to happen. Be careful."

"Thanks for the warning." She rang the order and placed the items in a paper bag.

"Don't pooh, pooh me, Miranda Rose. Something evil and wicked is going down. I feel it in my bones. I always trust my bones, you know." She reached out and grabbed Miranda's shirt sleeve, her gaze disconcerting. "You and your sisters need to be careful, too. And Aggie. There's something in the wind…"

Miranda doubted if Irene had read the signs correctly but decided to humor her. "I promise, I'll be careful. That'll be twenty dollars and fifty-five cents."

Irene placed several bills on the counter, along with the correct change. A shiver rippled through her as she glanced around the room, her gaze alighting on Max. She watched him for a moment as he perused the shelves, examining various items. "I haven't seen him around town before. Who is he?"

"A friend."

"You'd better warn him too. I'm not kidding."

"Thanks for your concern, Irene."

The woman had always been overly paranoid, but something about the look in her eyes made Miranda's skin prickle. Maybe she was more sensitive than Miranda realized.

Irene gathered up her bag and hurried out the door.

Max came back to the counter area. "That old bat seems to be in quite a hurry."

"She's always been somewhat eccentric."

"What did she mean about blood on the moon?"

"Irene's not an authentic witch, but she practices wicca. She's sensitive to natural events. She must have seen a ring of reddish color around the moon. It could have either been an atmospheric anomaly or it truly could be a warning."

"About what?"

She shrugged. "Could be anything. But just to be safe, I'll throw some salt over my shoulder and put a circle of it around the house when we get home. I'll also light a few candles to the goddess for good measure."

"You are a unique individual, Miranda." He held her chin in his hand and turned her face up. "One I should like to know better. If we had the time."

"That's the thing, isn't it?" Max's touch generated a thrill that tingled down to her toes. "We belong in different worlds."

He removed his hand. "Right you are. But I'd like to reassure you that after my time with you, I'll never feel the same way about a woman again."

The fact that he seemed sad about their parting made her feel guilty that she'd used him for sex. And unhappy that even if they had both wanted to stay together, the council would never allow it. "Max, you need to know that I never wanted to hurt you in all of this."

"I'll admit having you in my life has definitely upset the apple cart. Waking up in your world and having you reveal yourself as a witch hasn't been very easy." He began to pace, hands clasped behind his back. "But I realize you'd never intentionally cause harm to anyone. And I also realize this is no dream I'm in. Your automobiles, televisions, cell phones, and electric devices have convinced me. Along with the incident in the park."

She swallowed hard, anticipating making love with him again. It would be wonderful, but bittersweet, knowing all the while they would soon have to part. "You don't need any more proof?"

He shook his head. "No. I do require one thing, however."

"What's that?" Miranda's heart nearly stopped beating.

"Even though I understand you have a deadline, I'd like to stay a while longer. Before you send me home, I should like to see more of these wonders that exist in your world."

Disappointment rippled through her. Not because Max wanted to see more of her world, which would delay her search for Balthazar and the Philosopher's Stone, but because he only wanted to see more scientific advances. He didn't want to be with her. What a fool she'd been all this time, hoping and wishing she meant something to him. Of course, she didn't. And she shouldn't. They'd only get in trouble if they tried to have a relationship.

She cleared her throat, which had become strangely dry and tight. Her fingers went numb as she began to straighten up things on the counter—anything to keep from looking at him.

"Ah, sure, we can hang out for the rest of the day. There's plenty to keep you busy. We don't have a big mall here, but there's a large department store with an escalator and an elevator that I'm sure you'd find fascinating. We could also take in a movie and visit the museum. Since you like ships, we could go down to the docks by the Columbia River. You could have a look at some of the fancy yachts…"

Feeling large hands gripping her shoulders, she stopped fussing with the paperclips, pens, and notepads, and looked up. Max stood there, his eyes full of emotion as he drew her into his arms. "It's not just your modern inventions I'm interested in, Miranda. I'm completely fascinated by you."

Tears prickled at the back of her eyes. "I thought you'd hate me after you found out what I was. I figured you wouldn't want anything to do with me."

A muscle in his jaw twitched and the pressure of his fingers intensified. "I could never hate you, Miranda. I know this disease has affected us both, but I would like to believe what I feel for you comes from my heart. Do you think there might be a future for us?"

"As much as I'd like it Max, it could never work out. The witch's council will have my hide. They'd hunt me down and imprison me for disobeying their stupid rules." She sighed. "Besides, I've worked hard to become a high witch. I don't think I could give up that dream—"

He pressed one of his index fingers against her lips, effectively silencing her. His thin voice made him sound crushed, deflated. "I understand, Miranda. It was a wild idea to begin with. Neither of us should have to give up anything. But we have right now, this moment."

He crushed her against his chest and claimed her lips.

Back in his cage, Jacko flapped his wings and called out, "*Ra-a-a-k!* Two little lovebirds sitting in a tree, k-i-s-s-i-n-g!"

Chapter Seventeen

As Max held Miranda's pliant body, his head swam with desire. Her lips tasted like honeyed wine, sweet and exhilarating. Need coursed through him, urging him to take her. Flames of intense need licked at his soul, and he knew only she could quench the inferno with her silken offerings.

As many times as they'd made love, this seemed like the first time all over again. His penis became engorged, and blood moved sluggishly through his veins as she pressed her supple curves against his hardness. His once well-ordered world had now become a complicated place full of confusing events. One thing, however, had become clear.

He needed Miranda. Here and now.

The fire within leapt to new heights, fueled by expectation. His kiss intensified as he thrust his tongue deep into the velvety cavern of her mouth. She moaned softly and began her own exploration of his mouth with her tongue.

Groaning, he swung her into his arms. From the corner of his eye, he noticed people walking back and forth past the shop, along with the occasional automobile motoring down the street. A couple of individuals cast strange glances through the large shop window as they passed by.

"Where can we have privacy?"

"Upstairs," she muttered breathlessly. She hurried over to the door, clicked a lock into place and pulled down a shade.

When she returned, Max swung her into his arms and carried her toward the staircase. Before long, he'd reached the second floor and stood on the landing, looking around at the furniture.

"My aunt stores her antiques up here. Let's go over there," she said in a raspy voice as she pointed toward one corner.

Immediately he spotted the iron bedstead surrounded by tall potted ferns. Several quick strides later, he'd carried her over and laid her gently on a soft patchwork quilt.

Sitting on the bed beside her, he ran a hand down her smooth curves, drawing in a sharp breath at the bare emotion shining in her blue eyes. A sense of humble thankfulness rippled through him. He and Miranda may not have long together, but for now, she belonged completely to him.

"You are superb," he whispered as his need throbbed anxiously. "Everything a man could want."

She licked her lips, tantalizing him with their moist, berry appearance. "Even though you know I'm a witch? You still find me desirable?"

"All women have their charms and bewitching ways, Miranda." He smoothed mussed golden tresses away from her heart-shaped face, noting the tears shimmering in her eyes. "Yours happen to be top notch."

Miranda began to tug off her clothing. When she took off her top, revealing the creamy skin of her belly and her full breasts, he noticed her breasts were encased in a white band that encircled her rib cage. It was much different than the corsets women wore in his time. What his gaze really devoured was the sight of those tantalizing orbs, the tips of which were teased by scallops of lace. Eager to stroke her skin and thrill to the feel of her soft skin beneath his fingertips, he helped her remove the rest of her clothing, piece by piece, until she rested completely naked beneath his hungry gaze.

He noted how her breasts ended with rosebud nipples, how her waist curved with perfect proportions and how her rounded hips and luscious thighs aroused him.

"Take me, Max. I want to feel you inside me again." Tears welled in her lovely blue eyes. "I need you."

He couldn't deny himself any longer. Standing, he quickly shed his jacket and unbuttoned his shirt, slipping it from his shoulders. He kicked off his shoes and peeled away his socks. Next, he tossed aside his trousers, chuckling as his penis sprang eagerly from its confines.

Encouraged by her silken legs spread open for him, he stretched out beside her, drawing her naked, warm flesh into his arms. His manhood lay heavily on her thigh, throbbing with desire as he lowered his head down to claim her mouth. When her lips fused hotly with his, he thrilled to the fact she wasn't at all ashamed of her sexual needs.

He recalled the picnic they'd enjoyed, back in his world, and the first time they'd made love. Her willingness to give him her body had been surprising since most young ladies of gentle rearing fiercely guarded their virginity. It had been rather enjoyable not to have to coax and cajole her into sharing her favors. He'd known even back then she was no typical society debutante, which made her all the more exciting.

"Miranda, Miranda, Miranda," he said when he pulled back, his mouth still warm from her kisses. She smiled, and his whole world exploded with sunshine. How could she have captivated him so completely?

He loved her appearance and her unique laughter. He loved the way she walked, talked, and even how she tossed her golden hair over her shoulders and wet her lips with her small pink tongue. Did the disease have that big a hold of him, or were feelings genuine?

I love her.

The fact that he'd thought those words didn't surprise him. He knew it in his heart and his mind, even if he hadn't said it out loud.

Miranda moaned and began to stroke his phallus with her velvety palm. She arched her hips against his and said breathlessly, "Take me, Max. I can't wait much longer."

"Neither can I, sweetheart."

Cupping her buttocks, he pulled her against his throbbing cock. Her reaction was to wrap her legs around his abdomen, making his mind explode with raw passion. When he met her gaze, he recognized the need burning in her eyes.

He parted her nether curls and inserted a finger into her moist cavern. Then he drew one of her nipples into his mouth, sucking the rigid flesh.

She moaned and began to pant. "Max, don't tease me!"

Chuckling, he stroked the moist nub of her desire. Inhaling sharply, she arched into him, moving her hips urgently against his touch.

"You can't keep me waiting like this," she pleaded. "Take me, please."

"This is our last time together. I want you to remember it."

"Believe me, I won't forget."

He kissed her again, then thrust two fingers inside her and began to mimic what he would do with his penis before long.

Kaboom!

Windows rattled in their frames and the building shook fiercely. Screams erupted outside and the sound of confused voices sounded in the street. Pulling Miranda even tighter against his chest, Max removed his lips from hers and looked up in surprise. His ardor cooled as his concern flared.

"Bloody hell, what in the world was that?"

Her pale brows drew together in concern. "I don't know…"

"If I didn't know better, I'd think we were at sea and an enemy ship has fired a volley at us."

Another explosion sounded outside. Once again, the building shook, windows rattled. More screams, more shouting.

"Damnation." He jumped up, slid on his trousers, shirt and shoes, then went to the window. Miranda came up behind him, tucking the quilt around her curvy figure.

Billowing smoke marred the blue sky with jagged black streaks. People down in the street scrambled to safety inside buildings. Cars and trucks screeched away from curbs and swerved down the street.

"What could be causing this?" He raked a hand through his hair, chasing possibilities around in his mind.

"Son of a monkey," Miranda exclaimed as she hurried to put on her undergarments and sweater.

He walked over and gripped her shoulders. "Tell me what's wrong, Miranda."

"Remember Balthazar the wizard, that punk who's got the Philosopher's Stone? I would never have believed he could track me here, but I'm afraid he did…"

Kaboom!

When the building rocked again, the window glass blew apart, shattering into a million pieces and falling to the floor in a rain of sharp pieces. Max grabbed Miranda and leaned over her, shielding her with his body.

Youthful laughter filled the room, reflecting off the walls. Magical words rang out, *"Larfor, pranxtor,* south and north. Bring the witch forth!"

***

At first, Miranda saw nothing, then a shimmering mist descended. When it cleared, a small form emerged. *Ah, ha.*

She'd guessed correctly. Balthazar in his black, star-covered cloak and pointed black cap emerged, his hands shoved insolently on his hips. His dark tousled hair fell into his eyes, and a pair of round, horn-rimmed glasses rested crookedly across the bridge of his freckled nose. His eyes sparkled as though possessed, and the skin on his face had become tinged with gray.

He pointed at Miranda and held up a primitive-looking doll with yellow yarn hair. "I've been looking for you, witch! Now I'm going to take you back to my tower so the dark lord can deal with you."

Miranda grimaced. "Who is the dark lord?"

"He's taught me everything I know in order to keep the Philosopher's Stone in safekeeping. That's why the dark lord and I won't allow you to steal it."

"Balthazar, you've got to listen to me," she said, hoping to reason with him. "You don't know what you're doing."

Ignoring her, the boy produced a long pin and jabbed it into one of the doll's legs.

Intense pain shot up her right calf. She crumbled to the floor.

Max roared with outrage and knelt at her side, gathering her protectively in his arms. "Miranda, are you all right? What's going on?"

Through her pain, she managed to say, "He's got a poppet. Anything he does to the doll...will happen to me."

Rising up, Max strode toward Balthazar with a stormy expression. "I say, young man. I insist you stop your nonsense this instant."

"Hah!" An evil grin crossed Balthazar's face as he pointed his wand at Max.

For a moment nothing happened. Then Max's body slammed back against a wall. With a groan, he slumped over and slid to the floor.

Miranda's heart lurched. "Max!"

As Max tried to stand, beads of perspiration glistened on his forehead. He struggled to free himself from what appeared to be invisible bonds.

Balthazar grinned mischievously. "Don't worry, dude. It's only temporary. I need you to leave me alone so I can take the witch with me."

"If you even touch one hair on her head, you'll regret it," Max warned.

"You're not the boss of me," Balthazar shot back. "So stick it in your ear and blow it out your nose."

The boy wizard dangled the poppet by its arm. Miranda's arm jerked up, nearly ripping from the socket as she hung there. She tried to stand firmly in one spot, but as Balthazar pulled the poppet toward him, she, too, was dragged in his direction. The soles of her bare feet scraped across the hardwood floor.

"Stop this!" she cried as her body became a slave to Balthazar's twisted magic. "What you're doing is wrong, and you'll be punished. It's against all the laws of nature to harm someone with your powers."

"Not if that someone is bad. The dark lord told me all witches are bad." He lowered the doll's arm. Miranda dropped onto the floor at his feet.

She pushed onto her knees and looked up, her backside aching. "He's lying to you."

"You're trying to confuse me." He sniffed haughtily.

"I'm trying to tell you the truth. Magic can be used for good or bad, and you've been taught to use it for all the wrong reasons."

He frowned and seemed to consider her words for a moment.

She recalled what she had heard about the Philosopher's Stone.

Many wizards have held the stone over the centuries—all named Balthazar. Typically, the wizard winds up using the stone for evil purposes. The council has tried for eons of time to obtain it...

An idea began to form in her mind. She just hoped she could convince the boy wizard to believe her. "Balthazar, you need to listen to me. This dark lord must be using the stone's powers to try and foil all the good deeds witches accomplish on behalf of mankind."

He shook his head vehemently. "That can't be so. I have the stone. Not him."

Despite his reticence to listen, she continued. "I think the dark lord has created an elaborate hoax. Over the centuries he's tricked young boys into believing they were real wizards, when all he taught you were simple parlor tricks. He claimed you were holding the Philosopher's Stone in safe keeping when more than likely the stone you and the other boys held were fakes."

He frowned. "Why would he do that?"

"He did it so that when individuals come looking for the stone, they wind up pursuing the decoys. Meanwhile, the dark lord has been using the real stone to wreak havoc in the mortal world. It's like a game for him."

A sinking feeling came over her as she realized how easily she and all the other witches had fallen for the ruse. Over the centuries they'd relentlessly chased these boy wizards and their fake stones. The dark lord must have had a good laugh each time they tried, and failed, to retrieve the prize.

"He's been using you to do his dirty work, Balthazar. I bet if you questioned him about it, he wouldn't allow you to stay in the tower any longer. He'd probably send you home." *Or worse*, she thought. But she didn't tell him that—she didn't want to scare him. Despite all the stunts he was pulling, he was still just a kid.

"No, he likes me," Balthazar insisted in a whiny tone. "He's my friend. And I've never had any friends before. I get to eat anything I want for dinner and stay up as late as I want. I don't have to go to school, and he gives me all kinds of candy. He even sent the other boy home so I could rule the tower all by myself."

"What other boy?"

"The dark lord called him Balthazar, too. He was a lot older than me, though.

"It's like I told you. Over the centuries he's bribed young boys to watch over the fake stone while he uses the real one to instigate trouble."

"Nuh-uh." The young wizard shook his head vigorously.

"You've got to listen to me, Balthazar. When the boys get old enough to wonder what's going on, he gets rid of them. He'll get rid of you, too."

Balthazar's mouth twitched. It looked like he might cry. "No, he wouldn't do that!"

"He doesn't care about you," she explained in a gentle voice. "But I do. I don't want to see you get hurt."

"You're lying," Balthazar shouted. "You don't know what you're talking about."

"Balthazar—"

"I'm not listening to you anymore. You can't make me!"

He waved his wand and Miranda felt herself sucked into a void of darkness. Cold wind whipped past her body, pelting her skin with stinging needles. A weightless sensation swept through her, and she began falling...

***

"No!" When Max saw Miranda vanish into a shimmering mist along with Balthazar, a wave of panic washed over him. The pain of losing her made him angrier than he'd ever been in his life. With renewed strength, he struggled once more to free himself.

With Balthazar gone, the force that had held him dissipated. He pushed to his feet, but his body felt like a lead weight. Moving as though he trudged through deep mud, he made his way over to the area where Miranda had disappeared. Facets of light still shimmered like a chimera, lending an ethereal quality to the air.

"*Jump into it,*" a small voice urged.

An eerie numbness twisted through him, his heart pounded. Before all of this, he'd never even considered the possibility that magic existed. None of that mattered now. The woman he loved was in trouble.

He had to find her.

Gritting his teeth, he plunged into the iridescent swathe of light. The floor disappeared, and he tumbled head over heels into a void of blackness. Down, down, down he went. *This can't be real,* he thought. Yet he sensed differently.

A rippling sensation surged over his skin and his body seemed light as a feather. He could still feel himself. This was happening. Glancing around, he decided some peculiar chamber hurled him toward an unidentified destination.

In the cocooning emptiness someone cried out. *Miranda.* He would recognize her voice anywhere.

"Sweetheart, where are you?"

No answer.

He clenched his fists and the hair on the back of his neck bristled. That wizard had better be prepared to deal with him. He intended to put an end to this nonsense if it was the last thing he did. More ebony nothingness rushed past him and he sucked in a ragged breath.

Have I died?

Reaching down, he examined his arms, legs, and then his whiskered face. No, he still had a body. The Sunday school classes he'd attended in his youth had taught that the body stays on earth while only the soul transcends to heaven. For some reason, he doubted he was heaven bound.

The inky space began to clear, and a circle of brightness began to expand above him. Light meant hope, so he reached up, trying to grab hold of it. A rushing sensation washed over him, and he had difficulty breathing. Overcome by dizziness, he closed his eyes and fell to his knees.

Stillness surrounded him. The falling sensation had stopped.

Searching desperately for something solid and real, he pressed his hands on a flat surface. Bloody hell, had he been encased in some sort of coffin? A horrible vision of scratching the lid and choking for air took root in his mind. He did not want to suffocate.

Somehow, he summoned the courage to rise to his feet and glare into the darkness. "This will stop now! I demand it!"

Intense heat pressed against him. His shirt had become soaked in sweat and his face was damp with perspiration. It felt as though his skin had caught fire. Ignoring the discomfort, he narrowed his gaze and looked hard into the fathomless void.

"Miranda, where are you?"

With no idea of what would happen, he began walking toward the bright area. At first his feet wouldn't move. Finally, he managed to lift them, first one, then the other. It seemed to take forever as he walked through the inferno of heat, but he was determined to find Miranda.

Chapter Eighteen

Miranda sat huddled in a giant cage Balthazar had locked her in. Having taken her to his tower, he'd mouthed off some more about the dark lord, then he'd disappeared. She had no clue when he would return or when the dark lord would show up in order to deal with her.

What more could happen to her now?

She felt like giving up. Practically devastated by this turn of events, she wiped away the tears that had splashed across her cheeks and down onto her sweater, now riddled with burned areas from the time travel. The material was fire resistant, but the intense heat of the time transfer had still done serious damage.

Why am I worrying about this stupid sweater?

She could care less about it. What she needed to do was find a way to free herself. A million thoughts marched through her mind as she tried to decide what to do. Every plan she thought of seemed useless. Without her powers, she was helpless.

Get off your duff and quit moping.

The voice in her head was right. She couldn't give up, no matter how much she wanted to. Sniffing, she pushed to her feet. A thick chain attached to her foot rattled. Her heart sank at the sound. She was a true prisoner.

Nevertheless, she gripped the iron bars and shouted, "Balthazar, please. Let me go…"

Her words echoed in the silence. Brave, foolish requests from someone locked up tighter than Harry Houdini in a steamer trunk. At least Harry had secret ways of escaping. She, however, had nothing. *Think, Miranda.*

She frowned. What could she do now? Before Balthazar left, he'd boasted how the dark lord would arrive soon to deal with her, and that she was in big trouble.

She leaned back against the bars and closed her eyes. Only the gods knew what would happen when he showed up. She had no means of defending herself.

Despair gripped her. She feared she may never see Max or her family again. *Max.* She could have sworn she'd heard him call to her a short while ago, but that was crazy. He was back in Wysteria in her aunt's store. Maybe she was losing her sanity along with everything else.

She tried to summon the nature spirits and plead with them for help. Her efforts were half-hearted, and she doubted they were in tune with her right now. When warmth filled her, she opened her eyes and looked around. Tables, chairs, and other objects in the room shimmered with a glimmering light. Hope surged, then fell flat. No doubt it was only the dark lord making his appearance.

"Hoot, hoot!" Balthazar's owl began flapping inside its cage. Its yellow eyes had widened to the size of saucers.

A rush of air swept through the room and a tall, thin man in a black cape and black clothing appeared. He strode toward her, the long-jagged scar running along one side enhancing his evil appearance.

"*Noxius menendi,*" he said and waved a hand around the room. The shimmering dissolved. He turned to Miranda, eyes snapping with irritation. "You are a troublesome wench. Much more so than the others who have come to steal what belongs to me."

"I assume you're the dark lord."

He lifted a brow and looked her up and down, as if undressing her with her eyes. Though in reality, she wasn't wearing much that he would have to bother to remove. A shiver crawled up her spine.

"Correct," he returned in an insolent voice.

"You're not fit to walk this planet," she snapped, feeling very self-conscious that she wore only panties, a bra, and a sweater. "And if I get my way, you'll be banished to the Neverlands forever."

He threw back his head and laughed, then pierced with a glare. "Big threats from someone locked in a cage."

"I swear I'll get out of here somehow. And when I'm through with you, you'll regret what you've done."

He narrowed his gaze. "What are you talking about?"

"Tricking little boys into believing they are real wizards and having them stand guard over a mere chunk of obsidian. Meanwhile, you wreak havoc with the real Philosopher's Stone."

"You are as astute as you are beautiful. You're much more persistent than the other witches who've come here to find this. An unfortunate thing for you." Reaching into a pocket, he fished out a glittering crystal about the size of an apple. "It didn't take long for the others to admit defeat and return to their homes."

"I don't give up easily."

"Indeed," the dark lord said. "Balthazar told me he's watched you for months as you searched for this tower. It's a pity you finally found it."

Her throat tightened like a tightly drawn rubber band. "What are you going to do with me?"

He snapped his fingers and the stone disappeared. "I haven't decided yet. I do have a question, though."

She shrugged, feigning irritation. He pressed on.

"Why aren't you fighting back? You obviously have very strong powers to have even found this place."

Irritation shot through her. She and Max had been so close to making love before Balthazar interrupted them. If only the kid had shown up a little later, her powers would have been restored and she could have dealt with the dark lord on a level playing field.

Without her magical abilities, she was weak and ineffectual. It was important not to let him know this, so she'd have to deal her cards carefully. Summoning all her courage, she prepared to pull off the biggest bluff of her life.

She shrugged, mimicking his nonchalance. "I haven't decided how I want to handle you yet. A wise mortal once said, 'Know your enemy.'"

"Hmmph." He scratched his chin, watching her closely. "Why don't I believe you?"

"Because you're a fool." She forced a mocking laugh. "What in the heck kind of name is *the dark lord?* It's ridiculous. Sounds like you stole it from a Harry Potter movie."

He looked miffed. "I've had this name for centuries. Actually, it was stolen from me."

"Whatever. I still think you're lower than a dung beetle."

"Enough!" His eyes flared with anger, and he stomped his foot.

"Temper, temper. Sticks and stones may break your bones, but names should never hurt you."

The dark lord's nostrils flared. It looked like he wanted to wring her neck.

Inwardly, she flinched. Yet she forced herself to smile and square her shoulders. Maybe if she could goad this creep into making a mistake, she could outsmart him. Deep down, she knew she was playing with fire.

"You're disgusting," she snarled.

His face darkened with rage. "Someone needs to teach you a lesson. You are far too haughty."

"I dare you to use your magic against me. Because if you even try, I guarantee I'll bring down the wrath of the ages on you."

"Maybe I'll use something else to subdue you." He walked over to the owl's cage and opened it up. Reaching inside, he removed a key hanging from the perch on a leather loop. He stormed over to Miranda's cage, unlocked it and threw open the door.

Stuffing the key in his pocket, he grabbed her and said, "It's been a long time since I've had a woman, especially one as bold as you."

She cried out as he crushed her against his chest and kissed her fiercely, bruising her lips. Jerking away, she spit in his face. "Gods above, you even taste like a dung beetle."

"Filthy little witch!"

He threw her back against the cage with such force her teeth rattled. Every bone in her back felt as though it had been shattered. She wiped away a trickle of blood dribbling down the side of her mouth. A chant rose within her, and she spoke it aloud.

"Peace with the gods, peace with nature, may the winds bring deliverance…"

A breeze rose within the room, quickly gaining in intensity. It began to whip around the room, knocking over items and sending paper swirling through the air.

He laughed. "That's all you have? Where is this wrath of the ages you mentioned?"

"Right here." Max appeared behind the dark lord, his face covered in soot. Wisps of smoke rose from his clothing as he hefted a large silver candlestick. He smashed it against the back of the dark lord's head.

The master wizard staggered around, howling with pain. A second later, he fell onto the floor with a heavy thud. His hands twitched for a moment, then were still.

Max dropped the candlestick. In two strides, he reached her side and gathered her in his arms. He kissed her over and over, and she kissed him back.

Finally, she managed to say, "How did you get here?"

"I don't really know. I just jumped into the shimmering place where you disappeared."

"Thank the goddess." She couldn't imagine what he, a mere mortal, had gone through to get to her. It spoke of his regard for her. By the looks of his clothing, he'd nearly been fried to a crisp. She was humbled.

He gently gripped her upper arms. "Are you all right? Did he hurt you?"

She licked her dry lips, tasting the salty tang of blood. Everything she owned ached, yet she said, "I'm fine."

"You're not a good liar, Miranda."

She buried her face in his smoky-smelling shirt. Relief filtered through her, but she realized they were still in grave danger. "Don't worry about me, worry about the dark lord. The only way you bested him is because you caught him off guard."

"The element of surprise usually works."

"We've got to get out of here before he comes to."

Max released her and hunkered down to examine the chain holding her captive. "Bloody hell."

"He's got a key." Miranda nodded at the master wizard. "It's in his pocket."

Max walked toward the dark lord and rolled him over. The gash on the back of his head left blood on the flagstones. His arms flopped to the side. Hunkering down, Max reached into the dark lord's pocket and produced the key.

He hurried back over to Miranda's cage and wedged it into the padlock. When it fell apart, she stepped out of it. Max escorted her out of the cage. Then he dragged the dark lord inside and locked him in.

"That won't hold him for very long."

"Hopefully he'll stay passed out while we restore your power. You'll be able to take him on then, won't you?"

She nodded. Love for this mortal, who had braved overcoming odds to find her, flooded through her. "You risked a lot coming here. I cringe to think about what the dark lord would have done to me if you hadn't shown up."

He took her hands in his large ones, concern filling his chocolate-brown eyes. "I should kill that bastard right now before he wakes up."

Miranda shook her head. "You can't do that. It's a sin against nature to take another life. Just help me regain my powers, and I'll deal with him."

He kissed the backs of her hands. The sensation of his lips brushing against her skin filled her with warmth.

His gaze met hers. "Only for you, sweetheart, I'll let him live. Where should we go?"

She led Max from the room and down the narrow stone staircase. Outside, she guided him into the quiet green forest, stepping carefully with her bare feet. Her anticipation at making love with Max again, for the final time, nearly unnerved her. It was the only way to get her powers back, but it marked the beginning of the end for their time together. Tears welled up and she choked then back.

Breathe, Miranda. Just breathe...

She urged Max toward a leafy glade practically hidden by low, overhanging tree branches. The grass was cool and inviting, but her blood ran with sluggish warmth.

Shrugging off his jacket, Max laid it down on the soft ground and pulled her into his arms. Words between them remained unspoken, but it seemed as though she could read his mind.

He wanted her, she wanted him. Nothing else mattered.

She ran her fingertips along his jaw, studying him. She desperately wanted to remember how he looked. In the future, when he'd become merely a memory, she could conjure his beloved image to keep her warm.

"Miranda," he whispered. "I thought I would die when you disappeared with Balthazar. You mean so much to me. What will I do when we have to part?"

She swallowed a sob, and a pang of longing shot through her. "You'll be fine," she said in a low voice. "I'll cast a spell of forgetfulness on you. You'll never remember our time together."

"Don't do that." His voice became raspy. "I don't want to forget you."

"It's the rules, Max. I don't make them, but I have to follow them."

His expression was somber. He didn't look happy, but he did look accepting. He rubbed methodic circles on her back, then moved his hands down to her waist and even lower to cup her buttocks. As he pushed his hard need into her hips, his gaze smoldered.

Moisture gathered between her thighs. Gods above how she wanted him. She decided he was the most handsome, tenderhearted man she'd ever been with. The fact that he possessed strong feelings for her was enough to make her want to defy the council and try to run away with him.

Yet, she realized that trying to flee their wrath would be fruitless. It would have to be enough for her to simply cherish their time together.

"Miranda," he whispered huskily in her ear, his breath warm and moist on her cheek. "I love you. I always will."

Tears spilled freely down her cheeks. She couldn't stop them. "I love you, too, Max. I could never feel about anyone else the way I feel about you."

Lowering his shaggy head, he drew her lips into a kiss as gentle as the brush of butterfly wings. Hungry for more, she opened her mouth to his gently probing tongue. Her mind reeled with the smell of him and the sensation of his body pressed against hers. She wished they could stay locked in each other's arms forever.

Max swore his body was on fire for the second time that day, though these flames were much more pleasant. He needed Miranda like a plant needed sun. She gave him sustenance and bought meaning to his existence. How could he live without her? How could he live without even the memory of their time together?

It didn't seem right, but he had to accept it.

With shaking fingers, he helped her slip off her panties, then ran his hands under her tattered sweater and pulled it off. When he fumbled with the strange white band holding her breasts, she chuckled and removed it herself, tossing it into the bushes.

Within minutes he'd shed his clothing. Once they stood naked before each other, they lowered down onto the jacket. He suckled on each of her rosy-tipped nipples, which pebbled with hardness beneath his mouth. When she spread her legs invitingly, his need built to unbearable proportions. Hungry to taste more of her, he sprinkled kisses across the creamy skin on her chest, then moved down to her stomach and lower to her triangle of fluffy golden hair. Parting the damp curls, he found her nub of pleasure. Licking and laving at it, he inserted an exploring finger into her moist center until she bucked and writhed with gratification.

"Gods Max, take me! I can't wait any longer."

He wedged himself between her hips, gripped his penis and teased her glistening nether lips with the tip, swirling it around and around. Grinning with evil satisfaction, he dipped it inside a short distance then pulled it out.

"Ahhh!" She gripped his thighs and glared at him. "I need you—"

Propping himself on his elbows, he finally plunged himself inside, burying himself to the hilt inside her hot tightness. She arched her hips to meet his, and a groan of satisfaction escaped her parted lips. Lost in sensation, he thrust his pulsing erection in and out, in and out. He knew he was close to reaching his pinnacle, but he held himself back, wanting to enjoy this as long as possible. This would be the last time he would ever be able to make love to her.

She wrapped her legs around his waist, drawing him closer. Perspiration dotted his brow as he increased the tempo and intensity of his strokes. His peak of release hovered right there, just out of reach, but still he held back.

Her nostrils flared and her neck tightened. Her long dark lashes lay against her cheeks as she focused on her pleasure. Then she opened her eyes to watch him drive inside of her, her breaths coming in small pants, sounds of contentment escaping her lips.

A few more spine-tingling moments passed, then she lifted her hips and cried out. Her body tensed and gripped onto his penis. As ecstasy gripped him, he groaned and exploded inside her, feeling his seed spill readily into her velvety warmth.

Moments later, when the heat between them dissipated, and their frenzied movements quieted, he leaned down to bury his face in her fragrant curls. He clung to the sensations and emotions rushing through him. He'd never felt this strongly about a woman in his life. It nearly killed him to think she would soon be beyond his reach.

The realization tore him into pieces. To hell with that bizarre witch's disease that had brought them together. He wanted her now and forever. Bittersweet emotion ripped through him and he held her tight, refusing to surrender her to her supernatural world.

"I don't want to leave you," he finally whispered against her neck.

"I won't send you back until you're ready," she murmured.

He maneuvered himself back down beside her and they held each other tight, neither of them willing to relinquish the simple magic of being together.

Chapter Nineteen

Kaboom!

The ground rocked fiercely, and black streaks shot through the blue sky. The same thing that had happened back at Aunt Aggie's shop had started once again. Miranda cursed softly, wishing she could spend more time with Max. Obviously, it wasn't going to happen.

"Balthazar is on the war path again," she said.

"Bloody hell, but he's a little tyrant."

He helped Miranda to her feet, then quickly dressed.

She started to put on her sweater. Dizzy all of a sudden, she stumbled backward. An unusual sensation swept through her, and her insides trembled. She felt frozen to the spot, unable to move and unable to speak.

When Max looked over at her, the color drained from his face. "By Jove, you're glowing! You're surrounded by white light. What's happening?"

"I...don't...know," she finally managed.

The second she finished speaking, she felt herself lifted off the ground. Humming filled her ears, and a cottony softness cushioned her skin. As wind whooshed past, her skin prickled, as though covered in tiny sparks. At last, the noise stopped, the wind quieted. Her body lowered back down to the ground.

Max stared at her. "You look different, even more beautiful, if that were possible. It's as though you changed from a cocoon into a butterfly."

Glancing down, she realized she wore soft slippers and a long silk lavender robe. When she reached into her pocket, her fingers closed around her wand. The second she withdrew it, she realized what had happened.

"I believe my powers have just been restored." Pointing the wand at a rock, she said, *"Aphibius transformus!"*

The rock exploded with a small poof. When the smoke cleared, a frog had replaced its solid form.

"Ribbit, ribbit," it croaked, then hopped into the bushes.

"Hot damn, I'm back!" She twirled around gleefully.

When another streak of black smoke hammered the ground not too far from them, she grabbed Max's arm. "It's dangerous for you to be here. I need to send you home."

He pulled her close. "Not until I know you're safe."

"Max, I'm a witch. I can handle myself."

"Then why were you wearing smoldering rags the first time I met you?"

"I honestly didn't know how powerful Balthazar was. I thought he was just some punk kid. I held off because I didn't want to hurt him."

"I understand, but now it's time someone put a stop to the boy's foolishness. I want to help you."

Kaboom!

This explosion hit so close it covered both of them with clods of dirt. When the dusty haze cleared, Balthazar appeared, a foolish grin on his freckled, bespectacled face. His wizard's cap tilted crazily to one side.

"Nah, nah, nah, I found you Ms. Witchy Poo. Now I'm gonna take you back to the dark lord. He's pretty upset at what you guys did to him."

"I've been lenient up until now," she warned, her patience having worn to a thread. "But the gloves are off, kiddo. I won't tolerate your nonsense any longer."

"S'cuse me? For being a witch, your powers are pretty lame." He stuck out his tongue at her. "I'm not scared."

"Take a seat, young man." She waved her wand, and a chair appeared next to Balthazar. As though someone had pushed him, he flopped down into the seat with a shocked expression.

"What the heck?" His brows drew together as he struggled to stand. "You can't do this to me!"

"I just did."

Max chuckled and shoved his hands on his hips. "Jolly good, Miranda. Now all the little upstart needs are his parents to help him understand the error of his ways."

They looked at each other at the same time. "That's it," they both exclaimed at the same time.

Lifting her hands toward the heavens, she said, "Gods above, you above know this boy's growing, but he needs his parents to instill more knowing!"

As a man and a woman shimmered into view, Miranda waved her wand across the area where she and Max stood, creating a circle of invisibility. Once Balthazar's parents completely materialized, they glanced around in confusion. But when they noticed their son seated on the chair, relief replaced all other emotion.

"Mom, Dad!" Balthazar studied them sheepishly, a shock of dark hair slanting across his forehead.

"Thomas Lee Coulter, where on earth have you been?" With a cry, the woman rushed to his side, knelt down and hugged him.

"We've looked everywhere for you, son. What happened to you?" The man's eyes filled with tears as he walked up beside Balthazar and placed a hand on his small shoulder. "Are you all right?"

"I'm fine, Dad," Balthazar confirmed.

"When you disappeared, it scared the death out of us! We've even got the police out looking for you." Wiping away tears of joy, Balthazar's mother glanced around. "Where is this place? And how did you get here? How did your father and I get here?"

"Shouldn't we explain?" Max reached out and squeezed Miranda's hand.

She shook her head. "I'll send them all back home and they won't remember anything."

He frowned. "Just as you're going to do to me, correct?"

She hated the disappointment she saw in his face. "I don't like it either, Max. But like I said before, I have to follow the rules. If I don't do as the council wants, they'll put Aunt Aggie in prison."

Frustrated by the complications that kept her and Max from being together, she waved her wand at the family and said, *"Nexus praxtor belivius forgetfulness!"*

In the blink of an eye, they disappeared. A sense of accomplishment rippled through her and she breathed a sigh of relief. "Well, at least that part's over."

Max hugged her to his side. She basked in his warmth, realizing how wonderful it was to feel like her old self again. That disease had certainly taken its pound of flesh out of her, but she swore she felt stronger than ever.

Turning toward the man she loved with all her heart, she reluctantly told him, "Now it's your turn."

"What about the dark lord?"

She forced a smile, though her insides trembled with the ache of losing him, an ache she sensed would never fade. "Dealing with him will be a piece of cake."

His brows knitted together. "A piece of cake? I say, what does that mean?"

"Sorry, that's more modern-day slang. It means I won't have any problems."

"Please, Miranda. Don't do this—"

"Good bye, Max." Her heart squeezed as she held up her wand. She hated doing this, but Max's safety was more important than what she wanted.

"Miranda!"

He reached out to grab her, but she stepped out of his reach, which took every ounce of strength she possessed. She longed to be held by him again, longed to feel his strong warmth. But that could never happen again.

"Don't forget how much I love you," she told him.

"Look!"

Tears burned at the back of her eyes, but she refused to give into his pleas. She began muttering, "*Nexus praxtor—*"

Something slammed into her. Air whooshed out of her lungs and she flew back against the base of a hill, landing in a crumpled heap. Unable to move for a moment, she finally gathered her wits and sat up. *Max!* She glanced around, but he was nowhere to be seen.

What she did see made the blood curdle in her veins. The dark lord had appeared, his cape whipping about him like a flag. His eyes glowed with reddish zeal, and steam billowed from his nostrils.

Still worried where Max had gone, she pushed to her feet. She'd find him later. For the moment, she'd have to deal with this idiot. Meeting the dark lord's angry gaze, she said, "Who pissed in your Wheaties?"

***

Max had scrambled up a hill a safe distance from the battling witch and wizard. Though hidden by the shrubbery, he could see Miranda and the dark lord circling each other, preparing for some sort of battle. What kind of battle, he couldn't imagine. He realized she held great powers, powers he had little knowledge of, yet he feared for her life. He wanted to do something to help her, but he wasn't sure what he, a mere mortal, could possibly do.

A loud crash shook the ground, and a bolt of lightning shot from the dark lord's hand. It hurled toward Miranda. She disappeared just as the fiery dart slammed into the place where she'd stood only seconds before.

The dark lord roared with outrage, raised his hands overhead and thundered, *"Paracelus agrippa!"* The earth shook again, and a crack appeared in the ground, issuing forth steam.

Miranda reappeared behind him. As Max watched in amazement, several more Mirandas appeared, gathering around the dark lord and trapping him inside a circle. The Miranda figures began marching around him. They each raised a hand and pointed at him, their voices echoing as they said, "We are displeased by your actions. You are to be banished."

"You have no power over me, witch." The dark lord drew his hands into fists at his sides. *"Pywacket greedinue malkinwai..."*

The Miranda figures laughed. "Your evil forces have no influence here," they said. "We are of the light. We draw our authority from a source much higher than yours."

"Spirits of earth and air," the Miranda figures chanted. "We call upon thee to banish the dark lord's presence and restore a natural balance of events. Send this abomination to the Neverlands..."

Sparks filled the air above the clearing, raining down on the dark lord in a hail of light. The Miranda figures dispersed and only one remained. As she raised her hand, a ball of fire appeared, and she threw it at the dark lord. He ducked and it exploded into a million brilliant pieces.

As he dove toward her, she disappeared. He crashed to the ground and rolled over, writhing in agony.

Though she had rendered herself invisible, Miranda said, "You are finished, evil one."

She glimmered into view once again, her figure towering over the dark lord as it grew to an immense height. Her entire being began to glow. "Supreme witch power I invoke, the clan's prayers like sacred smoke. Cast this misguided soul into—"

"You're not going to cast me anywhere!" The dark lord reached under his cloak and produced a crystal that glimmered iridescently in the sunshine. Suddenly the sky filled with dark purple clouds.

**

Max felt like a coward hiding up here in the bushes. Worried about how to help Miranda, he glanced around for anything that could help. Then he spotted a large boulder. If the dark lord remained in his current position, he stood directly in the giant rock's path.

Hurrying toward it, he pressed his shoulder against the massive bulk. Teeth clenched, he pushed with all his strength. It took a bit of heaving, so much so that his shoulder began to ache. Finally, just as he was about to give up, the boulder broke loose. Situated at the perfect angle for gravity to do its job, it rumbled down the hill, grinding through the dirt. Just as the dark lord started to pitch the crystal at Miranda, he must have heard something hurtling toward him. He turned around in time to see the boulder. It knocked him down and rolled right over his chest. A scream of agony escaped him. The crystal flew from his grip and catapulted aimlessly through the air.

Max ran down the hill toward Miranda, who had transformed herself to normal size. She hurried toward the dark lord and knelt at his side. Pressing a hand to his shoulder, she muttered, "Peace with the nature spirits, send forth your healing balm upon this man, so mote it be!"

He rolled over and coughed. Before he could do anything else, she pointed her wand at him and he disappeared.

Max rushed up beside her and helped her stand. "You were magnificent."

"And you have magnificent timing."

"What will happen to the dark lord?"

"He will have to embrace the good side of magic. If the rulers believe he's been rehabilitated, they may eventually release him."

"What if he returns to his old ways?"

"He'll be hunted down and terminated. There will be no more chances for him to redeem himself."

Max whistled. "Though I honestly know better, I still keep wondering if all of this is an extraordinary dream."

"Tell me if this feels like a dream." Miranda gently drew his head toward hers and kissed him.

He never wanted to let go of her, but he knew he would have to. He would live out his life, never remembering the precious moments he'd spent with her. An ache wound through his heart when she finally pulled back.

A flicker of sadness crossed her face, then it faded. "I'm going to be plenty busy looking for the Philosopher's Stone," she said. "You didn't happen to see where it landed when the dark lord dropped it, did you?"

He shook his head. "Sorry. But if we look for it together, we should be able to find it sooner."

"Thank you," she said in a soft voice.

He stroked the side of her face with his knuckle. "It's the least I can do."

The sun had begun its descent in the sky by the time they'd thoroughly combed the area. Every nook and cranny had been explored. Unfortunately, the forested land refused to give up its secrets, and the stone remained hidden.

"Bloody hell." Max raked a hand through his thick hair. Bone-weary and disheartened, he shoved his hands on his hips. "I'm sorry we can't find it."

"It's not for lack of trying." Miranda brushed off her lavender robes, now dirty and disheveled from the search. "I'm not the first witch who has failed to retrieve the stone."

"Won't the witch's council lock away your aunt if you fail to return with it? And what about the war you said mankind would suffer?"

"The council won't lock up my aunt because I've honestly done everything I can to find the stone. Since the dark lord has been banished, and Balthazar is back where he belongs, neither of them can start any wars with the stone. Wherever it might be."

He looked down at his hands, then back up at her. "I suppose you need to send me home now."

She nodded slowly, her eyes burning with unshed tears.

"If you really must do it, do it now. It's killing me to think about it."

"I'll never forget you," she said in a quiet voice. "To keep from burning up on entry, you might want to ditch the clothes."

He lifted a quizzical brow.

"You saw what happened when Balthazar dragged us here." She pointed to the burnt and singed spots on his clothing.

"I think perhaps you only want one more look at what you'll be missing." Chuckling, he peeled off his clothes and stood before her naked, his glorious body like that of a bronzed god.

She swallowed hard, every nerve in her body strung taut. Clearing her tight throat, she continued, "I promise I'll do my best to send you back home to your bed. But you know as well as I do my spells don't always work out right."

A smile touched his lips, and dimples formed in his whiskered cheeks. "I'm sure you'll make jolly good work of it. After what I saw today, I'm convinced."

Her heart squeezing with love and regard for the man who would forever hold her heart, she pointed her wand at him. *"Nexus praxtor...belivius f-f-forgetfulness!"*

She glanced into his eyes one last time and saw regret glimmering in the chocolate brown depths. An instant later, he disappeared. Sobbing, she leaned over and scooped up his clothing. She buried her face in the folds of burnt material, her salty tears mingling with his scent.

The attire was a poor substitute for him, but at least it was some part of the man she'd known and loved. She'd cherish it forever, just as she'd cherish his memory.

Return his life to the way it was before so much personal tragedy struck.

Excitement whirled through her as she considered the idea. Since the dawn of time, witches had been forbidden to interfere with mortals' natural time continuum. Honestly, would it really hurt if she tweaked things to his advantage? Some of her misery lifted as she muttered the incantation that would ultimately alter Max's life for the better. What the heck if the council reprimanded her. Right now, she only cared about Max's welfare.

He would never remember her, but at least she could see to it that he had his family back. She knew that would make him happy.

Words formed in her mind and she muttered, "Heaven and earth's powers I invoke. Nature spirits that endow with breath, I beseech you! Return Sir Maxwell Chadwick's life to the world he knew before tragedy struck."

Intense, tingling warmth surged through her and she smiled, despite her pain. At least Max would be able to experience the joy he knew before his world fell apart with the deaths of his loved ones.

With a shuddering sigh, she snapped her fingers and Nellie appeared in her hand.

"Hey kiddo, long time, no see! Where have you been?"

Miranda rolled her eyes. As usual, the broom didn't remember much. "I've been looking for the Philosopher's Stone. Remember?"

"Oh, yeah. That's right. Well, did you find it?"

"No." Lifting her robes, she straddled the broom handle.

"What about that hot duke you met? How'd that work out with him?"

"I'd rather not talk about it right now, Nellie."

"Uh, oh. Got your heart broken that badly?"

"That's an understatement. But like I said, I'd rather not talk about it."

"Got it. Off we go!" Nellie lifted into the air and circled over the wizard's tower, gaining speed. Then she darted into the wispy white clouds.

Chapter Twenty

Max forced his way out of the cottony depths of sleep. He sat up in his bed and looked around, momentarily disoriented. After rubbing his bleary eyes, his room came into focus. Questions pounded his brain.

What in the world happened to me last night?

His body felt as though it had been trampled by a thousand horses and a pounding headache nearly blinded him. Trying to recall what he'd done to wind up in such a physical mess, he searched his aching brain.

Thinking perhaps speaking aloud might ground him, he said, "Let's see, I was at the pub with Edward. And I had a few whiskies."

A few whiskies shouldn't have disoriented him so much. There had to be more to it, but for the life of him, he couldn't remember what.

A knock sounded on his door and Henry called, "May I come in, sir?"

"Of course."

The butler entered cautiously and gave him a hard stare. "Another night on the town, I see."

"Don't nag, Henry. I'm not in the mood for it." Max rubbed his forehead.

"Someday I hope you'll mend your wandering ways." Henry shook his head. "But for now, you should eat. Breakfast will be served shortly. Do you plan to join your family, or would you like the cook to set aside a plate of food for you to have later?"

He looked up. "My family?"

Henry lifted a brow. "Of course, sir. Your mother and father are waiting for you as we speak. Your brother and his wife are here as well. And young master Charles."

"Charles?"

"Your nephew, sir. It's his birthday today. He's turning two."

Everything in the room seemed to fade in and out, then became clear again as he struggled to understand. "Is this some cruel joke, Henry? My family died years ago, and I was forced to assume the Duke of Pellamshire's title."

The butler's face blanched, and his pinched lips drained of color. "I assure you, sir, I'd never try to deceive you in such a cruel manner. I think perhaps you've had a terrible nightmare."

"If so, it was one hell of a nightmare."

"I'd say so." He rocked back on his heels. "So, sir, shall I tell your family you intend to join them?"

"Please do. I'll be down shortly."

After Henry left, Max jumped up and went to the nightstand that held a pitcher of water and a large bowl. He poured out a good measure of the liquid and splashed it over his face and body, attempting to sharpen his senses.

Could the terrible memories of what had happened to his family have been a nightmare? Had the dream that his parents and brother had succumbed to a fever been false? What about Catherine and the babe? Could it be true that she and the boy hadn't passed away in childbirth?

He could only dare to hope that it was so. But the pit in his stomach still made him question the possibility. Slicking back his damp hair, he quickly dressed and hurried down to the dining room. In the doorway, he gripped the wooden frame, his mouth falling open. He blinked several times.

Henry hadn't been lying.

His mother and father were on one side of the table eating breakfast, while Marley and Catherine sat on the other eating theirs. His mother and Catherine were discussing the latest fashions; his father and brother were arguing about politics.

A lavishly carved wooden high chair sat next to Catherine. A small boy with a mixture of both his brother and sister-in-law's features sat there with a spoon in his chubby fist. Intent on trying to feed himself, he scooped up scrambled eggs and put them in his mouth, none too gracefully.

But when he saw Max, he kicked his feet and cried, "Unc, unc!"

Everyone turned to look at Max, and his mother motioned for him to come and sit beside her. His limbs tingling with disbelief, Max pulled out a chair and sank heavily into it. Still stunned to find his family alive and well, he studied them closely, as though they might disappear.

His memories of their deaths must have indeed been a terrible, terrible dream. A nightmare he hoped to never suffer through again.

"Our apologies, Maxwell, for starting without you," his mother said. "We thought you might want to sleep in."

"You were out late enough," his father grumbled, stabbing a piece of bacon with his fork and plopping it into his mouth.

Max's mother patted his arm. "Now, now, Nathan, let him be. He's a young man, and young men will sow their wild oats, as we know."

"That's what worries me, Rebecca. Just where those wild oats might get sown."

"Shush," she retorted. "We're at the breakfast table, for heaven's sake. And there are young ears listening."

Marley and Catherine held up their napkins and snickered.

When Max's gaze fell on his brother's wife, he recalled how deeply he'd been in love with her. To his surprise, the overriding passion had been replaced by nothing more than respect and consideration. She was the mother of his nephew, after all.

He shook his head in amazement. How could his angst over her betrayal have disappeared overnight?

It was a mystery.

Max watched his family all throughout breakfast, making an occasional comment here and there, but still shocked to see them living and breathing. After the meal, his brother and father went off to the palace to take care of the courtly duties he'd so recently tended to. At least in his dreams, he'd done it.

Though he'd adapted to the demands of being the duke, it was nevertheless a relief to know his brother and father would handle them once more, and he'd be free to return to his military duties. He could set sail and enjoy the regimented life of a navy man.

For some reason, he felt as though something was missing. Something he couldn't quite put a finger on. *Something very important.* It continued to lurk at the back of his mind, taunting and teasing. No matter how he tried to concentrate, it remained elusive.

After Catherine took Charles home, Max and his mother went out into the flower garden. She slipped her arm through his and began to chatter. Her soft voice soothed his nerves. He found himself overjoyed, yet still awed, that she was indeed alive, as were the rest of his family.

"You don't seem to be yourself today." She met Max's gaze, her forehead lined with concern.

"I'm in a reflective mood is all," he told her, his heart warming at the love in her voice.

"That's not at all like you."

"I'm a changed man." While he didn't want to share the details of his imaginings with her, he realized he had a new appreciation for his family and home. Never again would he take them for granted.

"Oh look!" She reached out and gently touched a rose, caressing the velvety leaves. "I do so love the deep burgundy color."

As Max studied the rose, memories unfurled exactly like petals in bloom. The image of a beautiful woman flickered through his mind and he recalled laying a rose on her pillow. By Jove, what was her name?

Miranda.

As memories flooded his mind, making his temples pound again, he sat down on a stone bench and held his forehead in his hands. He remembered finding her in the empty field, the time they'd spent together, everything. And he remembered how deeply he'd fallen in love with her. Everything about her returned vividly.

But was he experiencing memories? Or only recalling more of his farfetched dreams?

No, he sensed they were real. He had to believe it because the love he felt for Miranda filled him utter joy. He decided he couldn't waste any time finding out who she was.

His mother sat next to him and put her arm around his shoulders. "Maxwell, are you not feeling well?"

"Something astounding has happened to me, mother."

She patted his back. "Tell me about it."

"You'll think I'm crazy."

"You're my son. I've never known a more solid, stable man in my life besides your father, of course. And Marley. All three of you have good heads on your shoulders and I trust each one implicitly. Now tell me, what is it?"

Taking a deep breath, Max started with his nightmare and his profound sadness at losing everyone in the family. Then he told her about Miranda's appearance and how she'd quickly become so important to him. He left out nothing—not even the fact that she was a witch and that she'd been battling a wizard to try and find the Philosopher's Stone. He explained about traveling with her to the future and then how devastated he'd been when she'd sent him back to his time.

"I desperately wanted to stay with her, but witches and mortals are forbidden to be together." Gripping his knees, he met his mother's gaze, searching her face to see if she believed him.

"This is quite a story," she murmured.

"It's real, I'm certain of it."

"How can you explain the fact that your father and I are alive again, along with your brother, Catherine, and Charles?"

"Somehow Miranda must have changed the past. She knew how miserable I was at losing my family."

She tucked a loose gray hair back into her bun and studied him closely. Her silence spoke of her disbelief.

"Bloody hell. You must think I've lost my marbles. I'd think so as well, except there's this voice inside me that assures me I haven't."

"I'm not discounting anything you told me, Maxwell. You are not the type of man to dally in fantasies and fairy tales."

"I know I sound like a raving lunatic, but I have this feeling right here…" He tapped his chest.

"I'm a religious person, son. I believe faithfully in God and the Protestant church. But I also know things beyond our ken often happen."

"What do you think I should do?" His throat felt ragged, his heart torn into bits. He had to find Miranda, but the question that ate at him was how.

"Let's examine the facts," she suggested. "You said the Philosopher's Stone flew from the dark lord's hand when the boulder hit him. Then you and Miranda searched everywhere but weren't able to find it."

"That's correct."

"The stone's still out there?"

He nodded.

"And a person who has it can perform all manner of magic?"

"Supposedly. What are you alluding to Mother?"

"I know you're distraught at losing the woman you love, Maxwell. But think about what you might be able to do if you had the stone."

Leaping to his feet, he began to pace next to the bench. Finally, he realized what he needed to do. "By Jove, you're brilliant! I must find the tower, then I need to look for the stone. With it, I'll be able to find Miranda."

Rebecca smiled. "Exactly, my son."

He sat back down beside her and took her hands in his. "I love Miranda so much. She makes me laugh and she fills my life with joy. I need her. And if there's even a ghost of a chance that we can be together, I'm willing to take it."

"Then what are you waiting for?" Rebecca dragged him to his feet. "Start looking for the wizard's tower and the stone. Now. There's no time to lose."

Filled with conviction, he hurried toward the coach house and retrieved his horse. A few moments later, he galloped toward the outskirts of London and beyond into the countryside.

***

Max spent a long time looking for the stone and the wizard's tower. People thought he'd become unhinged, and rumors flew about his endless quest. He didn't care. Determination to find a way back to Miranda made him ignore the fools.

Of course, his father thought he'd lost grip with reality, as did both Marley and Catherine. His mother continued to believe in him and encouraged him to continue the search. Every time he wanted to give up, she spurred him on.

After six months of riding out nearly every day, even spending nights at inns all across the land, he'd begun to lose hope. He'd become weary of his forays and began, once again, to seriously question his sanity. Perhaps none of his memories of Miranda had been real. Perhaps they'd been nothing more than a wild dream. Maybe he needed to accept that.

One cold winter day, just when he'd finally convinced himself he needed to put a halt to his search, he noted a break in the landscape. Freshly fallen snow dusted the trees, but a large gap existed between two of the oaks. The space between it seemed to shimmer.

He wheeled his horse toward the gap and began to travel down a narrow path. Even though he saw nothing amiss, he felt compelled to go deeper into the white-blanketed woods. Despite his leather gloves and coat, his hands and feet tingled with numbness. He wasn't certain if it was from the cold or excitement. Fearful he might have come here for no reason, he considered turning around.

Yet when he narrowed his gaze and scanned the horizon, his heart nearly leapt out of his chest. A familiar spire scraped against the foggy gray sky, tempting him to go farther. He urged the horse to continue through the thick trees until at last he could see the entire outline of a familiar structure.

The wizard's tower.

As he stared at the ruins, the horse pawed the ground and snorted, steam billowing from its nostrils. He slid to the ground, walking the horse closer. When he reached the place that looked like the area where Miranda and the dark lord had fought, he began searching the ground.

Before long, bitter cold gnawed his extremities. The icy weather wouldn't allow him to stay here very long. He poked and prodded for a while, then rode home. As soon as humanly possible, he would resume the search.

***

Max spent many cold winter days combing the landscape around the wizard's tower. Spring took its time arriving, but at last the frozen landscape around London thawed. With warmer days, he decided to move out to the tower to be closer to his work. One day he loaded a small wagon with clothes, food, blankets, and other items. Hitching his horse to it, he drove out into the courtyard.

His parents stood there, waiting to talk to him. It was a beautiful, sunny day. Birds sang in the trees, flowers bloomed brilliantly. Yet Nathan and Rebecca didn't seem to appreciate it. Concern filled their expressions, and his mother held her hands tightly as she always did when she was upset.

Max drew the wagon to a halt and stepped down, not eager to hear what they had to say.

His father sent him a thunderous look. "Where in God's name do you think you're going again?"

"For a ride."

"A ride where?"

"To look for something, Father. Just as I've been doing these past months."

"Why do you have all the provisions?" Nathan glanced at the stack of things in the back of the wagon.

"I'm moving out for a while. Hopefully I'll find what I'm looking for. Mother knows all about what I'm doing and why."

She nodded and glanced down at her feet.

His father frowned. "What have you two been plotting?"

"Nathan, calm down." She placed her hand on her husband's arm. "Max simply has some unsettled business he must take care of."

Nathan yanked his arm away and turned to face Max again. "You've always been an impulsive boy, and now you're an equally impulsive young man. First you resign your commission, and now this. I fear you're going to get yourself in trouble. What irresponsible nonsense are you up to now?"

Max rubbed the thick whiskers on his chin and cheeks, the rasp echoing in his ears. He hadn't shaved in weeks. His beard had grown long and needed a good trim.

"This is something I have to do," he insisted. "Please try to understand."

"Crazy fool." Nathan stomped back toward the house, went inside and slammed the front door.

"It's too bad he feels that way," Max said.

"Don't worry. He'll calm down later." Tears spilled freely down Rebecca's face. She hugged him. "Godspeed, Max. I'll be praying for you. Just as I have this whole time."

Max kissed the top of her head. His mother had always understood him. He swung into the wagon, settled into the seat and flicked the reins. As he rode away, his spirits soared, just as they always did when he searched for the stone. Only through it could he find his way back to Miranda.

Of course, his father thought he'd lost every lick of commonsense. And his mother was obviously worried about him. Until he'd exhausted every possibility of finding the stone, he wasn't going to stop looking. Months ago he'd plotted the land around the wizard's tower and since then he'd been methodically going over every inch. Surely, by doing it this way, he'd eventually locate the blasted thing.

Once he reached the tower and unpacked, he cleaned out the wizard's room enough to make it habitable. From that day forward, he worked from dawn till dusk, searching. Sometimes he forgot to eat and he had to force himself to do it. He also remembered to occasionally bathe in a nearby stream.

Spring turned into summer, then into autumn. Red and gold leaves fluttered on the trees and the landscape took on golden hues. As the nights became cooler, Max closed the window shutters, built a fire on the hearth and piled more blankets on his cot. Those measures, along with memories of Miranda, kept him warm. Once bitter winter snow began to fly, he'd probably have to return to London, a prospect he didn't look forward to.

One morning a loud noise awakened him. He jumped to his feet and looked around. A second later, he stood face to face with an impeccably groomed elderly man wearing a dark, expensive-looking suit and hat. The man's nostrils flared, and disgust spread through his expression.

"I don't allow transients to camp out on my property, sir. Please remove yourself from the premises." He held out a cane and prodded Max in the chest. "Now."

"I'm not a transient. I mean no harm."

"You're a filthy beggar, sir," the man said.

Max looked down and realized he did indeed look like a tramp. But he couldn't leave yet. He still hadn't found the stone.

"I'm warning you. Vacate now or I'll have you forcibly removed." The man scowled, and his thick gray brows drew together.

"Just give me a few moments and I'll collect my things." He knew he'd have to leave before the man brought out the constables to arrest him and lock him up. That would embarrass his family. Needless to say, he didn't want any part of that.

His mind raced with a million questions about what he was going to do as he gathered his belongings in a knapsack. As he reached for his jacket, movement caught his eye. Glancing up, he noted his reflection in an old mirror that had become smoky with age. The haggard gauntness of his heavily whiskered face stared back at him. Deep, dark hollows resided under his eyes. He'd become so thin his ribs showed beneath his shirt, and his trousers hung loosely on his hips.

Something shining caught his eye. Narrowing his gaze, he watched as a ball of light glittered behind the glass. A second later, the brightness became even more pronounced.

"I don't have all day," the man grumbled.

Max ignored him. He had to know what was behind the glass.

"I say, this is my last warning," the man said impatiently.

"*Find out what it is*," a voice urged Max. Unable to resist, he smashed a fist into the mirror. The glass shattered. He winced as the shards ripped his hand and clattered onto the cobblestones.

"What the bloody hell do you think you're doing?" the man shouted. He thumped the end of his cane on the flagstone floor.

Max barely registered anything around him when he saw what had caused the glittering in the mirror. In a hollowed-out area sat the Philosopher's Stone, its crystal facets shimmering with brilliance. All of these months of searching the perimeter of the tower had been a useless waste of time. All the while, it had been inside, tucked behind this mirror. Somehow, before Miranda sent him off, the dark lord must have hidden it in here.

Max pulled down the stone and cradled it reverently in his hands.

The man glared at him. "That is my property; therefore, I demand you hand it over."

"My apologies, but I can't do that."

"How dare you deny me?"

"Because I need this much more than you do. And I'll even pay you well for it." Filled with a combination of relief and exhilaration, Max reached into his pocket, withdrew all the money he had and handed it over. The old man stared at him in disbelief.

Max knew he must appear to be a complete idiot, but he didn't care. "Listen closely to me. Please return the horse pastured outside to Sir Nathan Chadwick and his wife, Rebecca. Tell them I'm alright and that I'll visit them as soon as I can."

"Yes, yes, I know who the duke is. But I don't understand." The old man's face turned red with irritation. "You're not making sense. Who are you?"

"My name is Max. And I'm going on a long journey."

He rubbed the stone, which had grown warm simply with his touch. "I have no idea of what mumbo jumbo spell to utter," he muttered to its glittering surface. "I only know I need you to take me to Miranda."

An odd sensation twisted through him and he rose into the air. Everything in the room disappeared as he stuffed the stone in his jacket pocket. He didn't know what was going to happen, he just knew he was willing to risk all to find the woman he loved.

A gust of wind sucked him into a swirling pool of blackness.

Chapter Twenty-One

"Attention ladies and gentlemen." Mistress Violet Silvermoon, the potions professor, rapped her wand on her carved wooden lectern and lifted a knowledgeable brow. "Today we're going to study basic spells. Manifesting, banishing, blessing, and honoring…"

Seated at her desk in the classroom, Miranda yawned with boredom. Every time she came to class, her mind wandered shamelessly. She couldn't help it. Having heard the subject matter many times, she wanted to scream at the idea of hearing any more. But she'd started the process of becoming a high witch once again, so she couldn't avoid the lessons. She glanced outside at the fluffy cloudscape, amazed at the way the azure sky stretched into infinity.

It had been an ingenious decision by the Supreme Witch's Council to build Wysteria's College of Magic up here, suspended in the heavens, far from any mortal's sight. Nevertheless, as beautiful as the place was with its lofty marble halls of learning, she'd grown weary of coming here. Since she'd failed to complete her seventh task for the council, she would have to repeat all of her lessons over again. It would take another hundred years for her to be eligible for promotion.

She'd sat through so many witchcraft lessons, she felt certain she'd be able to stand up there and utter them nearly verbatim. It wasn't her intent to be disrespectful but come on. How could any of the instructors expect her to remain engaged, when she'd been through all of this so many times before?

"Miss Rose. Are you paying attention?"

To her dismay, Mistress Silvermoon had stepped from the lectern and now stood at her side. The woman's face radiated disapproval, and a thick black hair sprouting from a beauty mark on her upper lip trembled. Her black robes swished as she folded her arms across her chest.

Miranda scrambled to remember what the professor had been talking about. "Excuse me?"

"Miss Rose," she said sharply, tapping a long fingernail on Miranda's desk. "You have already been censured by the Supreme Witch's Council for your outrageous actions of changing the time continuum for Sir Maxwell Chadwick. Would you also like to be reprimanded by the college's Board of Education? Perhaps they'll suspend you. Permanently."

"I don't want that, ma'am." She squirmed in her seat. This was ridiculous. She felt like a child, and everyone was staring at her.

"You are dangerously close to it, young lady. However, if you answer my question, I'll let this incident slip. Can you explain to the class what a charm is used for?"

"Sure."

"Please go up to the front of the room and enlighten us."

Embarrassed beyond belief, she approached the blackboard. Whispers and subdued laughter rose from the other students. With difficulty, she ignored them. *The gods know I don't belong here*, she thought with a sigh.

Taking her place at the lectern, she began. "A charm can be part of a long spell, or it can be a spell all by itself."

A thundering boom interrupted her speech, rocking the college's foundations. Grabbing the edges of the lectern, she held it tightly as it wobbled back and forth. Cries of surprise rose from the students, and they hurried to the windows.

She shouldered her way through the crowd and looked outside. Her eyes widened when she saw dark, billowing smoke rising from a plume slicing through the atmosphere. As the clouds parted, her heart nearly stopped. The activity seemed to come from the area around her home.

"Son of a monkey," she muttered in disbelief, realizing if something had happened to the mansion, no one would be around to take care of it. Aunt Aggie was in the Swiss Alps skiing with her parents. None of her sisters were at home either.

Mistress Silvermoon rapped her wand on the wall and said sharply, "Everyone, please return to your seats. "Whatever it is, there's nothing you can do about it."

Students shuffled back to their seats. But Miranda could hardly sit by while her house burned down.

"*I need you.*"

She looked around, but no one stood near enough to be talking to her.

"*Miranda...*"

"Max," she whispered, now recognizing his beloved voice.

It had been so long since they'd parted—more than a year now. Could he really have found a way to communicate with her or was she losing her mind?

"*Come to me.*" His voice sounded weak and distant.

"I've got to go," she called out as she raced into the hallway, not caring what Mistress Silvermoon or the administration thought. Let them throw her out for all she cared. Max needed her and that's all that mattered.

Her locker wasn't far, so she raced down the hall toward it and yanked it open. Grabbing Nellie, she rushed outside the tall brick building.

Nellie's bristles rustled. "What's up, kiddo?"

"Max is calling me."

"Max? Oh, that's right. Your duke. Didn't you send him back to his own time?"

"Yes." She straddled Nellie's handle. "I need to go to home right away. Something's happening."

"You got it." Nellie swooped through the misty clouds and flew toward the mansion.

**

Max slammed like a cannonball onto the ground. Excruciating pain radiated through him. When he pried open his sticky eyes, he saw a canopy of leaves above, along with thick billowing smoke. The impact had been terrible, and he swore his body must have splintered into a million aching pieces. Intense heat pierced his skin and he feared it had melted his bones.

He tried to move an arm. *Nothing.* Then a leg. *Still nothing.* Through the paralyzing pain, he managed to mutter, "M-miranda, where are you? I…need…you…"

Bloody hell, what had he been thinking? He'd been insane to try and use that Philosopher's Stone to get back to her. Insane and desperate. What good had it been to risk all if he'd killed himself in the process?

As his heart filled with love for the woman who consumed his every waking and sleeping thought, another wave of agony washed over him. His life had been crazy since he'd met her. But he wouldn't change any of it. The happiness she'd brought him, even for the short while he'd known her, was more than worth it.

At least as he lay dying, he could allow his thoughts to dwell on her—his wonderful angel. Memories of their time together filled his mind and heart. Her beautiful face, framed by familiar golden curls, appeared before him. By Jove, she seemed so real.

He tried to reach out to stroke her shimmering locks of hair but couldn't. It hurt too much. He'd become boneless. He couldn't even lift his hand.

Wetting his dry lips, he stammered, "You look just...just as I remember..."

A cry escaped her as she stroked the side of his face. Tears squeezed from her eyes and fell on his cheeks. "Oh, my goddess, Max, what happened? How did you get here?"

At the sensation of her gentle touch and her warm tears, he swallowed hard, his mouth dry and gritty. He stared hard at the vision. Could she actually be kneeling at his side? Had the Philosopher's Stone really transported him to the future?

"Are you r-real?"

"Yes, Max. I heard you calling for me."

Razor-sharp agony raked his spine and he winced. Summoning what strength he still possessed, he said, "L-look in my j-jacket pocket. The stone, it's for y-you. They'll promote you now..."

She reached into his pocket and withdrew the crystal. A gasp escaped her as she held it up. The stone's iridescent facets shimmered in the sun, just as the tears on her cheeks.

***

Miranda shivered as she studied Max's twisted and burned body lying in the meadow behind the Rose mansion. Shocked and saddened, she could barely think straight. Max had come here to find her. To see him dying from the time transfer broke her heart.

Time seemed to have completely stopped, and she couldn't think of anything but how cruel fate was to have brought him to her, then to take him away. Again. She tossed aside the stone as though it had burned her. After this, she wanted nothing to do with the damn thing. If she'd known at the start of all this that it would hurt Max, she would never have gone looking for it. Becoming a high witch wasn't worth his life.

She carefully lifted his limp hand, kissed the back of it, and laid it against her cheek. "Only a high witch or wizard can use the stone without harm, my love. It's a dangerous tool if it isn't used correctly."

Through the soot and grime on his face, which had been scraped raw, he grinned wryly. "Obviously."

"Max, oh, Max…" Her lower lip trembled, and she sucked it in. "I can't believe you did this for me."

"I n-needed…needed to see you…" He coughed, and something in his lungs rattled. His chest rose and fell erratically, and it seemed to take everything out of him to speak.

She flinched as though she'd been smacked across the face. He didn't sound good at all. She couldn't lose him again, not now. Pleading with the nature spirits, she asked them to heal Max. She chanted and cajoled, but he remained in his sorry condition. He was slipping away before her eyes, and she felt helpless to change that fact.

Why didn't any of her spells work? What was she doing wrong?

"Oh, Max," she cried, frustrated at not being able to save him. "Why did you come here? I gave you back your family, you should have been happy."

"Th-thank you for that. But I had to f-find you again…"

"Crazy man—"

"Now I can d-die in…peace…"

"No, you are not going to die!" Her blood boiled with anger. It couldn't end between them like this. It had been difficult enough when she'd had to send him back to his time, but at least she'd known he was alive. But this—this was unacceptable.

His chocolate brown eyes, hazed with pain, met hers. "I f-found you. That's all that m-matters."

Damn it all. There had to be something she could do. Thoughts raced through her brain—anything that would help. She didn't even have enough time to stir up a healing potion. This was terrible. The man she loved laid before her, dying from his wounds—wounds he received while trying to return to her.

It's my fault this has happened. I should have continued to search for the stone until I found it. That way, it couldn't have harmed anyone ever again.

"Kiss me…" he managed.

"But—"

"P-please…"

Trembling with sorrow, tears running down her cheeks, she leaned down and pressed her lips to his. They were so cold, like clay. Suppressing her sobs, she kissed him for as long as she could, then sat back to look at him again.

"Max, I…Max!"

He didn't answer. He laid very still, his face unmoving, his eyes closed. Around him, she saw the shadows of death, waiting to snatch him away.

***

Miranda didn't know how long she sat there next to Max in the meadow, holding her head in her heads, rocking back and forth in grief. When she looked at him again, a peaceful expression filled his face. In contrast, her emotions were in turmoil. All she could think about was how much he'd meant to her. Nothing mattered any more. She didn't want to live if he was gone.

"The Philosopher's Stone can bring Max back," Ursula said.

Miranda sat up straight and wiped tears from her bleary eyes. She looked over at the old witch who had appeared in the meadow. In her hands, she held the stone, which had transformed into a glimmering golden sphere and emitted sparks.

"I'm not a high witch, so it won't work for me."

"You have the knowledge, Miranda. You've been instructed in the magical arts for longer than any witch I know. Not even the council has as much training as you."

Miranda stood, her hands trembling at her sides. She dared to hope but feared doing so would only lead to more disappointment. "Won't the council be livid if I use it? Especially to restore life to a human who has passed on?"

Ursula shrugged. "Too bad. The old biddies need to learn they can't control everything."

Gripping the stone in her left hand, Ursula stepped around Miranda and Max, enclosing them in a circle of protection. Then, walking clockwise, she conjured a shimmering wall and handed Miranda the stone. "Search your heart, my child. Speak your feelings aloud, and your love will be returned to you."

Miranda was confused at first. Then, amazingly, she knew exactly what to say, as if she'd been waiting her entire life to do this.

"The sacred circle is cast, and I am between two worlds," she said. Lifting the stone skyward, she continued. "Earth, air, water, and fire, I call upon you to lend your influence. Aphrodite hear my invocations, for you know the power of love. Restore Max to me, blessed be!"

Sparks exploded from the stone and surrounded the duke. His body, imbued with a shining glow, lifted up, then lowered back to the ground. Amazingly, his wounds began to heal and finally disappeared. To Miranda's relief, his chest also began to rise and fall with even breathing.

The light swirled around and flowed back into the stone, which resumed its normal crystal appearance. Max stirred and coughed, then propped up on his elbows and met Miranda's gaze. "Bloody hell, what happened? I feel incredible."

Uttering a cry of relief, she sank down beside him. As he gathered her into his arms, she clung tightly to him.

Nothing could have surpassed her joy at feeling his living warmth.

She looked up, intending to thank Ursula for her help, but the old witch had disappeared. Someday she'd catch up with the crone and tell her how much she appreciated her intervention.

Glancing back at Max, she said, "Thank the goddess you've come back to me."

He chuckled. "By Jove, what did you do? I feel like a new man."

"I used the Philosopher's Stone to heal you."

His expression became somber. "I assume that's not allowed, me being a mortal and all."

"I should have asked permission from the council. But there wasn't time. You were…dying." She didn't want to tell him he'd passed. That might have wigged him out.

"Always bucking authority, aren't you sweetheart? I suppose that's why I love you so much. You keep things exciting." He brushed hair away from her forehead, his gaze twinkling with admiration.

"You need to know this, Max. I'll probably be punished for this. The council could even imprison me if they're angry enough."

"Then I'll go there with you."

"But—"

He pressed two fingers to her lips. "Promise me we'll never be apart again, Miranda. I love you."

"I love you too, Max."

"Now that I've found you again, I'm never letting you go. It would take all of heaven and earth to keep us apart."

She smiled. "I believe you."

Max's lips possessively captured her mouth, and she closed her eyes. Her spirit soared as she enjoyed his soul-stirring kiss.

Chapter Twenty-Two

Miranda and Max made their way to the mansion to rest. Barely a half hour had passed before a Supreme Witch's Council messenger appeared in the parlor where they sat on the couch holding each other.

A red-winged, heavily-scaled creature with glistening fangs, the baby mote dragon hovered above Miranda. It explained how the council members, with their highly attuned senses, had picked up on the stone's powerful electromagnetic activity. They knew she'd used it, and why.

Miranda shouldn't have been surprised. She'd known she couldn't slip anything past the council. A cold pit developed in her stomach as she listened to what the baby dragon had to say.

"Miranda Rose, because of your unauthorized use of a magical object, you are to appear in the council's chambers at sunrise tomorrow." The tiny dragon snorted a few orange flames before disappearing.

She and Max spent most of the night talking, dreading the unknown, but prepared to face it together. When the sun peeked over the horizon, Miranda dressed in her ceremonial lavender robes. She loaned Max one of her father's shirts, along with a shirt and tie, so he would have fresh clothing. Both men were close enough in size that everything fit pretty well.

Once they were ready, Max and Miranda climbed onto Nellie who flew them to the Supreme Council's palace, located in the heart of the Persephone Mountains. Max waited out in the vast marble hallway on a bench, while Miranda was admitted by a bespectacled troll with blue hair into the council's inner chambers. Scores of other witches stood in line to receive their sentences for breaking council laws.

Miranda took her place behind them, tapping one of her feet waiting for her turn to speak with the council. The idea of explaining why she'd saved the man she loved greatly angered her. Yes, she knew there had to be rules and guidelines for witches to follow. But for Pete's sake, she was in love. Mortal or otherwise, Max was the man for her. To be true to her heart, she'd had to save him. And she'd do it again, to heck with what anyone said.

When it was her turn to bat, she stood in front of the twelve council members seated at the high table, situated on a dais at the front of the room. Hands clasped behind her back, she studied the head priestess, Atlantia Southmore, who'd taken a seat at one end.

The distinguished witch stared at her with a sharp gaze, as did the other members who sat with their hands clasped before them. All wore black robes and black pointed hats with gauzy black veils that made them look like crows on a cornfield.

The air practically vibrated with their disapproval. Gods help her, she knew she was going to get her butt royally chewed. Tensing her jaw, she prepared for the onslaught.

"We find your recent actions regarding your mortal lover, Sir Maxwell Chadwick, most distressing. And we'd like to remind you this is why the council recently banned all witch/mortal relationships. They typically lead to trouble." Mistress Southmore frowned at Miranda. Her long dark robes swished as she rose and began to pace.

Refusing to be intimidated, Miranda stared straight ahead. She'd decided long before she ever entered this room that no matter what the council decreed, she would hold herself proudly.

Face darkening with rage, the head priestess continued. "By using the Philosopher's Stone to save Sir Maxwell Chadwick's mortal life, you have defied our laws. What do you have to say for yourself?"

Miranda summoned her courage, well aware she may be signing her own punishment orders. "Surely, you've been in love, Mistress Southmore. If you have, then you understand why I risked everything to save Max. Given the opportunity, I'd do it again without compunction."

Whispers rippled amongst the council as the witches bent their heads together, discussing what she'd just said.

"Furthermore," Miranda added, "Maxwell Chadwick risked everything to travel here and present the witch's council with this—something we have searched high and low for."

Reaching into her pocket, she held up the Philosopher's Stone. It glittered magnificently in the sunlight pouring in the widows, as though imbued with inner fire. She placed the stone on the council's long table. It illuminated the surface with golden rays.

The council members stared at the stone, then began bantering with each other in excited tones.

Miranda went on. "I would ask the council to remember that witches throughout time have been taught first and foremost to harm no one. Therefore, I'll put this question forth to all of you—would I have been upholding our time-honored values if I had stood idly by, watching the life drain from Max's broken and bruised body? Especially after he risked his life to bring this magical object to the council?"

Now the council's voices rose in heated debate. Mistress Southmore returned to her place at the head of the table and pounded a gavel. "Silence!"

Everyone stopped talking and stared at her.

"Obviously, we need to discuss the situation in more depth," the head priestess declared. "Miranda, please wait outside until you are summoned again."

She nodded, more than happy to leave. In the hallway, she walked toward Max. He rose when he saw her. When she reached his side, he pulled her into his arms and kissed the top of her head.

"Well?"

She sighed. "They're still trying to make their decision."

"Perhaps that's a positive sign."

"Hopefully. But deep down, I'm afraid they're simply adding more charges to my list of wrongdoings. I really let them have it in there."

A muscle twitched in his square jaw. "Do I dare ask what you said?"

She gazed into his handsome face and smiled. "I refused to admit that I was wrong for saving your life. I swore I'd do it again because I love you so much."

"You are a firebrand if I ever saw one." Max gave her a kiss of encouragement and pulled her down on the bench beside him.

They must have waited for close to an hour before the council's chamber doors opened and the troll appeared again.

"You will return to council chambers for sentencing." The troll's gaze fell on Max. "Bring the mortal with you."

Miranda stood, her knees quaking. Her mouth went dry, and her skin became cold and clammy. Max's large warmth as he rose up beside her was comforting, though it did little to dispel her sense of foreboding.

Gently taking her elbow, Max guided her through the double doors. He draped his arm protectively around her shoulders as they stood together in front of the council members.

Mistress Southmore propped a pair of glasses on the bridge of her nose, then rose. Picking up a piece of parchment, she began to read.

"Miranda Rose, novice witch of the Wysteria Hedge Haven Clan..."

Max's grip on Miranda's shoulder tightened.

"...the Supreme Witch's Council finds you innocent of all charges," the head priestess droned. "Because of the tremendous humanity you have shown, you are hereby promoted and will take your rightful place in the clan as a high witch."

When she heard those words, Miranda nearly collapsed. Instead, she met Mistress Southmore's gaze with honest surprise. "Really? I'm being promoted? And I'm not in trouble?"

The head priestess smiled and lowered the parchment. "You have long sought the position of high witch, Miranda. You could have easily allowed the mortal to die and turned the stone over to us. Instead, you showed extreme bravery by making the choice you did. You have reminded this council of why the gods placed us here in the first place—to protect mankind from harm and promote their wellbeing."

The witches on the council nodded and muttered their agreement.

"We only ask one favor of you. As you know, the power from the Philosopher's Stone can be difficult and dangerous to wield, yet you did a phenomenal job of handling it. Will you train the council how to work with the stone?"

"Yes, of course." Miranda smiled at each one of the members, then up at Max. This was better than she could have imagined.

"However, there is the matter of your affair with this mortal man," Mistress Southmore added. "That deeply concerns the council."

Miranda's heart thudded to her feet. She held tighter onto Max. "I won't do anything unless he's at my side."

"Just as we thought. Therefore, we'd like to grant him a reward for the great risk he took in bringing the council the Philosopher's Stone. We'd like to offer him immortality. Then the two of you will be free to live your lives together."

"What do you think, Max?" Excitement bubbled over into Miranda's words.

"I'm honored," he said with a smile. "What about my family? Will we be able to travel back in time to visit them?"

"As often as we'd like."

He nodded. "Jolly good then. Let's get on with it."

Mistress Southmore handed Miranda the Philosopher's Stone. "You can do the honors, my dear."

Heart hammering with joy, she closed her eyes, summoning the spell from the depths of her memories. She walked toward Max and held up the stone. *"Nimbus resurrectus eternus!"*

Max's body shimmered with a golden light. He faded nearly of sight then reappeared. A rosy aura radiated from his skin. A second later, it was gone.

"That's it?" He grinned. "I'm immortal?"

"Yes." Miranda handed the stone back to Mistress Southmore, then turned to hug Max. Claps and cheers rose from the council.

"All right now, hurry along you two." The head mistress sat down in her chair, her gaze turned toward the couple. "But Miranda, we expect you back here in the morning. We have much work to do."

"Yes, ma'am."

Max and Miranda hurried outside where jagged, misty mountains surrounded the palace. Blue sky, filled with wisps of cottony clouds, arched above. A warm breeze blew across the land, rustling trees and bushes. Max danced with Miranda across the lawn, twirling her around and around until they were both breathless. Then he pulled her close and tenderly hugged her.

"By Jove, this is the happiest day of my life." He stroked Miranda's cheek with the back of his hand and looked deeply into her eyes. "I'll be with the woman I love for the rest of my life. Actually, forever."

"Forever is a long time," Miranda reminded him. "Believe me, I know. Aren't you afraid you'll eventually grow tired of me?"

"Never, my love. Never." Max gave her the sweetest kiss imaginable.

About Cindy Keen Reynders

www.cindykeenreynders.com

Cindy was born in Portland, Oregon and has lived all over the United States and in Misawa, Japan. She has visited Canada, the Philippines, Samoa, Hawaii, both the western and eastern Caribbean and New Zealand.

Over the years, she has won or placed in various writing contests. She has also written for and edited numerous newsletters. Additionally, she has sold several non-fiction magazine articles to "True West" and "Wild West." She is also a book critic for Storyteller Alley.

Cindy works for Laramie County School District 1 (LCSD1) in Cheyenne. She is a marketing specialist in the district's Community Relations department where she is a contributing editor and writes feature articles for the LCSD1 Public Schools Chronicle, which has a circulation of approximately 46,000 readers.

Social Media

Facebook https://www.facebook.com/cindy.k.reynders

Twitter https://www.facebook.com/cindy.k.reynders

Blog https://wyomingfreelancemuse.blogspot.com/

Website http://www.cindykeenreynders.com/

Instagram https://www.instagram.com/reynders.c/

Acknowledgements

Thank you to the Greater Power that has blessed me with the ability to have my way with words. Also, I appreciate that Solstice Publishing has allowed me to join their publishing team.